BLACK RUBBER DRESS

BLACK RUBBER DRESS

A SAM JONES MYSTERY

LAUREN HENDERSON

CROWN PUBLISHERS ... NEW YORK

Published by Crown Publishers, 201 East 50th Street, New York, New York 10022. Member of the Crown Publishing Group.

Random House, Inc. New York, Toronto, London, Sydney, Auckland
www.randomhouse.com

CROWN is a trademark and the Crown colophon is a registered trademark of Random House, Inc.

Originally published in Great Britain by Hutchinson in 1997.

Printed in the United States of America

DESIGN BY KAREN MINSTER

Library of Congress Cataloging-in-Publication Data
Henderson, Lauren, 1966–
Black rubber dress / Lauren Henderson.
p. cm.
I. Title.
PR6058.E4929B53 1999
823′.914—dc21 98-52335
CIP

ISBN 0-609-80438-3

10 9 8 7 6 5 4 3 2 1

First American Edition

To my darling
Giacomo,
with thanks
for all the love
and support
he has
given me

Acknowledgments

With many thanks to Andrew (fight arranger), Lisa and Sandy, PJ (inside information), Sue, a great editor, and Dawn and Nicky for services to fetishwear.

BLACK RUBBER DRESS

1

"I can't do this any more," Hawkins said with an air of manly resolution. He was sitting on the end of the futon, his back to me, pulling on his shoes. One of the shoelaces was in a tangle and he dragged on it as viciously as if he were garrotting me.

"Well, my cervix'll be glad to hear that," I said from a semi-recumbent position on a pile of pillows. "It's not what it was. I think it needs a rest cure."

He turned a look of loathing on me, his jaw set. "Why do you always have to make a joke of everything?"

"Please. I *hate* rhetorical questions."

He tied the other shoelace and stood up.

"I mean it, Sam," he said seriously. "I can't do this any more."

"Is Daphne beginning to suspect?" I found the name of Hawkins' girlfriend exquisitely amusing for some perverse reason.

"It's not that so much as the guilt." He was looking around for his jacket.

"Maybe you should try not to enjoy it so much. Then you'd feel less remorse."

The glance of loathing returned. "If that's all you can think of to say. . . ."

He started rummaging around on the bed, presumably hoping to find his jacket buried in the mess of duvet and blankets. Instead he uncovered a part of me by mistake; he stared at it, unwillingly fascinated, for several moments before throwing the covers back over it as heavily as if he were attempting to tamp out a fire.

"One of the reasons I like you is that you make me feel such a scarlet woman," I observed. "A temptation to be resisted as long as you can possibly bear it."

"That's because you are," he snapped. He had now found his jacket, which was a shame, because it was a nasty brown leather blouson which did nothing for him whatsoever. "And this is positively the last time I give in to it. You."

"That's what you always say."

His eyes narrowed with rage. Hawkins' blue eyes were his one claim to handsomeness. Around them was one of those solid, unpretentious faces, Spencer Tracy crossed with a knocked-about prizefighter, which would be craggy in later life and gave you the impression of total reliability. Which was ironic, considering his profession.

"Well, this time I mean it." Despite himself, his voice softened. "Can't you just try to understand how difficult it is for me, Sam? I've been living with Daphne for four years now. And it's not as if you'd take me in if I left her."

"God, no. I'm not cut out for domesticity. Besides, it would ruin both our careers at one go."

"Exactly." He looked very hangdog.

"Oh, piss off, Hawkins," I said impatiently. "Most men would be bloody grateful for what you've got. You can try to shag what's left of my brains out when the mood takes you and then pop home to Daphne and a nice home-cooked shepherd's pie—"

"How the hell do you know what Daphne cooks?"

"Anyone called Daphne knows how to do shepherd's pie. It wasn't even a guess."

"*God*, you piss me off!" Hawkins glared at me, arms folded across his broad chest in best macho style. For a moment I thought he was going to have his way with me again, and I braced myself against the headboard in anticipation; but he limited himself to swearing violently and then swung over the side of my sleeping platform, on to the ladder which led down to the main studio. I scrambled out of bed and hung over the edge, shouting:

"It was you who came round here, remember? I didn't even ask you!"

"I wouldn't come back even if you begged me!"

"Yeah, yeah. Same time next week, then?" I yelled vindictively.

He made what sounded like a snarl and slammed the door behind him. It would have rocked on its hinges if I hadn't put on the extra-strong ones. Men often seemed to leave me this way. I attributed the phenomenon to my winning charm.

Well, I was awake now. I should be; it was three in the afternoon. I got out of bed without bothering to huddle under the covers first. There were only a few months of the year warm enough for me to wander naked round my studio—a tacked-on warehouse extension in Holloway, and even less glamorous than that description makes it sound—so I might as well make the most of it. Pushing aside the big screen, painted with colourful and rather rudely cavorting people, which stood at the foot of my bed, I rifled through the contents of my clothes rail, pausing for a moment at my little blue linen suit: it would be perfect for this evening, which was precisely why I wasn't going to wear it. People might take me for an off-duty merchant banker.

I looked across the platform for a moment at the Thing, a large silvery mobile which hung smugly from the central steel joist in the ceiling. Attempts had been made by Duggie, my agent, to call it something more saleable, but I had resisted them. To me it would always be the Thing; its personality wasn't good enough for it to deserve a more poetic moniker. It was demanding, pushy and it positively revelled in attention, which was why it had become a mobile in the first place. It loved hanging above people's heads, in the most literal sense being looked up to, while it basked happily, feeling admired and superior.

It was because of the admiration provoked by the Thing that I was now facing a clothes decision. An American couple had commissioned one like it, but on a larger scale. I had wanted to call the second one Thing II, but this time Duggie had stood firm, and it now answered to "Undiscovered Planet." The husband of the couple was otherwise known as Mr. Big of Consolidated Drilling; he had shown the mobile to a mate of his, a.k.a. Mr. Big at an investment bank called Mowbray Steiner, who happened to be looking for something to hang in the bank's front hall and wanted this to be slightly more original than ceramic flying ducks. So he placed an order for "Floating Planet," which he had requested on a scale that made its forebears look the size of ball bearings. Duggie predicted that all the smartest five-mile-high marble atria would be wearing one next season.

I had spent the past few months sweating over the wretched thing (literally: welding masks are hell on the skin. I used a mud pack after each session to draw out the impurities) and the past couple of weeks assembling it in the aforesaid marble atrium. I'd made it in segments, like an orange, otherwise it would never have got out through the door of my studio, let alone into my van. The committee who commissioned art for the bank had thought it would be a great idea for me to work at night; that way the mobile wouldn't be seen in the stages of assembly and thus lose its mystique. Fortunately their acquisitions budget had forked out enough to allow me to afford something substantially stronger than ProPlus to keep me awake. And so from midnight onwards, under the frankly incredulous gazes of various cleaners, Bill the night guard and the occasional late office-leaver, I had screwed the planet together, wrapped sheets of ripped chicken wire round it and attached the huge silver metal contraption, like a Victorian wire petticoat, which hung over the whole thing in irregular rings.

This evening it was due for the ceremonial unveiling at a cocktail party of carefully selected staff, together with the kind of guests who were likely to be impressed enough by the image of Mowbray Steiner as an artistically forward-looking, cutting-edge sort of place to deposit in its coffers the odd million or two. I of course had to be present, so they could talk to me about my creative vision and feel, for a few brief, shining moments, slightly less like people who had to wear suits to work. The money they had paid me required me to look, at least, as if I were enjoying myself during this process.

My hand alighted on my newest and thus favourite frock, the one I had really known I was going to wear all the time. It was sleeveless and Empire line; the bodice was black bouclé and the skirt, which had a slight flare so as not to cling too vulgarly to my hips, was black rubber. A wide border of more black rubber trimmed the neckline, which skimmed my shoulders flatteringly. I pulled it on and stared at myself in satisfaction. At least I didn't look like an off-duty bond trader. Nor did I look like someone who was having an affair with a detective sergeant—whoops, detective inspector, excuse *me*. I kept forgetting about Hawkins' promotion.

It suddenly occurred to me to wonder whether he had turned up in a squad car this afternoon. Shit, I hoped not. My image was already tarnished enough with the neighbours.

...

The giant block of granite and marble that was the Mowbray Steiner Investment Bank dominated the corner of Liverpool Street and Broadgate, looking heavy enough to crack its foundations and sink imposingly through the pavement. Not an observation I should share with any of its occupants; the IRA bomb a few years ago had exploded just a block away, down Broadgate, taking a couple of Mowbray Steiner–sized buildings with it. Bill had told me that his mate on the night shift in the building next door had returned to his desk just after the blast to find an enormous lump of Tuscan marble squatting exactly where he would have been sitting if he hadn't had to have a pee at the critical moment. Or perhaps this was just a story Bill had made up to justify his habit of leaving his post every so often to have a whisky in the storeroom. He'd clocked me as someone who could be corrupted into keeping silence; the fee for my silence had been a couple of beers. I come cheap. Ask anyone.

It was seven o'clock on a glorious Friday evening in full summer. Mellow evening sunlight refracted off the myriad glass buildings silhouetted imposingly against the Wedgwood-blue sky, making them look magical for an enchanted moment, modern temples to something spiritually a little higher than Mammon. The streets were teeming with life forms dressed in grey suits, their heads down, hurrying towards the station, like a modern version of *Metropolis*. Walking at a normal pace made me a hazard; the human traffic converged behind me and when there was a gap in the oncoming bodies passed at high speed, without signalling that it was pulling out. I manoeuvred across a number of lanes and then took a right turn into the Broadgate complex which massed above Liverpool Street station.

The sludgy-rose granite walls loomed up on either side, making me feel pleasantly tiny and insignificant beside the scale on which they were built; they would have made even Arnold Schwarzenegger look like Dustin Hoffman. The sculptures that dotted the complex were equally colossal. My favourite was the Richard Serra, two towering sheets of metal tilted against one another in what looked a precarious balance. Standing between them and looking up was a guaranteed adrenaline rush: equal parts claustrophobia and dizzying excitement. My least favourite was the enormous naked woman. Bloody typical of all these bankers. In the interests of balance, they could at least have commissioned a naked man facing her with all his little vegetables draped over his thighs.

I circumnavigated what in the winter was a skating rink (London's would-be answer to the Rockefeller Center, how sad) and headed towards the Mowbray Steiner building. The reception would have started by now; it was time for me to sing for my supper.

Bill, who came on at seven, was already ensconced behind the desk. His eyes widened flatteringly when he saw me for the first time dressed smartly, rather than clad in layers of stained black rags. I had put my hair up in a high chignon and cut in a short fringe, Audrey Hepburn style, though somewhat less waif-like by necessity. To aid the effect I wore sheer black tights, high heels and an abbreviated cut-off bouclé jacket to match the dress, with demure little rubber collar and cuffs. I was spending the Mowbray Steiner Art Acquisitions Committee advance like there was no tomorrow.

Over Bill's shoulder I could see the shape of the mobile, which had been winched up last night and now hung in the air from a central chain which bore its weight; smaller chains radiated out like bicycle spokes, holding it in place so it couldn't sway in the breeze of the air conditioning which Mowbray Steiner had in place of a normal climate. The effect was marred only by the large piece of green felt which was draped over the mobile, obscuring its contours.

"They're through across the hall," Bill said, indicating.

I found myself curiously reluctant to go in and face the throng. Instead I leant on his desk and started bitching about a common enemy of ours. He had been one of our main topics of conversation over the last few weeks, and I saw no reason to tinker with tradition now.

"I bet you as soon as I get in there David Stronge will start nagging at me. He's been fussing about this unveiling all week like it was the raising of the *Titanic*."

My status here was rather like that of a governess in a Victorian household; I didn't belong below or above stairs. But nowadays having an indeterminate class position meant that people talked to you more freely, rather than less. Bill was nodding.

"I know what you mean, he's been messing around with the cord on that bit of felt all this afternoon. Worse than my old ma making curtains."

My heart sank. "If it gets caught and doesn't come off the mobile when it's supposed to, it'll be his fault. I never wanted to cover it up in the first place. That felt could easily get stuck on the chicken wire." I shrugged. "Oh well, it's his problem now."

I looked at Bill, and noticed for the first time how preoccupied he seemed, inexpressive as his face was. It resembled a potato, dented and knobbly, though with only the human amount of eyes, tiny ones sunk into his flesh so far that you would need your sharpest knife to prise them out. Despite a body now as monumental as the great slab of gold-studded mahogany desk behind which he sat, he still convinced the occasional unwelcome visitor that he could handle himself if he needed to; and as a reminder of his glory days, in the little nook behind the desk where he made endless cups of tea (topped up, as the night wore on, with something stronger) was proudly displayed a photograph of himself as a young, strapping sergeant-major with a chest like a barrel and a no-nonsense stare.

I had a lot of time for Bill. Over the fortnight that I was assembling the sculpture he had been a considerable asset, not only in helping me haul its component parts out of the van, but also, with an unexpectedly good eye, by providing shrewd judgements on how the work was going. And he knew exactly when I needed a break. Over frequent mugs of milky tea and whisky we had long chats about the state of the world (Bill Conservative, me Labour, conversation reasonably amicable, all things considered); passing on to the personal, he had told me all about his wife (sadly passed away), his daughter (a great girl) and his son-in-law (a stupid git). He kept threatening to set me up with nice young sons of ex–army colleagues but fortunately for them, nothing so far had come of it.

So now I stared at him, concerned, and saw that my first impression had been correct. He looked as if he had something on his mind, something unpleasant; his shoulders, instead of being pulled back in his usual erect posture, were slumped forward and his forehead was creased with worry.

"Bill, is everything all right?" I said.

Immediately, he looked hunted. "What do you mean, Sammy?"

"I don't know. I'm asking you. You don't look like your usual cheerful self."

His eyes wouldn't meet mine. Instead he nodded in the direction of the reception room.

"I'm fine, Sammy, just fine. Hadn't you better be getting in there?"

Let no one say that I can't take a hint. Sighing, I straightened up off the desk.

"All right, I'd better go through and face the tumbrels. Want me to smuggle you out a glass of something?"

"Nah, I don't like that champagne. Fizzy stuff gives me wind. I've got my own poison right here." He tapped one of the desk drawers, giving me a big, exaggerated wink. This worried me still more; it was such a parody of Bill's normal behaviour that I could only see it as an indication of how much he wanted to hide whatever was worrying him.

I gave him a steady look. "You can talk to me, you know, Bill. It won't go any further. Think about it, OK?"

For a moment I thought he was about to say something; then, muttering "You'd better get on," he turned away and pretended to be busy at the console. There was nothing more I could say.

It was the first time I had worn heels on the inlaid marble floor of the atrium; they made a ridiculous clicking noise, signalling my passage like Morse code. Taking a deep breath, I pushed open one of the heavy mahogany doors. The cocktail-party sound of clinking glasses, murmured conversation and the occasional male guffaw flooded out and enveloped me. I paused for a moment on the threshold. Heads turned and across the thick green carpet of what would have been the banqueting room hundreds of years ago came David Stronge, chairman of the Art Acquisitions Committee and my personal nemesis, to greet me.

"Samantha, how lovely to see you, my dear!" He looked me up and down. I had never actually been crawled over by a giant slug, but, strangely enough, at that moment I could imagine exactly what it would feel like. "What a delightful vision you are out of those work clothes of yours. Do have a glass of champagne."

Beside me had materialized a smooth-faced waiter with a silver tray. I took a glass gratefully. Half my brain was still occupied with trying to work out what could be worrying Bill; I'd drop in to see him in a few days and tease it out of him over a cup of tea. Ten to one it was much less important than he thought. Men were so prone to exaggeration. But I wanted to help him out. He had let me moan on while I was assembling the mobile, always the worst part of the job for me; he had been a tower of strength. And I like to return favours. All part of the Sam Jones code of ethics.

Meanwhile, David Stronge was leading me over to a group of men, though most of these looked so similar I wondered how he could tell one from another. Most of them were overweight and every single one was wearing a suit—dark navy or grey—their ties subdued, their haircuts sensible. The occasional woman stood out like a hummingbird among crows, as did my agent Duggie Sutton, who beamed at me cheerfully as we approached. He was small and tubby, with his ubiquitous fob watch, bow tie and ratty tweed jacket. Someone ought to use Duggie as the prototype for a cuddly toy; they'd make millions.

"Richard, let me introduce you to Samantha Jones, our artist-in-residence," David Stronge was saying.

"Richard Fine. Pleased to meet you." He shook my hand with a firm grip. I was buoyed up by the knowledge that this must be Sir Richard Fine, chairman of the bank, and that you pronounced his surname, not as it was written, but "Feen"; at least I wasn't going to put my foot in anything too squashy. Not at once, anyway.

"Call me Sam," I said at once. Samantha sounds much too like the kind of person who has herself photographed wearing a fishnet thong, a thick gloss of body oil and a bright smile.

"Don't understand this vogue girls have now for shortening their names," Sir Richard barked, but in a friendly sort of way. "Both of mine are at it, silly little mares, they had perfectly good ones to start with. Where *are* Susan and Belinda?" He turned to look round the room. "They'll be about somewhere. Anyway. Duggie you already know, of course. And this is Akis Georgios and Ikimura-san. Bit of the United Nations, eh?"

Both men politely shook my hand.

"I'm very much looking forward to seeing your sculpture," said Mr. Georgios in the purest of Oxbridge accents. "Richard tells me it's just what he was looking for."

"Jim Ashley showed me some snaps of his," Richard Fine said. "He's taken it back to the States, of course. But we've wanted to put something in the atrium for yanks. Something different, y'know, not just one of these classical statues that they've got outside: woman with thighs as big as B-52s. David here was thinking of a fountain, which would have been OK, apart from making us want to pee all the time, but then I saw what young Sam here did for Jim Ashley and I thought, well, why the hell not a mobile? Young British artist, too," he added as something of an afterthought. "We like to support that kind of thing."

That kind of thing smiled politely in acknowledgement while Duggie made approving noises. Sir Richard Fine was as imposing as his domination of the conversation suggested; a big, well-upholstered man with a reddish, slightly puffy face and clever eyes which saw more than the geniality of his manner suggested. He had thick grey hair, which was more than one could say for most of the men around here, and he ran his hand through it every so often with a satisfied air which suggested his pride in it.

"When are we due for the unveiling?" he said, looking at a watch which had probably cost him as much as my advance payment for the mobile. "Seven-thirty, isn't it? I want Henry to get here first, David. Make sure we wait for him, OK?"

David Stronge nodded emphatically and said: "Absolutely, Richard," in servile tones.

"Tell me," Akis Georgios said to me, "how on earth did you manoeuvre that monster through the doors here?"

"I assembled it here," I explained. "It's welded in parts, and the rest is screwed together."

"You welded it together?" Georgios looked at me disbelievingly; or not so much at me as what was signified by my little black dress and high heels. "You yourself?"

I tried not to roll my eyes too obviously. "It's easy once you get the hang of it."

"A girl of many parts, our Sam," Duggie added, not helping matters much; it made everyone, not just Georgios, stare at my parts. David Stronge patted my shoulder in a way that he doubtless told himself was avuncular.

"I dropped by a couple of times to see Samantha at work," he said over my head. "Very impressive it was too. Nice to see a young woman doing that kind of thing without losing her femininity, eh? Though you'd never have known she was female when you saw her all bundled up in her dungarees, I can tell you!"

I had finished my champagne and was finding it hard not to shove my glass into David Stronge's face and ask him if that counted as a feminine gesture. I never, *ever* wore dungarees.

"Could I leave my jacket somewhere?" I said as dulcetly as I could. It was the only excuse I could think of to get away before I injured someone. "Is there a cloakroom?"

David Stronge escorted me across the room, holding open the door for me. I had to flatten myself against the jamb to avoid touching him. His smile was as greasy as a cheap Chinese takeaway.

By now I was used to the toilets at Mowbray Steiner, so I didn't stop dead under the impression that I had just been shown into the chairman's private lavatory by mistake. In contrast to the reception room, which was modelled on an old-fashioned gentleman's club, the toilets were rigorously modern: grey granite sinks, slate flooring and light bulbs round the mirrors like a Bauhaus dressing table. The doors to the cubicles were opaque grey glass—at least I hoped they were opaque—and the toilets themselves looked as if only a very vulgar person indeed would dare to take a dump in them.

In front of one of the make-up mirrors a girl was touching up her lipstick. She performed the action with deft strokes, as if this were a ritual which was second nature to her. Lifting her eyes, she met mine in the mirror.

"Escaped from David, have you?" she drawled rather affectedly. "God, that man's a bore. Bet he was pleased to see you. He's sick of the usual faces—pawed them over for years."

"It's the dandruff I really object to. I keep expecting some of it to shake off on me."

"Ugh. Nightmare. I'm Suki Fine, by the way. I saw you chatting to my papa. You must be the artist."

Suki Fine seemed unaware of the inverted commas her tone had placed around the last word. She snapped the top back on her lipstick and put it into the tiny black bag which was propped in front of her. Extracting a gold powder compact filled with little pinky-brown spheres, she produced a brush and started dabbing powder over cheekbones, temples and even the tip of her nose.

"Bronzing pearls," she explained, catching my eye in the mirror. "Givenchy is the best. Gives you some colour till you pop off to somewhere sunny. Look, this is where it goes." With the brush now unloaded she indicated the correct areas of the face for application. "See?"

Later I was to realise that, to Suki Fine, giving advice was as natural as breathing; she couldn't cross the road by your side without pointing out how to look left and right properly. She had a special smile for it, too, a knowing little smile which at the same time was friendly, because she meant well. And in fact her advice was almost always correct. In a way that was the most annoying part.

"Right," I said, nodding politely. I had a Barry M fuchsia lipstick in the pocket of my jacket, and not to be outdone I pulled it out and poked at the edges of my mouth with it. I didn't need to bother, but neither did Suki Fine need any of the highly expensive stuff she was applying to her face. It looked as if she were constructing a mask for herself, though her skill was so subtle that the effect was not as artificial as that implied. Tall and slim, she was nearly beautiful, and would have been so if she hadn't had a trace of what her enemies might call smugness and her friends something more polite, but comprised that veiled knowing smile and a slight hauteur in her manner. Her hair was straight and streaky blonde and hung almost to her waist; her eyes were blue, her skin rosy-pale. She wore a light pink Chanel suit (a woman knows these things) with a low-cut black body underneath to avoid looking like a lady who lunched. That she would be one of that sorority in ten or twenty years' time was obvious.

"What's your name?" she said. "Daddy told me but I forgot."

"Sam. Sam Jones."

"I love your outfit."

"I'd better take off my jacket. It was my excuse for getting away from David."

Suki was now spraying some perfume on her wrists. I hung the jacket on the rail which had been thoughtfully provided by the management.

"God, what a great frock," she said, sounding genuine for the first time. "Where's it from?"

"This little shop in Camden Market . . ."

My voice tailed off as I saw Suki's blank expression. She had probably never been further north in London than Hyde Park Corner. It was

, she hadn't asked me what brand my lipstick was. She might have .ainted on the spot.

"Well, it *looks* lovely," she said, obviously making a great effort to be charitable. "You'd never know, honestly."

Just then a sudden scrabbling noise made us both jump and turn around. It had come from inside one of the toilet cubicles, which I had thought unoccupied. From the surprise on Suki's face she had obviously assumed the same thing.

The noise stopped as abruptly as it had started. Suki and I looked at each other, unnerved. There had been something not quite human, and definitely not quite right, about the sound. Tentatively, Suki advanced on the one opaque glass door which was shut, tapping at it. I stood well back. The last time I had investigated a closed toilet door I'd found a dead body behind it, and frankly I thought that experience would last me for some time to come.

The faint thud as the door swung fully open and knocked against the cubicle wall caught, stupidly enough, at my throat. Or maybe it was simply the sight inside; a girl, slumped on the toilet seat, as fragile as a handful of sticks wrapped in white tissue paper. Her long fair hair hid her face, her hands were as loose by her sides as leaves fallen from the twigs of her wrists, and for a terrible moment I had such a wash of déjà vu that I couldn't hear anything but the blood drumming in my veins.

Then the hair tumbled back, the body straightened out as if pulled by an invisible string in the top of her head, and a face as naughty as a demon child's looked up at us, the blue eyes wickedly aware that she had given us a scare. Suki, who had been frozen to the spot, came to life as if someone had flicked a switch to turn her on.

"Bells! Did you faint again?" Her voice was full of concern, the self-conscious society butterfly tone forgotten. She rushed forward, obscuring my view of the girl. "Poor darling! Can you stand up?"

She guided the girl to her feet, one arm protectively around her waist, and helped her out of the cubicle.

"Maybe if you splashed your face with cold water—"

"God no. I don't want to ruin my make-up. I'm fine, Sukes, really. Do stop fussing."

"This is my sister Belinda," Suki explained to me, superfluously enough, as the resemblance was so strong the girl could have been no one else. She was the spitting image of Suki, but so much thinner that she made Suki's cheeks seem positively plump, her figure curvaceous in comparison. Belinda, on the other hand, looked as if she had fallen into the hands of an over-enthusiastic liposuctionist.

"Bells has anaemia. That's a lack of iron," Suki explained importantly, as if this fact were an arcane piece of medical information. "Every so often she gets weak and faints. Bells, this is Sam Jones, who made the sculpture. She'll say hello properly when she feels better. I'm so sorry," she added sotto voce in my direction.

I blinked: I couldn't see why Suki was apologising, nor why she felt the need to act like a hostess in the middle of a ladies' toilet. Perhaps she considered that we were on her father's property. Still . . .

Belinda had shaken off her sister's arm impatiently and was leaning into the mirror, staring at her extraordinarily pretty face.

"God, I look like a hag," she commented, clearly talking to her reflection rather than to either one of us.

"Do you want some blusher?" Suki said, eager to help.

"No thanks, I've got mine. . . . Shit! Where's my bag?" Belinda looked around frantically, her expression changing in the blink of an eye from complacency to panic. "Where *is* it? It's got to be around here somewhere. . . ."

I went into the cubicle and retrieved the bag, a little suede pouch embroidered with bugle beads, from beneath the cistern. The scrabbling noise Suki and I had heard must have been Belinda searching for it. What she had been doing while Suki and I were talking was anyone's guess; but I ruled out the possibility of a faint. It amazed me that Suki hadn't too. No one looked that wide awake and aware of the trouble they were causing just after a blackout—iron-deficiency induced or not.

I handed the bag over to Belinda, who snatched at it ungraciously, nearly ripping it out of my grasp.

"Bells! How rude!" Suki exclaimed.

Belinda turned her back on me and her sister pointedly, proceeding to open the bag and rummage inside.

"Just leave me *alone* for thirty seconds, can't you, Sukes?" she complained over her shoulder. "I need some peace and quiet."

Suki, extraordinarily, accepted her sister's request at face value.

"Of course, darling, you must still be feeling a bit wobbly. I'm sure you didn't mean to snap at Sam. Come on," she said to me, readopting her bright, superficial, hostess voice. "Let's go out and face the world. I'll keep David off you if I can."

I was glad that Suki made no further comment on the scene that had just taken place; I had the feeling that anything I said would have mortally offended her. The cocktail party was now in full swing. Faces were getting flushed and some of the men had even unbuttoned their jackets; they'd have let their hair down if they'd had any. David Stronge was hovering near the door of the toilets but Suki favoured him with a hundred-watt smile while heading ruthlessly in the opposite direction. I followed obediently, looking neither to left nor right. Now that my jacket was off, the dress was garnering frank stares on all sides.

Suki led me over to a group of young men whose focal point was a blond Adonis, Belinda Fine's male counterpart, all blue eyes and gold hair and manicured fingernails. His impeccable suit was navy blue and fitted his long, lean figure in a way most Englishmen would avoid for fear of being misunderstood.

"Everyone, this is Sam Jones, the sculptress," Suki announced, rather with the air of someone introducing a rare breed of iguana to a gathering of zoologists.

"Charles de Groot," said Adonis, shaking my hand and smiling at me, the whites of his eyes and teeth almost blinding me. "Nice to meet you. We're all looking forward to the unveiling."

A couple of other young men, who beside the handsome Charles faded rather into the woodwork, murmured similar comments and shook my hand; they told me their names but I forgot them at once.

"Isn't something supposed to happen now?" Belinda said from behind us, her voice high and spoilt. Making an entrance into the middle of the group, she stood there like a model, her hands on where her hips would have been if she'd had any, as if thrusting them forward to show herself off to photographers. She was wearing a peach suede dress which matched her bag and required little more material than the latter to cover her chicken bones.

"Your father said he wanted to wait for someone called Henry to turn up," I volunteered. Glances were exchanged; everyone seemed to know exactly who that was.

"Planes, trains and automobiles," said one of Belinda's swains.

"Daddy's courting him like mad," Belinda said.

"Well, they should just jump into bed with each other and get on with it, if you ask me," said Charles de Groot. "God, where are my manners? You girls haven't got anything to drink." He turned round and snapped his fingers. "Over here," he said loudly, "some champagne and quick about it."

I made a point of thanking the waiter when he arrived, though I doubt he gave a damn. I was feeling more uncomfortable by the second; worried that the uncovering of the sculpture would go wrong, uneasy at the company in which I found myself. There seemed to be more undercurrents here than tugged beneath the Cornish sea at high tide. Just then a buzz ran round the room and someone clapped his hands for silence. It was David Stronge. Raising his voice he announced:

"Ladies and gentlemen, we are about to proceed into the atrium for the ceremonial unveiling of our latest acquisition. In accordance with Mowbray Steiner's policy of supporting young British artists we have specially commissioned this work, called 'Floating Planet,' from Miss Samantha Jones. Miss Jones is here tonight and I'm sure we all agree she deserves a round of applause."

To my horror, David Stronge proceeded to forge a path across the room and put an arm around my waist. I averted my head. All the faces duly turned in my direction and there was a polite sprinkle of clapping. David Stronge was by now rather sweaty and excited. This was foul.

"Shall we head outside?" he said familiarly in my ear. I detached myself from his grasp and finished my champagne in one gulp.

"Be with you in a moment," I said, smiling, and wriggled away into the crowd. When I exited, armed with a full glass, David was, as I had hoped, on the other side of the room, fiddling with the cord. Sir Richard Fine strode over to him manfully.

"Believe that's my job, eh, David?" he said. "Everything ready? Come over here, Henry, you'll get a better view."

Henry of the planes and trains was a tiny man with a pleasantly wizened face. He stood next to Richard Fine as the latter said loudly: "Well, bless this ship and all who sail in her!" and pulled the cord.

For a horrible moment the material seemed to have snagged on something and I held my breath, hoping that Richard Fine, who by now had had quite a bit to drink, would realise and stop tugging before he tore off a piece of the chicken wire. But then, in one smooth rush, to an accompaniment of oohs and aahs, the green felt came free and cascaded neatly at Sir Richard's feet, as I imagined most things did sooner or later.

Thing III, a.k.a. Floating Planet, hung majestically in the centre of the atrium, perfectly proportioned against the octagonal walls which surrounded it. Just above the mobile was the balcony which ran high around the atrium, and from this hung clustered banks of light fittings, sending streams of pale golden light to catch the different planes of the mobile, leaving some parts in shadow like craters of the moon. The rings around it shone bright silver and from this distance the chicken wire was a filmy, mysterious mesh, casting its outline irregularly against the polished surface of the mobile. It was like seeing a stage set, garishly painted, which in the glow of the footlights becomes magical, the forest of Arden or a ship wrecked on Caliban's island. Thing III was a meteor that had crashed into this most proper of places, invading it with quite unconventional beauty; as I stared up at it I felt a lump in my throat.

It was wonderful, and I had made it. And it was going down well, goddamnit; the exclamations and comments around me sounded genuine. The lump had grown so large I had to choke it down with the rest of my champagne.

2

It was all wrong, of course. The mobile and its setting went about as well together as a lifelong teetotaller in a Hemingway novel. The only point in favour of the atrium was the balcony, which had provided a useful place from which to haul up the mobile. Still, the balcony with its elaborately curved brass balustrade and shiny gold sprays of lamps, let alone the green and white marble pavement of the atrium, inlaid with brass like the floor of a particularly showy cathedral, clashed horrendously with Floating Planet. If they'd been trying to coordinate they would have asked me to run them up something gold-plated and tastefully symmetrical.

"Would you like another drink?" It was a pleasant voice, low and easy. I turned my head in its direction to see a young man who had appeared next to me with two brimming champagne glasses in his hands. "You seem to have finished that one."

"Please," I said, trying not to sound too enthusiastic.

Deftly he handed me a glass and removed my empty one almost simultaneously, depositing it on the tray of a passing waiter.

"Your dress is wonderful," he said. "I'm sorry if that sounds familiar."

I took a sip of the champagne and looked up again at the mobile, still unable to believe that I had made it.

"It's brilliant," he said, following my gaze. "Though something of a fish out of water."

I turned to look at him properly for the first time.

"Why do you say that?"

"Oh, well . . ." He seemed embarrassed now, but ploughed on bravely. "The styles are completely different, aren't they? I mean, this place is conventional to the nth degree, and your sculpture isn't. It doesn't look as if it had been made to go here—more like it fell through the ceiling, don't you think? Like a shooting star."

He was only the second person who had ever compared any of the Things to a meteor. My interest grew, fed considerably, I had to admit, by his good looks; he was just as handsome as Charles de Groot, but without the latter's eerily perfect grooming, which made him seem at first glance superhuman and shortly afterwards extraordinarily vain. This one had grey-blue eyes and straight brown hair which fell over his forehead in a schoolboyish way, and from time to time he would run his hand through it, pushing it back on reflex. He had long eyelashes and rather full lips and looked like an E. M. Forster hero. If he ever happened to meet Ralph Lauren he'd be off to America before the ink was dry on his modelling contract; the physique was as perfect as the face. He looked as if he worked out regularly in the company gym, and doubtless played cricket on Sundays just to round things off.

"I'm Sebastian Shaw," he was saying. "I hope you don't think I was being rude about your sculpture."

I snapped out of a brief reverie which involved the unsuspecting Sebastian on a running machine, clad in shorts and a T-shirt, the sweat beginning to dampen it to his chest, his thigh and calf muscles swelling as they pounded away at the conveyor belt. . . .

"Not at all," I said with compensating formality. "In fact I agree with you." I held out my hand; it seemed to be what one did here. "I'm Sam Jones."

"Nice to meet you," he said. His aftershave was light and dry, like his hand. "The dress really is amazing."

"Thank you," I said demurely, and took another sip of champagne.

"I saw David Stronge heading in your direction just now, so I thought I'd cut him off at the pass."

"Thank you again, in spades. The best thing about finishing this job is that I won't have to peel him off me any longer."

"Oh, you mean you won't be needing to come back here?"

"Not unless they don't pay me and I have to come round to beat up David to get him to sign me a cheque."

"It's hard to imagine you beating anyone up."

"Believe it," I said. It came out more sharply than I had intended.

Sebastian looked at me. "I'm sorry, I seem to have put my foot in it." He drank some champagne. "Well, steering smoothly away from that subject," he continued, "how did someone in a rubber frock get involved with a staid old bank like this in the first place?"

I gave him a brief résumé of events, which I enjoyed chiefly because it allowed me to look at him while I was talking. His suit, navy with the faintest pinstripe, was as well cut as Charles de Groot's but hung more loosely around his well-toned body; classic English style, compared to Mr. de Groot, who was definitely Eurotrash. Even his tie, silk with splodges of purple and mauve, was as tasteful as one could hope for in the circumstances, which were quite bad enough. Never would I have thought to find a man in a suit attractive.

". . . Thus delivering you into the hands of David, who hasn't got enough to do with his time and farts around sitting on committees to make himself look busy," Sebastian Shaw finished for me.

"What does he actually do?" I asked. "He never seems to be hard at it."

"Quite. Well, he's the head of compliance."

"That sounds *much* more interesting than the image I have of David."

Sebastian Shaw raised his eyebrows slightly at me and continued:

"Which means that he ensures that—well, to put it simply—"

"Thank you."

"—he ensures that what the staff do complies with the appropriate City rules and regulations. I could go into more detail, but something tells me that you don't want me to."

"And what do you do, Mr. Shaw?"

"Sebastian, please." He pushed back the lock of hair that had tumbled down over his forehead. His fingers were long and elegant. "I'm in corporate finance. I suppose you could say that I advise companies on buying each other."

"You mean mergers and acquisitions?"

"Yes, actually. Well done."

"Don't patronise me, Sebastian." I rather enjoyed saying this. As I had hoped, it threw him into confusion.

"Oh, I wasn't—I didn't mean. . . ."

He was saved by the timely arrival of Suki Fine, who said to me in her best rich-girl drawl:

"Well, I see you've met the best-looking man in the place. Or he's met you. I like your sculpture, by the way. This hole needed something to liven it up a bit. How are you, Sebastian? Haven't seen you in ages."

She kissed both his cheeks and then stood more closely to him than her casual salutation would seem to warrant.

"I've been warding off the in-house arsonist from Sam," Sebastian said.

"The *what?*" I said.

Sebastian leaned down a little so he could speak more quietly; he was a good eight inches taller than me, even with my heels on. This offered me another waft of his aftershave. It was so long since I'd met a man who wore aftershave that I was perhaps over-impressed by its presence. "David torched his car recently." He was visibly enjoying my disbelief. "It was a company car, OK? Five-series BMW. Once you've picked the car you want they won't let you replace it for four years, and David was sick of it. So he set it on fire. They've just given him a Corvette instead."

"You're *joking*."

Sebastian grinned, happy to have shocked me. "I'm not. I swear."

"So what do you drive?"

"Only a three-series. I'm still a humble assistant director."

"That doesn't sound very humble to me." I laid a slight emphasis on the word and looked straight into his eyes, or rather up. They were as wide and innocent as ever and I thought I detected a faint blush on his cheeks.

"Oh, you'd be surprised," he said.

"I don't know what you want with that old banger, Sebastian." Suki Fine broke in with more unsolicited advice. "You should have got a TVR."

"Not really me."

"You must see my new Honda. It's got a T-bar and the roof goes right back into the boot. Just press a button. You have to see it to believe it. I'll give you a ride some time, just you and me. It's a two-seater."

She smiled at him seductively, her lips drawing together in a V for victory. So much for the solidarity in the ladies' loos; out here in the real world it was clearly every woman for herself. And yet, despite the way she was flirting, I didn't think Suki Fine actually had designs on Sebastian; behind her words there had been all the charge of a flat battery. Instead, my instinct told me that she was the kind of girl who liked to hunt down men other women were chatting up—the kind who needed to feel more attractive than everyone else.

It would be a shallow victory, though, because she'd hardly ever come across. Suki was a trophy collector: once she got a man, all she'd do would be to hang him on her wall. I knew this because I could remember someone just like Suki from art college. Different class, different style, different words, but the moves they made were identical.

"You don't work here yourself, do you?" I asked her, firmly inserting myself back into the conversation.

"God, no." Suki's beautifully made-up eyes widened. "Much too thick. Left school with just the one O-level—well, if it's good enough for Princess Di. . . . No, I cook. Directors' lunches, at the moment. Two doors along from here. It's quite fun—they're all old pets really. I did plenty of cordon bleu courses, you know, as one does, so one day I just thought, well, why not? Keeps me busy."

"And Belinda?"

"Bells? Oh, she's doing a secretarial course in Kensington. Then she's going to be a PA to one of the fashion editors at *Mode*."

"She'll be lucky," I said, unable to keep a shade of dryness out of my voice; those were the kind of jobs girls like Belinda risked their Chanel-varnished nails scratching up each others' faces to get.

"Oh no, it's all lined up." Suki was happy to correct me. That little I-know-more-than-you smile flashed again. "Daddy knows the director of the publishing company."

"Oh, I *see*."

Out of the corner of my eye I thought I saw Sebastian looking at me with amusement.

"The terrible twins," he said.

"Twins?" I said, baffled.

"Sebastian means me and Bells," Suki said rather coldly. "Though why we're terrible—"

"You two are twins?" I exclaimed. Certainly, if Belinda put on a stone she and Suki would look as alike as peas in a pod, but their behaviour contradicted this completely. Belinda was the naughty baby sister, Suki the hyper-responsible older one. As far as that went there could have been ten years between them.

Fortunately, Duggie Sutton appeared at my elbow before Suki could ask me why I was so surprised.

"Can I just whisk this clever girl off for a moment?" he asked, and drawing me slightly aside, he whispered to me confidently:

"Darling, what a success! It looks *wonderful*. I hope you're thrilled. Of course it's all wrong here, but we'll be able to take some *lovely* pictures." He smiled at me conspiratorially. "I see you're networking, so I won't keep you. That's one of the daughters, isn't it? Good for you. I hear they've settled down a bit since their wild-child days."

"Wild child?" I echoed.

"Oh, they used to take all their clothes off and dance in nightclubs while deviating their septums, the usual spoilt brat routine, you know, darling. Anyway, their daddy seems *terrifically* pleased, which is much more to the point. We must talk about an exhibition. What do you say to lunch on Monday? You can? Super. I'm off now, sweetie, so see you then. Come to the gallery about one-ish? Big kiss."

He buttoned up his jacket over his firm little tummy and toddled off across the hall. I turned back to Suki and Sebastian, who had been joined by Belinda, her arm proprietorially linked with Charles de Groot's, and the other two men in suits. One of them barged up to me and said, with the air of someone pronouncing judgement:

"You must be jolly clever, I should have thought. Congratulations on the, um, sculpture. Rather striking, isn't it? Give us all something to talk about, anyway."

"Thank you," I said. "I think."

"I'm James Rattray-Potter. Expect you didn't catch my name earlier."

He was tall and broad, with classic Sloane good looks: thick dark hair above a pink, fleshy, strong-featured face whose nose was already beginning to swell slightly from drink. James Rattray-Potter struck me as being one of those men who were uncomfortable being young and came into their own from about forty onwards, from which time they collected a swathe of non-executive directorships and, thus financially provided for, spent their time lounging around their clubs smoking large cigars and making haw-haw noises.

"So you work here as well?" I said politely.

"That's right. On the trading floor. Got a loud voice, don't you see? It helps."

He laughed loudly. It was indistinguishable from the neigh of a carthorse.

"I thought it was all nineteen- and twenty-year-olds nowadays."

"No, no. That was strictly an Eighties phenomenon. They were mostly FX dealers—that's foreign exchange to you—but it got computerised, don't you see. Well, that was it as far as they were concerned. They're all mobile phone salesmen now. About time too. They were lowering the tone of the City. Load of riffraff, speaking frankly."

"Right." James Rattray-Potter was going down with me about as well as a barrel of cold vomit; the irony was that I could see from the way he was puffing out his front like a peacock on heat that he thought he was—as he would doubtless have put it—charming the knickers off me.

"Are we heading off, then?" Belinda said, pouting prettily. She fidgeted on the spot, calling attention to her legs, which in their pastel tights were as long and thin as a stork's; her knees looked even narrower than her calves. She cast a dazzling glance up at Charles de Groot from under her fringe. Duly prompted, he consulted his watch.

"The booking's for eight-thirty, isn't it? Yes, we might as well push off."

"We're all going out to dinner," Sebastian said to me. "Would you like to join us?"

I shook my head. "I've got to be somewhere about eight-thirty myself."

"Really? That's a shame," said Suki. "We hardly ever have any other girls. I can't imagine why. I always think the boys must be terrifically bored with just us two," she went on disingenuously.

A chorus of denial greeted this statement; under cover of the noise I excused myself and went to fetch my jacket. In the privacy of the toilets I checked myself out, pleased with what I saw. My lipstick was still on, but it damn well should be; I'd put enough sealer on it to cover the bows of the *QEII*. Exiting from the toilets, however, I ran straight into David Stronge, who was hovering just outside the doors like a would-be flasher not quite able to muster up the courage to bare himself to the world.

"Sam, how delightful," he said, leaning unsteadily over me. If I'd held a match to his breath it would have gone up in flames; he'd been at something harder than the champagne. Dandruff speckled his shoulders like talcum powder, only less perfumed. His aftershave had fought a battle with the whisky fumes and lost. "I wondered if you might be free this evening? I know a charming little French restaurant, most discreet. . . ."

The prospect flashed before my eyes. We would sit by candlelight on a red plushy banquette in the furthest corner and he would press my hand stickily. Then he would move up till his leg pressed mine stickily. After that my mind blanked out in a self-protective, anti-sticky mechanism.

"I'm afraid I'm busy," I said, not as curtly as I would have done if the second half of the money his committee owed me had been stashed safely in my current account. It was craven of me, but I had my eye on a pair of boots not unlike the ones Belinda Fine was wearing and somehow I doubted that my bank manager would give me a loan for that kind of investment.

"Well, perhaps we could fix another date?" David Stronge insisted slurrily. I mean that literally; he was like slurry. "We haven't really had a chance to talk, have we, just you and I?"

The company was beginning to thin out. I looked around rather desperately for a way of escape and saw Sebastian Shaw, his fringe in tumbling mode, approaching us.

"Sebastian!" I called. "Over here! Sebastian has kindly offered to give me a lift," I explained to David Stronge.

"I would have been only too happy—" he began, thwarted.

"The race is to the swift, eh, David?" Sebastian said with commendable aplomb. "Do you have everything, Sam?"

"Yes, thank you." I buttoned up my jacket and held out my hand to David. "Lovely to see you again."

I wondered whether to say that I'd be in touch about my cheque. Then I looked at David Stronge's pouty, baffled expression and decided that this might not quite be the moment.

"You don't really have to give me a lift," I said to Sebastian when we were safely out in the hall. "It was just to get away from David."

"All you did was pre-empt me. I was going to offer anyway."

"Well, if you're sure. . . ."

We crossed the hall towards the Fine twins and their various escorts, who were milling round the revolving doors, Belinda's high, piercing voice ringing out over the rest of the babble. I paused by the reception desk so I could say goodnight to Bill; Sir Richard Fine was there already, talking in a lowered voice to his mate Henry. As he heard us approach he looked up, frowning.

"Shaw? Do me a favour, will you, there's a good man—look out the chappie who's supposed to be sitting here keeping an eye on things and tell him this just won't do?" He made a sweeping gesture to Bill's unoccupied chair. "Station unoccupied. This is simply not good enough."

"I won't be a moment," Sebastian said to me, striding quickly round the back of the desk. For a moment I stood there, unsure of what to do, and from the doors Suki Fine called out:

"Sebastian? Where are you off to?"

It looked as if they were coming to see. Poor Bill, if a whole group of them caught him in his back room with the whisky bottle in his hand. . . . I ducked behind the desk too, after Sebastian, concocting plausible excuses for Bill's absence as I went.

But Bill wasn't drinking whisky, nor was he in the back room. Sebastian had found him in the cubbyhole just behind the desk, a blank small room where rows of video monitors hummed away. He was sprawled on the floor, clutching his chest and gasping for breath. His face was bright red, his eyes blind with pain.

"*Jesus*—"

Hurriedly I knelt down to take his pulse. Sebastian, beside me, was already on the phone.

"Emergency," he was saying, "we need an ambulance at once to the Mowbray Steiner building, Broadgate . . . someone's having what looks like a heart attack. . . ."

I could hardly feel a pulse.

"Bill?" I said urgently. "Bill, can you hear me?"

His eyelids flickered. Suddenly he was looking straight at me.

"Sammy . . ." His voice was so faint I had to duck my head right over him to hear it. His breath smelt strongly of whisky, which surprised me; but I was trying to concentrate on what he was saying and pushed the thought back. "I can't do it any more . . . even if . . . he tells them . . . I can't do it. . . ."

"What, Bill? What can't you do?"

Sebastian was putting the phone down, and behind me I could hear voices, people clustering into the little room. Someone pressed at my back.

"What is it, does he need CPR?"

"Probably," I said over my shoulder, "just hang on a minute. . . ."

"Sammy?" Bill was saying urgently, his voice rising slightly, "Sammy, I want to tell you . . . tell you about it. . . ."

But they were pushing me aside. Someone bent over him, mouth over his, and started working at his chest, the movements eerily regular and controlled in contrast to the panic around us.

"Bill," I said hurriedly, "I'm still here, can you hear me?"

Bill half lifted his head. "I can't . . ." he said again, and then he caught sight of something straight ahead of him. His eyes widened and he clutched at his chest with one clawed hand. "I won't!" he repeated, his voice raised, as if he were talking to someone in particular. "I won't do it! You blood—blood—" The word tailed off with a horrible choking noise.

I whipped my head round to see the direction in which he had been looking. The room was full of people: Suki and Belinda Fine, their father, who was talking quickly to a tall, well-preserved man in his forties with a smooth cap of black hair, David Stronge craning his head to hear what they were saying, behind him Charles de Groot and James Rattray-Potter. More people were jostling in their wake, but these were the faces I saw, the ones I thought Bill would have seen. Crushed next to me, still working on Bill, was the other man who had been in the Fine group. Then the bodies started to fall back, pressing themselves against the wall, someone calling from outside: "The ambulance is here, they're coming through. . . ."

Despite the cramped space, the paramedics managed to heave Bill onto a stretcher and out the door, one of them keeping up an automatic stream of "Out of the way, 'scuse me, move please, out of the way. . . ." I stood in the doorway of the cubbyhole, now cleared as if a wind had blown everyone back into the hall to gawp at the spectacle of poor Bill *in extremis*, and found that I was wrapping my arms around myself.

"Did you know him well?" Sebastian Shaw said. I had forgotten that he was in the room.

"He's not dead yet," I said curtly. Then I remembered that it had been Sebastian who had rung for the ambulance, and calmed down a little. "Not really well, no. But we talked a lot when I was putting the mobile together. He was a real help. Poor Bill. I never knew he had a bad heart."

"He drank a bit, didn't he?"

"A drop in his tea every now and then. Nothing much."

Sebastian was an employee of the bank, after all. It was useless to deny that Bill liked his whisky, but to cover his back I could minimise his drinking as much as possible.

"We'd better go," he said. "There's nothing more to do here."

"Someone should ring his daughter—"

"Sir Richard's already sent David to do it."

I grimaced.

"Why did it have to be him?"

"That's what David's for. Things no one else wants to do."

The hall was full of people, eyes excited, discussing what had happened in voices artificially lowered to denote respect for someone who might be dying; I was sure that most of them didn't even know Bill's name. They were like the crowds who collect round a car accident, peering ghoulishly at the police cars and ambulance, soaking up the worst details to give their friends the shudders. I walked straight through them and out the door without looking back. Outside the building the evening was warmer than it had been in the air-conditioned bank, and though the sun had set the sky was still light, a rich lavender-blue smudged with mauve.

"Where do you need to go?" Sebastian said, catching me up.

"Just Farringdon."

"Is that where you live? I mean, would you rather I took you home?"

I shook my head. "It's OK, thanks. I'm going to meet a friend for a drink, which is probably just what I need."

"Well, if you're sure. . . ."

We were walking round the side of the building now, towards the car park. The scale of the walls on either side of us was dwarfing; I could hear the humming of the giant electricity plant which ran the computers, the lights, the air conditioning. . . . From this angle, its industrial-sized machinery whirring away, Mowbray Steiner resembled a factory, which, in a way, it was. The car park, at the back of the building, was almost as well lit as the atrium, and so full of expensive machines that it looked like a car showroom in Berkeley Square. Sebastian stood back politely to let me pass through the barrier before him and then led the way to a navy BMW. Clicking off the alarm, he opened the door for me. The car smelt of leather and polish.

"You shouldn't open doors for me, you know," I said sarcastically. "I'm not suitably appreciative." Then I took a deep breath and told myself to lighten up: what had happened to Bill was scarcely Sebastian's fault.

Nor was there anything I could do to help Bill now. "Sorry," I said in a more reasonable voice. "I'm still a little tense."

He shot me a quick glance, shut the door nonetheless and went round to his side, swinging in his long legs.

"Nothing to apologise for," he said easily. "It wasn't much fun for anyone. Poor man. I hope he pulls through."

He inserted the key into the ignition but didn't turn it. I realised that he was waiting to see if I wanted to talk about Bill.

"I wish I knew what he was trying to tell me," I said slowly, grateful for Sebastian's thoughtfulness.

"I didn't hear. Was it important?"

"I don't know. Maybe. Because he was so desperately trying to talk, and you could see how much it was hurting him."

"You can go to see him in hospital as soon as he's a bit better, and ask him. He probably won't even remember what it was about. Some silly thing that was on his mind just before he had the attack. I know it's a cliché, but the mind does play strange tricks."

"He seemed to be looking at someone. Accusing them."

Sebastian stared at me. "Who?"

"I don't know. I couldn't tell. One of the people who was in the room."

"But that's just not possible. He must have been seeing things."

Perhaps he was right, but I didn't think so. Still, there was no point discussing this with him. I put it aside to mull over later.

"OK." I shook my head as if emerging from deep water and turned to look at him for the first time since we'd got into the car. "Thanks. I'm making too much of it."

"Shall we go?" He sounded relieved, and started up the motor at once. It purred with smooth content, like a glossy, well-fed cat; my van was a ragged, mangy old dustbin scavenger in comparison. "Do you drive?" he said, clearly wanting to leave the subject.

A weight was rolling off my shoulders. I relaxed back in the ridiculously comfortable seat. "Yes, I have a little Ford van. Red. Not really big enough now I'm making these huge mobiles. I was wondering whether I should spend some of the Mowbray Steiner money on a Transit or something, but they're so unwieldy for driving around town, don't you think?"

He slanted a glance at me, seemingly aware that I was teasing him.

"Where exactly in Farringdon am I taking you?" he said mildly.

"The *Herald* building, just up from the Clerkenwell Road. I'm meeting a friend of mine who works there."

"On the newspaper?"

"That's right. Not something I imagine that people read much in your circles."

He kept his eyes on the road.

"What do you want me to say, Sam?" he said with a touch of asperity. "No, actually, we do take the *Herald* and similar left-wing rags at the bank, but only when we run out of toilet paper?"

"OK, I was winding you up," I said meekly. "I expect I wanted to see if you felt guilty."

"If I was going to crawl to you, you mean. Oh, no, I always read the *Herald*. I don't really fit into this kind of life, I'm too sensitive to be a banker. I'm only doing this job to save up enough money so I can retire and fulfil myself by writing a deep and meaningful novel about the state of the world. . . ."

I was laughing. "All right," I admitted, "you've made your point."

"Are you sure? I like my job, you know. I don't have to defend it."

"All *right*. I said you'd made your point."

"Here we are." He pulled up outside the *Herald* building so smoothly I hardly noticed we'd stopped. Riding in that car was like being insulated from the world; almost noiseless, watching the streets flitting past in lofty unconcern. I was reluctant to get out, and not just because it meant leaving the car.

"I hope you're noticing that I didn't get out to open the door for you," he said. "I can take a hint. Look, this may be appalling timing, but would you like to have dinner with me sometime?"

He said this all in a rush, as if he had been nerving himself up for it. There was a second's pause, then I said: "Oh. OK," and kicked myself at once for not having responded with something a touch more suave and articulate.

"Good. I'll try not to take you anywhere that would offend your sensibilities," he said. "Would Tuesday suit you?"

"Fine. I'll give you my number."

He produced a leather diary with gold corners and opened it to the current week. I detached its little gold pencil and scribbled down my number. Then I swung my legs out of the car, keeping them together in an elegant, Kensington modelling school getting-out-of-Porsche kind of way. The occasion seemed to warrant it.

"I'll give you a ring Tuesday morning to confirm," he said, and then paused for a moment. "Will you be all right? Are you sure you don't want a lift home?"

"No, I'm fine now. But thanks. I'll ring the hospital in a little while and see how Bill's doing."

He nodded.

"See you soon."

The car pulled away and I stood looking after it for a moment in a sort of stupor. What on earth had I just done? Still, he seemed to know what he was getting into. I turned and went up the steps of the

Herald building, quite unable to work out what I felt. Which is unusual for me.

. . .

Tim was already waiting for me in the Cap and Barrel, an undistinguished little pub in the tangle of backstreets between the *Herald* building and the Clerkenwell Road. Set on a corner, its frontage jutted out as pugnaciously as an out-thrust jaw, and the atmosphere inside could be fairly similar at times. There was a much smarter pub right next to the *Herald*, with stripped pine floors, high green-painted stools and descriptions of fashionable snacks chalked on to blackboards propped against the walls, but Tim had never been in there. He cocked his nose and said disparagingly that it was full of journalists.

I saw Tim as soon as I walked in the door; tall and thin, with a face all bones and angles, he was hard to miss. He was wearing a big navy sweater, a faded shirt showing at the collar, and looked, as always, reassuringly reliable. I was aware how much easier my life would be if I could only fall in love with Tim; he'd already made it clear that he would be happy to take me on, and we'd make such a perfect media couple. We'd have an artistically decorated flat in Islington, from which I could commute to my studio, and Tim would take a sabbatical every now and then to write a piercingly incisive book about Labour Party policy or the State of the Nation which would immediately become recommended reading on every politics and sociology degree course in the country. We would holiday in Spain or Italy and perhaps in time even buy a cottage in a little village we had discovered in the Algarve. . . .

I shuddered. What a nightmare.

Sitting with Tim were a couple of women, a study in contrasts. One was perfectly turned out in an orange suit which looked wonderful against her dark skin, her short, very curly hair cut tightly to her head to accentuate the lovely shape of her skull. Small diamond earrings glistened in the dark brown lobes of her ears and around her throat was tied a silk scarf; she looked like an illustration from an Hermès catalogue. The second woman was an image of the first, only enlarged and lightened on a poor-quality photocopier. Her pale blue tailored suit did her no favours. Something looser in navy would have been kinder to her complexion, not to mention her figure. Her long, rather straggly brown hair was held back with a velvet Alice band, classic Sloane style: which was odd, because she didn't look like a Sloane.

"Sam!" Tim got up to kiss me as I arrived at the table. "This is Anne-Marie, our City editor"—he indicated the orange suit—"and this is Jordan, her deputy, the diary editor."

We all made polite greeting noises.

"I've talked to you on the phone," I said to Anne-Marie, "but you probably don't remember. Tim put me through and you let me pick your brains."

"I must have been feeling generous that day," she said, smiling deliberately at Tim. "Or someone persuaded me very convincingly."

"You got my note, then?" he said to me as I pulled up a stool and sat down.

"No problem. I even remembered where the pub was without having to ask."

"Unfortunately we've landed next to the worst elements from the Sunday magazine," Tim said, nodding his head at the group at the next table. "They're famed for general dissoluteness and degeneracy, and they seem to be doing their best to live down to their collective reputation."

I glanced over, not that I needed to look; the sheer volume of noise they were making was enough to confirm what Tim had said.

"Seems like fun," I said.

"If you like that kind of thing," said Anne-Marie superciliously. I was beginning to think that whatever category of thing Anne-Marie liked did not include myself.

"Look," Tim said, gesturing at a bottle of champagne in a plastic ice bucket on the table. "In honour of your opening." I hadn't noticed it before. It was easy to see that I was still upset. He looked at me hard, picking this up at once. "There's something wrong, isn't there? What is it?"

Briefly I told them about Bill. Everyone reacted differently: Jordan made gushing sympathetic noises, Tim squeezed my hand and Anne-Marie raised her eyebrows and stared, with the air of someone who is above mere news of births or deaths, at the opposite wall.

"Do you want me to take you home?" Tim said, letting go of my hand rather reluctantly. I felt Anne-Marie's stare snap off the wall and fix on to the side of my head, willing me to refuse.

"No, I'm OK, thanks. Might as well get drunk in company." I nodded meaningfully at the champagne bottle.

Tim promptly took the hint.

"To Sam, who's just got her first sculpture on public display," he announced, filling our glasses. "Congratulations!"

We all drank. Anne-Marie asked me where the sculpture was hanging and on hearing the name of Mowbray Steiner expressed interest in me for the first time.

"Did you meet the head of dealing?" she said. "Marcus Samson? He's supposed to be in line for a knighthood. My money's on him to get the top job when Richard Fine leaves."

"No, the only person I met on the trading floor was a noxious specimen called James Rattray-something. Potter, I think. I doubt you'd know him."

Anne-Marie crinkled her brow. At least I assumed this was what she was doing, as her skin was so dark and smooth it was impossible to see if any lines were forming.

"No, never heard of him," she said. "What about you, Jordan?"

"No, Anne-Marie," Jordan said obsequiously. She seemed to have all the personality of a turnip.

"You wouldn't want to, either," I said, dismissing Mr. Rattray-Potter. "Porcine is all too mild a word to describe him."

"Well, all that means is he's not your type," Jordan said with unexpected spirit.

I stared at her. She looked so nervous at having spoken up that I didn't have the heart to say anything but "You're right, I suppose," and was rewarded with a grateful smile. After that, seeming to have scared herself by her own daring, she retreated into a suitably turnip-like silence and scarcely said a word for the rest of the evening. Tim picked up the bottle and poured out more champagne for everyone.

"I met his daughters," I offered. "Sir Richard's, I mean."

"Oh really?" Anne-Marie raised her eyebrows. "That's a wild pair of girls, they say. Spoilt rotten. The mother walked out on him years ago and left them to their own devices. Apparently—"

I slipped away from the table, leaving Anne-Marie holding forth, and found the payphone in a cramped little nook beside the toilets. It took me a while to get through to someone at the hospital who could tell me how Bill was; they kept putting me on hold till I felt like slamming the phone against the wall. And when a female voice did finally tell me, I still felt like slamming the phone against the wall. It wasn't good news, she was afraid. She was sorry to inform me that Bill had died twenty minutes after arrival. She sounded even less interested in the subject than Anne-Marie had been.

3

"Tim and I were actually supposed to be going out to dinner, but it never happened. I couldn't face being on my own with him, because I knew he'd want to have a sympathetic talk, perish the thought. So I drowned my sorrows and we ended up staying at the pub till closing time, when someone from the Sunday magazine, which is a rough lot if ever I've met one—they probably crack stones between their teeth to sharpen them in their spare time—said why didn't we go to the pub a few streets down, because it was having a lock-in. Only we had to run across there before they closed the doors, which was a bit frantic, and Anne-Marie and Jordan, the business section people, didn't come with us, because, as Anne-Marie made very clear in a snotty way, they obviously thought it was a sad, sordid thing to do. Which I must admit it was. The second pub turned out to be a really squalid dive, the kind of place hardened drunks without homes go to. So of course we fitted in perfectly. There was a coven of girls in particular who were almost too much fun. We stayed till about two o'clock, when the landlord finally kicked us out, and then this girl who looked like Louise Brooks fell over in the doorway as she was leaving and ripped her trousers on the pavement and got very upset. She wouldn't move, she just lay there on her face, moaning: 'Oh God, I can't bear to look, I heard them tear and they're from Agnès B, oh no, why me, why now, it's all gone horribly wrong. . . .' Her friends had to haul her up and take her back with them. It was like a white trash version of *Absolutely Fabulous*. Poor

Tim, I hardly talked to him all evening. I wouldn't even let him give me a lift—I got a taxi home, now I'm rich for ten minutes."

"So it was a good evening, then? Apart from that poor man."

"Apart from him. Every time I think about it I feel so—so—"

One of the nice things about Janey was that she let you finish your own sentences.

"Frustrated," I said at last.

"Because of what he said to you?"

"Mmm."

"'I can't do it, even if he tells them. . . .'"

"'I can't do it any more,'" I corrected. "Meaning that he'd done it at least once already."

"'Even if he tells them . . .' what? It could be: 'Even if he tells them it's all right.'"

"Even if he tells who it's all right?"

Janey pulled a face. "Let me think. It could all be so innocent, you know: 'I can't let the cleaners go early, even if their supervisor tells them it's all right.' See?"

"God, you have a real gift for the mundane. Have you thought of writing a sitcom for Channel 4?"

"Easy, now. Don't mock the hand that feeds—"

"On itself?"

I was round at Janey's flat for dinner. She was my one really successful friend, a script editor working on a comedy series which was in the middle of filming but wasn't going too well, according to Janey, who on the subject of her work would have made Eeyore look like the Jolly Green Giant. Fortunately the evening was tête-à-tête, as Janey's awful girlfriend Helen was away filming a processed cheese commercial. I had been surprised to hear this; it was hard to imagine that Helen would have been considered sophisticated enough for the product.

I forked up some more ravioli with gusto. Janey was an excellent cook.

"This is delicious, by the way."

"Oh, it's from Marks and Spencer's. I couldn't be fagged to make anything."

Janey looked tired, but as pretty as ever. She was a classic English rose: big blue eyes and fair, fine skin which was already creased with a thousand tiny lines. Her long hair was pulled to the nape of her neck but strands hung down randomly around her face as they always did, even just after she had pinned them back.

"Are you seeing much of Tom at the moment?" she asked.

I shook my head. "He hasn't forgiven me yet."

Tom, a large and shambling not-very-successful poet, was one of my best friends, or he had been till the Incident.

"For what?" Janey said, surprised.

"Oh, I haven't told you!" I ate the last ravioli and washed it down with some red wine. "You know he always goes for these little blonde Bambi-looking girls, sort of helpless and fragile, right? Well, we were at a party and I told him one of my blonde jokes, and instead of pissing himself with laughter, as he usually does, he came over all austere and said he didn't think it was terribly amusing to make fun of something as superficial as other people's hair colour. You can imagine how well that went down with me. So when I noticed he was looking at this girl across the room in a rather soppy way, I said vindictively: 'Wasn't she the model on the Anaemia Research Society's fund-raising poster?' To which he snapped that I was too bogged down in a cynical sinkhole of my own making to be able to appreciate the pure and innocent charms of Alice, and then shot off and parked himself beside her for the rest of the evening. Someone else told me that he'd met her at a poetry reading a couple of weeks before and they'd been inseparable ever since."

"Tom couldn't really have said that about the cynical sinkhole," Janey objected.

"I swear to God. Alice has had a bad effect on his metaphors already. Just think what he'll be writing after a couple of months with her."

I poured myself another glass of wine. "There was something else he said, Janey."

"Tom?"

"No, Bill, the security guard. It was after the other stuff. He seemed to be looking at someone who had come into the room, and he said: 'I won't do it, you blood—' "

"Blood what? Bloody?"

"No. I know this is going to sound strange, but I think it was 'bloodsucker.' "

" 'Bloodsucker'?" Janey repeated. "As in blackmailer?"

"I know it sounds ridiculous. Everyone in that room was really well off—chairman of the bank, his daughters, a couple of directors and so on. The idea of one of them blackmailing a security guard is ludicrous."

"It's not enough to go on, is it?" Janey looked at me, frowning. "Sam, stop worrying about this, OK? A friend of yours is dead and you're upset. But there's nothing you can do. You don't have the faintest idea what he was talking about or who he was looking at."

"I know," I said gloomily.

"So leave it alone for once in your life. It's a storm in a teacup. The man was dying, for goodness' sake. Things come into your head when you're dying that have nothing to do with what's going on around you." She adjusted the gauzy scarf tangled round her neck, her hands as round and plump as a cupid's on a fresco. "Now I'm going to change the subject to stop you sinking into a pit of morbidness. Tell me which blonde joke, exactly, you regaled Tom with? Just out of interest."

I coughed guiltily. "You know I don't consider you a blonde, Janey, not deep down, I mean. Intellectually you're definitely a brunette—"

"Just tell me the joke, you pathetic coward."

I said unhappily: "How does a blonde turn the light on after sex?"

She shook her head, blue eyes wide and ingenuous; Janey was about as innocent as Mae West, but you'd never tell from looking at her.

"Well, um . . . she opens the car door."

"Right. For that you can wash the pans."

"But you made me tell you!" I protested. "It's not fair. . . ."

My voice tailed off. Janey fiddled with one of the several necklaces she was wearing and gave me a small knowing smile.

"Hang on a minute," I said, "if you bought the food from M&S there are no pans, right?"

The smile grew larger.

"Got you," she said.

. . .

I hadn't told Janey about Sebastian Shaw's dinner invitation. This was not an attempt to protect her sensibilities; Janey wasn't one of those lesbians who thinks that having sex with the male species is a betrayal of the female one, roughly equatable with the heinous crime of wearing black lace underwear and painting your toenails. I told myself that the reason I hadn't confided in her was because it would doubtless all come to nothing, but of course it was really because I was embarrassed about going on a date with a merchant banker in a suit. It all seemed so . . . *grown-up*, somehow.

Lunch with Duggie, however, was very successful. I met him, as requested, in his gallery, which he co-owned with his ex-boyfriend, Willie. Their tastes clashed appallingly, which was the point; the two of them fought like cat and dog and enjoyed themselves tremendously in the process. I caught the bus to Oxford Circus and strolled down Old Bond Street, basking in the sun and pretending that I was a lady who lunched, which made me think of Suki Fine for a moment. This was one of the few streets left in England where expensively coiffured women with their faces tacked up tightly over their bones dared to wear their furs without looking over their shoulders nervously for activist vegans armed with cans of red paint and nasty scowls.

The Wellington Gallery was something of a contrast to all the jewellers' shops I had just passed, their windows crammed to the gills with shiny baubles for rich men to give their mistresses as consolation prizes for not marrying them. Duggie's gallery was large and white and practically empty, apart from some giant oil paintings of plumbers' wrenches in lurid colours and a new assistant, a supercilious young man in a pale green suit and white *faux* crocodile loafers who was leaning against a desk as I entered and managed to sneer at me without moving a muscle. I was impressed; I had worked in a gallery for myself for a while and had always had to *do* something physically to convey disapproval.

"I'm here to see Duggie," I said. His features stayed in absolutely the same position, and yet the sneer intensified. I was watching a Zen master at work.

"Do you have an appointment?" he asked, garnishing the question with a veneer of politeness which I knew he had applied simply in order to strip it away when I hung my head and admitted I didn't.

"Yes, actually, he's taking me out to lunch. I'm Sam Jones. You must be new here," I added sweetly.

For a second his eyes tightened into slits and his mouth puffed out like someone having an allergic reaction. Then he pushed himself away from the desk and swivelled towards me, his smile as thin as if I'd just cut it into his face with a Stanley knife.

"Lovely to meet you," he said. "I'm Adrian. You do those fabulous mobiles, don't you? I've heard *all* about you."

"That's right."

"I'll just buzz Duggie, shall I? He didn't tell me he was busy for lunch, the naughty thing."

Now that it was closer to mine I could see that Adrian's face was preternaturally smooth. I wondered if he depilated his facial hair. Leaning elegantly over the desk, he pressed a button on the speakerphone and said when Duggie answered:

"It's Ms. Jones to see you, Duggie, your lunch appointment. Shall I ring ahead to the restaurant?"

He picked up the telephone. "Lucky it's Monday," he said to me confidingly, "they'll have a table. They would for Duggie anyway, but I think it's better to ring, don't you?"

Duggie emerged from his office at this point, wreathed in smiles. Due to the exigency of the season, he had changed the corduroy trousers he wore in winter for a pair of linen ones in roughly the same shade of dirty beige, and the waistcoat was slub silk rather than velvet. But the tweed jacket was unchanging, a secure point in a spinning world.

"Sam and I have been having a fascinating conversation," said Adrian, which I thought was pushing it a bit. But he was overridden by Duggie's exclamation of "Sam, *darling!*" as he hurried towards me. Duggie's feet were a little too small for his round, sturdy body; he always seemed to be on the verge of toppling over. "*What* a success Friday night was!" he went on. "I can't *wait* to get some photos done. I'm trying to book Tony at the moment, but you know how busy he is."

"Oh, Tony would be *wonderful,*" said Adrian in sycophantic tones. Duggie ignored him completely.

"And they all seemed terribly happy, didn't they? What a bunch of suits, though, darling! And not even *clean*, some of them—did you see that man from the committee with all the dandruff?" He shuddered theatrically. "Well, shall we be off?"

"I booked you a table at Luigi's, Duggie," Adrian said, a slight note of entreaty now entering his voice.

"What?" Duggie said. "Oh, good, good. Come on, my dear. What a lovely suit."

It was in fact my blue linen one with the short sleeves and equally abbreviated skirt, which I had rejected for the Mowbray Steiner cocktail party. I must have bought it at a very thin point in my life, doubtless a long-forgotten moment of heartbreak; it was so snug that if I ate anything more than a starter salad for lunch the seams, currently being tested to breaking point, would promptly burst under the extra pressure. Still, it looked good, which was really all that mattered. Duggie bustled me out the door. Safely on the street he turned to me and pulled a face.

"Frightful, isn't he? Smarmy little creep. But Willie adores him. He only does it to spite me; he knows perfectly well I like them more rugged. Bastard. He hired him in my absence, would you believe? *Pale green suits*, my God. And *Adrian*, what kind of name is that?"

"What kind of name would you prefer, Duggie?"

We had turned on to Old Bond Street now. Duggie bustled through the arcade, casting a wistful glance at the chocolate shop where each truffle cost as much as if it had been personally hand rolled by a member of the royal family.

"*Love* that place," he said, "but it's *too* wicked. What were you saying, sweetie? Oh. Boys." He looked even more wistful. "Brad would be nice," he said. "Or Chuck. American, ideally, but *not* a preppie. I prefer beach-boy looks. Rugged. Brawny. I love all those Australian boys on the soaps, but their *accent*, darling. We couldn't have one in the gallery. The clients wouldn't stand for it."

We had reached an Italian restaurant on the corner of Dover Street, shaded by a large apple-green canopy, which looked light and fresh and welcoming. Duggie ushered me through the door, tenderly kissed someone who was presented to me as Luigi, and sat down at a street-side table with an air of satisfaction. The sliding doors were open on to the pavement, the air on our faces warm and only slightly tinged with car exhaust. A queue of people waiting to be seated fixed us immediately with hostile stares, none of which were a patch on Adrian's. The tables were crammed into the small space tighter than battery chickens in a cage, and the menus Luigi duly brought us were so big and floppy that before I could get mine under control I had slapped the woman sitting next to me across the face with it twice.

"I'm on a diet, darling," Duggie said firmly to Luigi. "I could hardly get into my summer trousers this year. So I'll just have the fried mozzarella to start and the crab and leek risotto for a main course. And we'll have a bottle of Pinot Grigio. White all right with you, Sam?"

I nodded, frantically scanning the menu for something that looked as if it wouldn't argue too vehemently with the seams of my skirt. I picked a rocket salad to start and linguine with clams (starter size) to follow and spent the next hour trying not to salivate too obviously as I enviously watched every mouthful of Duggie's food being shovelled on to his fork. Despite his conspicuous consumption, he kept up a constant stream of chatter. I had long since learnt with Duggie not to bother saying anything unless it was absolutely necessary.

He had plans to give me an exhibition early next year; I must hurry up and start working for it now. We could get one really large mobile in the window, and then perhaps some smaller pieces in the side room? Up to me, of course, but since the mobiles seemed to be going down so well, maybe we'd better stick with those, didn't I think? Also, of course, we would have photographs of "Floating Planet." And he had a possible client who he wanted to take to see it *in situ*. Strike while the iron's hot. And talking of which, who was that *divine* young man I was chatting to at the opening? Yes, Luigi, dearest, he *would* like a tiramisù, wasn't he a naughty thing! What about me? Was I *sure?* What willpower!

By the time Duggie had scraped the last trail of mascarpone and flaked chocolate into his mouth, I was a nervous wreck who could think only about how much I wanted to eat something stuffed full of big juicy calories. That would teach me to buy clothes so exiguous that they only fitted me when I inhaled deeply and pulled my stomach in. As soon as I got home I stripped off the bloody suit, threw it petulantly across the room and then hacked free the Mars bar ice cream which I had been keeping at the back of the freezer for a special occasion. Half the stalactites in the freezer came out with it too, thus unbalancing the rather fetching icy jaws of death effect I had been cultivating in there for a while, but chocolate came before aesthetics. It was so wonderful that I had to restrain myself from eating the wrapper as well.

4

If Sebastian Shaw had been one of the kind of men I usually went out with—which category, incidentally, did not include policemen; Hawkins was very much a freak incident—I would have known roughly what to wear, where we would go and what we would do on our first date. If it went on classic lines, it would centre round Camden and comprise a drink or two at some small, trendy pub like the Crown and Goose, followed by a pizza or Chinese on Parkway and then, perhaps, a club. After that events would be left to our joint discretion. Even if for some strange reason we met up in Islington instead, say, or even the area non-Camdenites called central London (I'm not insular; I'm *selective*), the pattern would usually be the same, though perhaps with the inclusion of an arty foreign film.

But Sebastian was a Creature From Another World, the Man From Planet Suit, and all normal bets were off. For example, he actually rang when he'd said he would. I used my best cool voice on the phone, letting a trace of surprise shade through it when he identified himself and then catching it back at once. (Goodness, his voice was nice.) Yes, I was still free for dinner. (I tried to imply that this was due more to chance than to design.) About eight? Fine. No, I didn't really want to meet in South Kensington. (Gagging gesture performed at this point.) St. Christopher's Place sounded lovely. In the bar? OK, see you at eight.

I put the phone down and wondered if I had just made a horrible mistake—the mention of South Kensington had been pretty unsettling—but of course I was being much too cocky. I had forgotten how attractive Sebastian Shaw actually was.

. . .

The sun had just set as I got off the bus and walked down Oxford Street and the air was still warm and clinging, the sky that colour which in the 1920s they called ashes of roses. In London, with its myriad artificial lights burning all night long, the sky never went completely black. An hour or so before dawn it would be an even deeper mauve—cinders of roses, perhaps—till the sun started to streak it once more with gold. I should know. I had seen it rise more times than I could count.

The shops were shut now, the streets already quiet. Nearing Selfridges I ducked right into St. Christopher's Place, a narrow alleyway off Oxford Street which once, years ago, had been a backwater filled with antique shops—Japanese print galleries, war memorabilia, even a button emporium—and now was Designer Clothes Central. Halfway down it was a pretty little square and across this was the restaurant, tables spilling out over its steps and into the square with almost Continental abandon. I managed to work out that the bar had a separate entrance, but not that you pulled the two-inch-thick plate-glass doors instead of pushing them. Cursing, I reversed the procedure, nearly cutting my hand on the artistic wrought-iron handle, and finally made it in. Sebastian was already sitting at the bar; I hoped he hadn't noticed my pratfall. Suki Fine doubtless always had a man in tow expressly to avoid the do-I-push-or-pull dilemma.

"Sam!" He stood up when he saw me. I really had forgotten how good-looking he was. All the women in the bar, and quite a few of the men, had probably been staring at him wistfully for the past twenty minutes. I knew this assumption was correct when several heads turned to see who he was meeting; I just hoped they weren't thinking "*Her?*" in disbelief. Remembering how tall he was, I had put on my black suede boots with three-inch heels, a little black shift dress which made me look taller, all my hair, not just random bits of it, up (ditto) and a pearl choker which hopefully continued the resemblance to Audrey Hepburn. (I had just seen *Breakfast at Tiffany's* again and was currently obsessed by her.) I had regretfully discarded elbow-length black gloves as being rather OTT for a first date.

"You look lovely," he said with flattering emphasis. "Would you like a drink?"

"*Oh* yes." I hadn't struggled through those bar doors to refuse a cocktail on the other side. I settled myself on a bar stool and said "A White Lady, please" to the barman. My eyes met Sebastian's in the mirror behind the bar. This was what dates should be like, I thought; why didn't I always meet handsome men in American-style cocktail bars with high stools on which I could sit and cross my legs in a becoming and sophisticated sort of way?

"Did you have a nice dinner the other night?" I asked. "After you dropped me off, I mean."

"No, nothing special. Apart from the fact that James got very drunk again. Did you meet him?"

"The one who looks like a big pink pig?"

He grinned. "That'll be James. Well, we went to a Chinese restaurant in South Ken and they gave us one of those tables with the bit you can turn in the middle, you know, so you can all get at the food. And James just started spinning the wretched thing till the soy sauce fell off and splashed all over Charles. He nearly took a swing at James. Me and Minor practically had to hold him back."

"Minor?" I said.

"Oh, it's just a silly nickname from school. Simon's the younger brother, you see. We always used to call him Minor, and it just stuck."

"And what did you call the older brother?"

"You called him Grenville Major, sir," Sebastian said, grimacing. "And you were quick about it."

"Not a nice piece of work, I take it. I feel sorry for Minor."

"You needn't be. He's doing very well for himself: he got all the brains and Thomas—that's the older one—only got the brawn. Thomas went to agricultural college and is currently making a hell of a mess of the family estates while Simon's on a nice healthy whack at Mowbray's."

A thought occurred to me. This does happen sometimes.

"Is Simon the one who gave Bill the mouth-to-mouth resuscitation? He looked like he knew what he was doing."

"Oh, Minor's one of those quiet, competent types. Doesn't do anything unless he means it, and doesn't talk about it afterwards."

"You make him sound like a minor character in *Beau Geste*. Pith helmet, khaki shorts and a stiff upper lip."

"I don't think they wore pith helmets in *Beau Geste*, did they?"

"Don't be pedantic."

I grinned at him and found that he was already looking at me, laughter in his eyes. The gaze held for a long slow moment; then, as if remembering his duties as host of the evening, Sebastian looked at his watch and said, clearing his throat:

"Shall we go through and get something to eat?"

We went through into the restaurant, which was positively welcoming without being old-fashioned: yellow tablecloths and orange napkins and cherrywood panelling hung with great colourful Gauguin imitations. I hated those minimalist eateries with bare white walls, three-legged steel tables and chairs with holes in unexpected places;

portions might be bigger now, by popular demand, but the atmosphere made it impossible for you to settle in and get cosy. The only people who could date successfully in that kind of place were architects.

We ordered, Sebastian mercifully taking it upon himself to choose the wine. He picked something Australian which was supposed to be rather special. It was OK. I'm more a wine box kind of person. The waiter brought us a basket of assorted breads with a little glass bowl of olive oil to dip them into; I took some sun-dried tomato bread and bit into it. It went nicely with the wine, anyway.

The waiter withdrew, and suddenly I felt a little on edge. Sitting opposite Sebastian so formally, both of us dressed up (yes, he was wearing a suit) and on our best behaviour, made me want to wriggle in my chair and start picking my fingernails. I was saved by some basic remnants of good manners which reminded me that it was considered polite to ask people about themselves; I fired off various questions about his life to date, to which he responded with matching formality. Father a vicar, mother a housewife, education Rugby and Bristol (history degree), offered a job at Mowbray Steiner from university and never looked back. This was all fairly daunting, but it got us through our first course, and the food was delicious. If Suki Fine could produce half as good a soup as my tomato bisque with beetroot chips, I'd take back anything nasty I ever thought about her.

"Also Minor turned out to be at Mowbray's too," Sebastian was saying as the waiter cleared our plates. "I hadn't seen him since school, but we always got on very well. Played some cricket together," he added with a modesty which probably meant that he had captained the first eleven. "It was nice to see him again. He'd been there for a year and he rather showed me the ropes."

"And then you met Suki and Belinda?"

"All that lot, yes. Simon's known the girls for years."

"Is that the crowd you usually hang out with?" I asked, curious for any little tidbits of information about the people who had been in the room when Bill had made his accusation.

Sebastian, rather surprising, pulled a face. "You mean the people you met on Friday? I expect so, yes. Proximity, you see. I've got other friends, of course, but it tends to be easier to arrange things with people you see every day at work. Charles sits at the next desk to me and I've known Minor for years, so you see how it is. . . ."

"And James?"

"James just pushed his way in, basically, and it would take much more effort than any of us are prepared to expend to get rid of him again. He's an awful snob. I'm pretty small fry, but Charles is some kind of Dutch count and Minor's family own half of Yorkshire. Then there are the girls, of course. One can't underestimate the benefits of hanging around with the boss's daughters."

He said all this with a sarcastic inflection that I liked. The fringe had fallen forward over his forehead again and his grey-blue eyes were gleaming almost maliciously.

"James's real name, by the way, is just Potter," he added. "He decided it wasn't posh enough for the kind of circles he wanted to move in, so he called himself Rattray-Potter instead."

"God. I must say he didn't go down that well with me."

"You thought he was like a big pink pig. I remember. Well, unless you happen to find big pink pigs attractive—"

"Not desperately."

He grinned at me again. His teeth were clean and white without being as ostentatious as Charles de Groot's. Our main course arrived, on colourful, hand-painted plates that I immediately coveted. Not much point having nice plates when your idea of gourmet cooking is scrambled eggs, however.

"And what about the girls? Are Belinda and Charles an item?" I tucked into my filo cheese parcel, reflecting that other people are always a good neutral conversation topic. Besides, I had to admit to a sneaking interest in how Sebastian would refer to Suki Fine.

"You like to gossip, don't you?" Sebastian pushed back his fringe, raking his fingers through his hair to make it stay in place. "Belinda and Charles are going out, yes. I don't know how serious it is. Suki's rather aloof from that sort of thing. Loads of suitors but I don't think she lowers herself to consort with them. Belinda's just your typical spoilt rich girl, the kind who marries well. I don't know what Suki wants out of life. She was like Belinda years and years ago, maybe even worse. Then she got a shock and cleaned up her act. I think she's come to a bit of a dead end, doesn't know quite what to do with herself."

"She cooks, doesn't she?"

Sebastian shrugged. "They all do these cooking courses, these girls, that or dressmaking. Gives them something to do. Makes a change from shopping, I suppose. I don't think she has any intention of taking it seriously."

I grimaced. To me that kind of life sounded like something out of *The Wasteland*.

Head bent, fiddling as if absent-mindedly with his fork, Sebastian said hesitantly:

"Look, tell me if you don't want to talk about this, but I was just wondering whether—well, I assume you know about Bill. You said you were going to ring the hospital. I haven't seen you since, um, we heard the news."

"Yes. It's odd, but I was somehow assuming that he was going to die, though I know people pull through this kind of thing, and he wasn't that old. There was something about the way he looked—not that I know anything about it."

"And what he was trying to say to you? Have you worked that out?"

I shook my head. "I did ring his daughter, to see if he'd said anything to her, but she didn't get to the hospital in time. Poor girl."

"It was probably nothing at all."

"I'm not so sure. But I was talking about it to a friend of mine and she immediately invented something totally banal that would fit in with most of what he'd said." I didn't want him to think that the mystery surrounding Bill's heart attack was still on my mind; I hardly knew him, after all. And he was friendly with most of the people who had been in that room, maybe with the person Bill had been talking to. So I gave him my best limpid, suspicion-free stare instead. "I'm not worrying about it any more, if that's what you mean."

"It was, actually. I just wanted to make sure you were OK, in my clumsy sort of way."

"Thanks."

By now we had drunk enough wine to make us considerably more relaxed with each other. Cunningly pinching a ploy I had used earlier, Sebastian not only asked me about myself but managed to look interested in the answers. We had barely scratched the surface of that fascinating subject when I suddenly realised that it was the end of the meal and the waiter was saying:

"Can I bring you anything else?"

"Just the bill, thanks," Sebastian said.

When it came, he slipped a silver credit card into the folder and handed it straight back to the waiter. I felt just like a kept woman.

"Look," I said, "how much is it? I mean—"

"This is on me, Sam. I asked you out."

"Well, I'll get the next one."

"Oh," he said with a joking inflection, "you mean you want to see me again?"

I looked up to find him watching me with an almost vulnerable expression on his face which belied the lightness of his voice. His eyes were very wide and grey. I had the sudden urge to lean across the table, grab his tie, pull him towards me and kiss him thoroughly; I might even have done it if the waiter hadn't come back with Sebastian's credit card, ruining the moment.

The night was so mild Sebastian didn't even need to do up his jacket. We walked down the little alleyway of St. Christopher's Place in silence; the effect of the strings of fairy lights twinkling above us was so cornily romantic that I kept expecting him to stop and kiss me, but, extraordinarily enough, considering that he had just paid for my dinner, it didn't seem to have entered his mind. I couldn't believe that we would make it to the end of the alleyway in the same chaste condition in which we had entered it, but, unflatteringly, he didn't even take my hand. By the time we emerged into Oxford Street I was seething with frustration. A taxi idled towards us almost at once and Sebastian hailed it with the skill of long practice.

"I'll see you home," he said to me in the politest of tones. "What's your address?"

I told the driver, who double-took.

"You sure, miss?" he said.

"Absolutely. Look," I said to Sebastian pettishly, "you don't have to see me back. I'll be fine. It must be completely out of your way."

"Really? I mean . . ." His voice tailed off. The taxi ticked away behind us. I wanted him to insist, and was even more riled that he didn't. Obviously he didn't fancy me after all. I turned to get into the taxi.

"Hang on," he said, "don't you owe me a dinner?"

"Oh." I turned back to him. "I did say something like that, didn't I? Well—what about Friday?"

"Fine. Give me a ring at work."

"OK. Well, goodnight then."

I got into the taxi, feeling deeply confused. God, this dating shit was difficult. Now I realised why I usually avoided it like the plague. I never bothered with this sort of thing normally; we just jumped on each other's bones. The driver swivelled round to look at me impatiently.

"You made your mind up yet," he said, "or you going to let that poor sod sit out there all night?"

Sebastian was still standing on the pavement. I rolled the window down and leant out.

"You can see me home if you want," I said, feeling like an idiot.

"Oh. Are you sure?"

The taxi driver made a noise that sounded like a kettle overheating. I didn't know why he was making such a fuss—the meter was running, wasn't it? Still, I opened the door hastily and Sebastian got in. We sat with the width of the seat dividing us for the whole length of the journey from Oxford Street to Holloway. I had to direct the driver towards the end; he kept thinking I'd got the address wrong. Finally we arrived at the palatial Jones residence.

"You *live* here?" Sebastian said, astounded.

"Just what I was thinking, mate," said the driver. His sympathies were definitely with Sebastian; any moment now I expected him to add "Women, eh?" and spit out of the window. I couldn't really blame either of them. My studio is a beaten-up extension abutting on to a larger warehouse which thought it needed more space and then changed its mind. I admit the exterior doesn't look particularly promising. And inside the lack of promise is thoroughly fulfilled.

I got out of the taxi. Sebastian followed me, muttering something about seeing me to the door. I pulled out my keys and we stood for a moment on the steps, again in silence. This was awful. I had the feeling that we were about to start up with another round of goodnights. Anything was better than that. So I reached up and kissed him instead. He tasted of wine and whisky and smelt deliciously of a spicy aftershave, the lapels of his jacket silky under my hands. It transpired that he was only shy at the courtship stage. The things he managed to do to me, just with his mouth on mine, were quite spectacular. As I finally, reluctantly, let him go, I felt as drunk as if the whisky on his mouth had sent my head spinning.

"Do all public schoolboys kiss like you?" I said. "If so I've been missing out in a big way."

This was his cue to kiss me again, but instead he just smiled and said: "I'll see you Friday."

I reached up and pushed the fringe back from his forehead. His hair was the colour of bronze and it felt soft as satin running through my fingers. For a moment I debated holding onto it, dragging him inside and having my way with him, even though I might not respect him in the morning. Still, the morning was a long way away. . . .

"I'll ring you on Friday, then," I said, letting him go. As soon as I did I regretted it. Behaving properly was no fun.

Sebastian turned and went back down the steps to the taxi. I watched it drive away, imagining what the driver was saying at this moment: I bet he thought Sebastian was coming in with me. *I* thought he was coming in with me, goddamnit. How long before his principles would actually allow us to have sex? Did we have to wait till the third date? I wasn't even sure I could wait till Friday.

. . .

Normally the next morning I would have rung up Tom and told him all about it, but now there was a rift between us things were more difficult.

I wondered if I was expected to apologise for my implication that to call his new girlfriend a dishwater blonde would have been an insult to dishwater. Personally I thought I had been pretty restrained; there were plenty of worse things I could have said. After all, as Tom himself had commented, I dwelt in a cynical sinkhole of my own making. I longed to tell him that I had (a) been on a proper date and (b) kept my knickers on afterwards. That would be at least two impossible things for him to believe before breakfast.

I toyed with the phone and then put it down again. I wasn't going to crawl back to him. But his temporary absence left a gaping hole in my life; my other friends, like Janey, for instance, had proper jobs. Janey, with her ridiculously long working hours, was an extreme example, but it meant that I couldn't just ring them up whenever I felt like it to update them on the latest twists and turns of my love life.

I sulked for a while. Then I looked down at my bare thighs and after a while started squeezing my cellulite, which was so revolting that it quite distracted me from thoughts of Tom. I heaved myself out of bed. If I had a hot date on Friday I needed to hit the gym in a big way, and certainly depilate afterwards. And my toenail polish was more chipped than the outside wall of the warehouse next door. It was time to take myself firmly in hand before Sebastian did it for me.

5

Tony Muldoon, Duggie's pet photographer, was nearly an hour late when he staggered through the doors of the Mowbray Steiner building and only the fact that Joe, the security guard, knew I was expecting him saved him from being immediately and forcibly ejected. He was wearing a battered old khaki jacket with improbably bulging pockets, three cameras hung on straps attached to various parts of his podgy body, and he stank of beer. I would have looked on him with disfavour even if he hadn't been so late.

"You must be Tony Muldoon," I said coldly from my seat of authority behind the desk. To relieve my boredom, Joe had been showing me how the security cameras worked. "I'm Sam. Weren't we supposed to meet here at three?"

He waved his hand in a vague gesture. "Well, I'm running late, arn' I?" he said in a sub–David Bailey accent. "Is there somewhere I can dump me gear?"

I nodded over to the two black leather armchairs and glass table on the other side of the reception hall.

"Try there," I said.

"Right." He dumped all his cameras and various adjuncts on to the glass table with scant regard for whether he scratched the surface. All the photographers I knew had black nylon padded bags with side pockets and restraining straps made specially to carry their extremely valuable pieces of equipment, and they wore clothes that fit them, in black to match their bags. Tony Muldoon obviously modelled himself more along special correspondent lines. He stood back and looked around him.

"It'll be that, won't it?" he said, indicating Floating Planet. "What I've come to do, I mean."

"That happens to be Miss Jones's sculpture," said Joe, firing up. "I'll thank you to refer to it with a little more respect, young man."

"Don't you know who I am?" said Tony Muldoon incredulously. "You can't bloody talk to me like that."

The veins in Joe's neck swelled visibly. "I don't care if you're Jesus Christ himself, sonny boy! You'll be out on your arse in a minute if you keep that sort of thing up."

I put down my mug of tea and patted Joe on the hand.

"It's all right, Joe, but thanks." Getting up from behind the desk I walked round to Tony Muldoon, who was glaring at Joe in what was supposed to be a threatening way. This was a mistake on his part; his biceps weren't even as large as Joe's wrists.

"Come and see it from over here," I said in a pacifying way. "I thought you could get some shots of it without all that fancy gold lighting on the balcony."

Tony Muldoon squinted up at the mobile. "Nah, maybe I can get a bit of blur on them," he said. "Give it a bit of atmosphere, know wha' I mean?" He looked at me properly for the first time.

"You going to wear that?" he said, indicating my dress.

"It's this or my underwear," I snapped back. "What's wrong with it?" I smoothed down my black rubber skirt defensively. This dress had been doing so well for me lately it had seemed only fair to let it feature in my portrait.

"Yeah, it'll do, I s'pose," he conceded. He stared at me hard and nodded. "Arms're all right for the moment."

"My arms? What do you mean, 'all right for the moment'?" I said incredulously.

"Start to sag, don't they? I usually do young girls, know wha' I mean? These models, they start at thir'een nowadays. No sag there. . . ."

He reached out, grabbed my upper arm and pinched the tricep muscle.

"Work out, do you?" he said, releasing his grip. "Wise girl. It all starts to go so quickly, dunnit?" He narrowed his eyes into tiny slits. "Nose could be a bit of a problem," he said thoughtfully, looking at my face. "Have to angle it up. All right, you ready? I'll do you first, then I can piss around with the mobile, you know, do a bit of the arty stuff."

Squinting down at my nose in an effort to see what was wrong with it, I made my way to the spot Tony pointed out, at the edge of the atrium with the mobile hanging in the air behind me. He retreated to the extreme end of the reception area and squatted down, muttering to himself like a bag person.

"Take your hand away from your nose!" he yelled. "All right. OK. Turn your head round to the side. Yeah, all right. Now turn it back a bit . . . a bit more . . . look, follow me finger. Can you see it? All right, *look* at the bloody finger, then. Do something with yer 'ands, go on, fold 'em or something, don't just stand there. . . ."

I thought photographers were supposed to soothe you with sweet nothings and elaborate compliments. Tony Muldoon was modelling more than his accent on David Bailey. A few employees of the bank came in and out as he snapped away and stared at us in bewilderment. The lifts were on the left of the atrium, so these hapless people were in shot as they passed, thus drawing from Tony a long flood of curses which fortunately, after a menacing glance from Joe, he mumbled more or less under his breath. Finally he did some close-ups of me.

"Move over next to that wall," he commanded, "that'll give us a nice background. No, further over. Right, now turn round and look back at me over yer shoulder, yeah, that's right . . . hang on, I've got to change the film. . . . All right, now get yer head down so yer nose looks straight . . . not like that . . . look, follow me finger, all right . . . no, you're crossing yer eyes now, for God's sake . . . all right. . . ."

At last it was over. I didn't much like having my photo taken at the best of times, and there was something about this cold-eyed professional scrutiny that was paralysingly unpleasant, even apart from the insults. I slunk away to check my nose in the nearest toilet, in a passageway just next to the lifts. Apart from the atrium, the ground floor of the building was mostly composed of the grand reception rooms, with administrative offices tucked away out of sight; hardly anyone ever came in here. Thus I could spend a good ten minutes twisting myself round in profile and three-quarter view to see what was wrong with my nose. There was a slight bump, but nothing I could see that would require the kind of fuss he had made about it.

Finally I exited. Tony Muldoon was nowhere to be seen. At last I spotted him, hanging over the balcony at a dangerous angle. I took the lift up to the first floor and tiptoed unobtrusively up behind him, thinking evilly how easy it would be to tip him off it; that would teach him to make people sensitive about their perfectly normal-looking, only slightly bumpy noses. His saggy bottom was tilted precariously high in the air, one foot completely off the floor. I could just lift it and twist. . . .

"Hiya," I said just behind him. He jumped like a nervous rabbit. Instinctively I grabbed at the back of his jacket to pull him down.

"Fuck, you scared me!" he said belligerently.

I smiled sweetly. "Just came up to see how you were doing."

"Well, watch it next time, all righ'? Could of given me a heart attack."

From a doorway behind us emerged a man with black hair Brylcreem-smooth to his head. The red silk handkerchief in his breast pocket was folded as sharply as a razor cut. I recognised him at once. He was the man Richard Fine had been talking to as Bill was having his heart attack.

"Is everything all right?" he inquired. "I thought I heard something of a frahcaah."

His accent was the most upper class I had ever heard; even Tory Cabinet ministers weren't allowed to talk like that any longer, because they would put off the voters. He could have given Prince Charles lessons in clipping his words.

"Fine, thank you," I said politely before Tony Muldoon could start complaining again about having had a fright, the big girl's blouse. "We're just taking some photographs of the sculpture."

I gestured to it, hanging below us, glittering in the lights like a Christmas tree ornament. The man's face cleared.

"You're the artist gel, aren't you? Jolly good show. Saw you at the do last week. One couldn't forget that dress in a hurry, what!" He held out his hand. "Marcus Samson," he said, only it came out as "Sempson." "Delaighted to meet you."

"Sam Jones." I shook his hand.

"Thet the photographer johnny?" he said, indicating Tony with disapproval. "Rather scruffy, isn't he? Tell you what, young man, take a tip from me. You'd do better snepping this pretty gel here than a chunk of metal, eh? Well, I'll leave you cheps to it. Happy snepping!" He disappeared along the balcony. Tony's face was swollen apoplectically.

"Pompous old bastard," he muttered, leaning over the rail again and focusing intently on the side of Floating Planet. "Where's he get off, talking to me like that?"

"Apparently that's the next president of the bank," I said, remembering what Anne-Marie had told me about Marcus Samson. In line for a knighthood, she had added. I stared in the direction Marcus Samson had taken. "So I dare say he gets off roughly when—and how—he wants."

. . .

Tony Muldoon finally finished, rehung his various pieces of equipment on his unattractive body and slouched out of the building once more. I was putting off going to the gym, and made Joe and myself another cup of tea instead. We had a pleasant bitch about Mr. Muldoon, segueing smoothly to bitter generalisations about pretentious would-be arty types (Joe's word here was a little more spirited).

"That wanker was lucky it was me here and not Bill," Joe said. "Shouting at you like that. Bill would've kicked him out on his ear for that kind of language. He thought a lot of you, Bill did."

There was such affection in his voice as he mentioned his dead colleague that I made an instant decision.

"Look, Joe," I said, putting down my mug, "can I ask you a question? Bill tried to tell me something before he died. I didn't get it too clearly, but it sounded like somebody was making him do something he didn't want to do. He used the word 'bloodsucker,' I think. I know this sounds melodramatic, but does that ring any bells with you?"

Joe stared at me, his face completely blank, and for a moment I thought he was going to tell me to mind my own business. Then, slowly, he stood up and went to a drawer in the desk. From it he took a crumpled piece of paper, which he handed to me.

"The cleaner found it behind one of the monitors in the back room, all crumpled up," he said. "Must've fallen there when Bill had his attack. I didn't know what to make of it."

I unfolded the paper. "Has anyone else seen it?"

"Just me and the cleaner, and he can't hardly speak English anyway."

It was a typed note, only a few lines long. "Don't be a fool," it said. "You have no choice. Do what I tell you and no one will ever find out. If not, you know what will happen."

I stared at it, images running through my brain. Had Bill already had this note when I talked to him? Or had someone given it to him later, someone who had been at the reception? That made more sense; it explained what might have triggered the heart attack. I imagined the person slipping Bill the note, as if he or she were saying a friendly goodbye as they passed the desk; Bill would have read it and poured himself a stiff drink, which would account for the fresh, strong smell of whisky on his breath. And then the shock, or the strain of whatever he was being asked to do, had proved too much for his heart. He had died refusing to do it, trying to accuse his blackmailer.

Who, logically, must have been one of the people in that room. Only it still didn't make sense. And it wouldn't, not until I could find a reason why one of those people, with all their money, their connections, their privileges, would have bothered to blackmail the night guard at the bank.

I looked at Joe. He was shaking his head.

"I've thought and thought," he said. "It's beyond me. I've got no idea what this could be about."

"Neither do I. But I'll find out, Joe."

"Be careful," he said, and now he looked worried. "Bill wouldn't have wanted to see you in trouble."

"I can look after myself, Joe."

He stared at me, not seeming notably reassured by this statement. "Just be careful," he repeated.

6

I left it till Friday afternoon to ring Sebastian, hoping that he would have suffered all morning waiting for my call, but I was disappointed: he sounded annoyingly laid-back.

"So am I still taking you out to dinner tonight?" I said.

"Actually," he said, "I know it's supposed to be on you, but I wondered if you'd like to come to mine instead."

"You mean you're going to cook me dinner?"

"Well, I'm not inviting you round to eat Indian takeaway," he said with rather more sarcasm than I felt was warranted. He gave me his address.

"Oh well," I said, "it could be worse. I was dreading it would be Battersea."

"Someone who lives in an incredibly unsalubrious disused warehouse shouldn't cast stones at other people's nice mansion blocks. For all I know yours doesn't even have running water."

"You mean you have running water in your flat?" I said incredulously. "Really? I bet you've got an inside toilet, too. You yuppies don't know you're born."

...

I reached the South Kensington/Earl's Court border without mishaps; no one had turned me back at a checkpoint for wearing too much black or having on bright red lipstick. I stopped briefly at an Oddbins. It was full of people buying wine to take to dinner parties, wearing the oversized cable-knit sweaters, stripy shirts and faded green corduroys which are considered *de rigueur* around these parts. Sloanes wear corduroy seriously, rather than in a spirit of satire. You could tell the men from the women easily enough; the latter wore navy court shoes.

I noticed what plump faces they had, and how clean they all seemed to be, as if their nannies had bathed them, brushed their hair, pinched their cheeks to bring some colour to them and sprinkled them with toilet water before allowing them out of the house. One of the reasons I preferred Camden is that no one there felt obliged to be jolly; we were allowed to slump around looking cadaverous and terminally depressive. In SW postal districts, however, people found it necessary to slap each other on the back and bray cheerfully, no matter how they might be feeling. I bet the suicide rates here were much higher.

I emerged from Oddbins clutching two bottles of a Spanish Rioja which the sales assistant, in the cut-glass tones of one who knows, had assured me was extremely drinkable. This was not my previous experience of Spanish Rioja, but, quite frankly, as long as it got Sebastian drunk enough for me to take advantage of him I wouldn't be complaining. I felt like a stranger in a strange land. I had heard one of the people in Oddbins, presumably female (I hadn't had time to check her shoes), being addressed as Muffy. This was definitely not my world.

"I feel like a tourist on a day trip," I said cheerfully when Sebastian opened his flat door. My heart rose. I had been dreading having to bear the sight of the ubiquitous Sloanes-at-play uniform draping his attractive figure, but instead he was wearing white linen trousers and what looked like a cricket sweater, white with big blue stripes at the neck. It wasn't my particular fantasy but he looked very nice in it. There was also an apron tied round his waist.

"Hello," he said. He looked as if he were going to kiss me, but the wine bottles were in the way, so instead he led me into a large sitting room with a built-in kitchen, complete with what I believe is called a breakfast bar.

"I'm just finishing the cooking," he said. "Do you want something to drink?"

He gestured at a shelf across the room which seemed to be the bar. I made us each a gin and tonic—when in Rome—and strolled around, frankly eyeing up the place. It was very much a pad for a bachelor who didn't express his personality through interior decoration; comfortable but anonymous. The view from the window was beautiful, the sun just setting, bathing the tops of the buildings in a diffuse tangerine light; we were on the fourth floor, high up enough so that in the distance I could see the green lawns of Brompton Cemetery, which was more attractive than it sounded. It made a lovely walk if you didn't mind the fact that large areas of it were staked out by gay men cruising for company. Personally I found the experience rather dispiriting: it's not particularly flattering to round a tree and bump into a large, expectant-looking, well-built man on the other side whose face falls visibly in disappointment when he sees you.

Sebastian was busily chopping vegetables into matchsticks at the counter. I wandered over to have a look.

"What are we having?"

"Crostini to start, then grilled marinated tuna steaks with a black bean salsa," he answered as casually as if he had said "Hamburgers."

"Jesus. You'd better not come round to mine for dinner unless you like toasted sandwiches."

"Oh, do you have one of those special sandwich makers?"

"No. I don't have a toaster either. I do them in the oven. They're all right if you're not fussy." I paused. "Perhaps you'd better not come round to mine for dinner at all."

Watching him at work was having a bad effect on my libido. I had never been a particular fan of celebrity chefs, but there was something about having a handsome man engrossed in preparing a delicious meal for my personal delectation, his slender fingers expertly stripping down spring onions and chopping them fine, his head bent in concentration with its fall of bronze hair tumbling over his forehead. . . .

"Shall I push your fringe back for you?" I said. "Your hands must be all oniony."

"Oh." I thought I saw him blush slightly. "Yes. I mean, um, why not? Thanks."

I reached out and pushed back his hair, very slowly. It felt as soft as if it had just been washed. He looked up at me, his lips slightly parted, as handsome as something out of a shampoo commercial and a good deal more available.

"Is that better?" I said.

He cleared his throat. "Yes. Thanks." Then he bent his head to the chopping board again. "What about making another gin and tonic?"

I went over dispiritedly to top up our drinks. Something had to be done, or we were going to have to eat crostini and slabs of tuna and God knew what for dessert before a decent interval had elapsed and we could jump on each other. I needed to cut through the red tape. Then I had a brilliant idea.

"Do you fancy a line of coke?" I said, having remembered that I had half a gram in my wallet. Usually coke was way out of my income bracket, but, as previously mentioned, the Mowbray Steiner commission had bumped that up for a brief, shining moment. I had been saving it up for a special occasion, and tonight certainly fell into that category. I fished around in my bag till I found it.

"What, now?"

"Why not?"

He grinned at me unexpectedly, looking for a moment in his cricket sweater like a head boy being tempted off the straight and narrow.

"OK, go on then. It's nearly the weekend, after all."

I sat down on the carpet and put my little make-up mirror on the coffee table, cutting two lines on to it with my gym membership card. Then I put the card away quickly before he could see my photo, which was distinctly unflattering. Rolling up a five-pound note, I did a line. He promptly followed suit. I had cunningly picked the coffee table because it meant he had to kneel down next to me. He raised his head and gave me another lovely grin.

"Not bad stuff, this."

"Journalists' special."

I ran my finger over the glass, collecting stray crumbs, and then rubbed it over my gums. He did the same.

"My tongue's gone numb," he said, looking at me.

"Completely?" I said, raising my eyebrows.

"I'll have to try that out. If you don't mind. . . ."

He leant over me and kissed me very slowly, touching me only with his mouth and the very tip of his tongue. Then he pulled back a little. This time I was the one who had to clear her throat.

"How was that?" I said.

"I'm still not sure. There seems to be some sensation, but I can't tell how much yet. . . ."

He kissed me again, delicately nipping, biting my bottom lip, teasing me with promises he didn't quite keep. When his mouth released me I was burning with frustration. This time his grin looked positively wicked.

"I hope that helped," I said, with a slight edge to my voice.

"I wouldn't want to take advantage of your generosity," he said archly. "But if you wouldn't mind my trying just once more. . . ."

"Maybe it would help if I knelt too," I suggested, suiting the action to the word till our faces were almost level. He looked down at me, his long lashes brushing his cheeks, and I felt my own eyes closing in anticipation as his mouth came down on mine. This time when he kissed me it was the release of all the energy from the coke and quite a lot of other things beside. We couldn't let go of one another. Still kissing me, Sebastian started slipping off my shirt, his long fingers just as agile as they looked, one hand holding me tightly while the other caressed me so cleverly and delicately that I bit his full lower lip with pleasure.

"Christ," I said, trembling from head to foot. "Sebastian—"

"What?" He did something unmentionable that would have made me jump into the air if he hadn't been holding me down.

"Is our dinner burning?"

"Do you care?" He increased the pressure.

"Not much. In fact, not at all." I bit his lip again. Shivers of excitement were running down my spine so fast I wondered if he had plugged me into something without my knowing it.

"So tell me something, Sam. Am I the first public schoolboy you've had?" he said, kissing me on the neck. The electricity turned up several notches further. I tilted my head to one side, trying not to moan too loudly.

"I haven't had you yet," I pointed out, just managing to keep my voice level.

"Just hang on." He manoeuvred me neatly down on to the carpet and started to unzip my jeans. This was surely not the kind of behaviour one expected from a head boy lookalike. Or maybe it was. "It won't be much longer now."

. . .

Some time later I raised my head from its uncomfortable position under the coffee table and squinted around me. Night had fallen and the room was relatively dark. Beside me Sebastian was stirring.

"I have carpet burn," I announced, wincing. "And I'm hungry."

"God, you're spoilt," he said drowsily. "Am I expected to cook dinner now?"

"We could get the Indian takeaway previously referred to," I suggested. "I don't really mind what I eat as long as it's food."

"Not on your life." He sat up sharply and cracked his head on the coffee table. "Ow! Fuck!" He massaged the back of his skull tenderly.

"Shall I rub it better?"

"You've done quite enough of that kind of thing already." He stood up slowly and went over to close the curtains. His silhouette against the window was like something Praxiteles might have knocked up for personal consumption.

"Right," he said, "put your clothes on and we'll have dinner."

"You're not serious."

"I bloody am. I didn't go to a lot of trouble preparing a gourmet feast just to chuck it out because some young woman's strolled in, drugged me and had her way with me on the living-room carpet." He switched on the main light to blinding effect.

"Ow! Stop that!" Eyes closed into slits, I scrabbled around for my clothes. "Where's the bathroom?"

He raised his eyebrows. "You're prepared to have sex with a near-total stranger before you even know where his bathroom is?"

By now I had pulled on my shirt.

"That speech would have come out better if you weren't delivering it stark naked in the middle of your living room," I retorted with a degree of asperity. He had the grace to look down at himself. It was a tempting prospect for me as well, but I really needed to go to the toilet.

"Second on the right," he yelled at me as I left the living room.

The bathroom was very clean and stocked with twice the amount of toiletries I used myself, none of them with dry crusted bits around the rims of the jars. There were hair creams, aromatherapy bath oils, dental floss, toothpaste *and* mouthwash, let alone the peanut butter and rosehip face mask and selection of moisturisers. I cleaned myself up a bit, washed my face, and then put on some more lipstick and dabbed on some of his aftershave in lieu of perfume. It seemed the least I could do. I pulled on my jeans and headed back into the living room, padding on bare feet. How lovely to be in a place with fitted carpets.

Sebastian had opened a bottle of red wine and poured out two glasses. On the dining table was a plate of sliced French bread, warmed in the oven, spread with goat's cheese and decorated with matchstick vegetables. I ate three, one after another.

"This is very nice," I said with my mouth still full. "Better than toasted sandwiches."

He brought over two plates of the grilled tuna and black bean salsa, which was delicious. I proceeded to demolish it as fast as I had the crostini. Occasionally I stared at him across the table, taken aback; it was easy to forget how handsome he was unless I kept looking every so often.

"Afterwards we can have some more coke," I said. "Helps you digest." A thought struck me. "Do you know, on Tuesday night I thought you didn't fancy me?"

He nearly choked on his wine. "Why on earth did you think that?"

"You didn't start kissing me passionately in St. Christopher's Place."

"I thought you were going to do that! I've never been out to dinner with a feminist artist before. I didn't want to do anything to make you call me a chauvinist pig."

I sighed. "Well, I thought I'd better wait for you to start. I didn't want to shock your sensibilities."

"And now you know better."

"Absolutely."

Our eyes met across the table. Pleasant shivers of anticipation started to run down my spine.

"You look like the captain of the cricket team in that sweater," I said irrelevantly.

"Oh, that reminds me: what was the verdict on public schoolboys, by the way?"

"A bunch of smart-arse sexual perverts, if you're anything to go by."

"Is that a yes?"

"It's a definitely."

7

Next morning—despite the fact that it was Saturday—Sebastian, who was putting together some bid or other, went into work at the usual ungodly hour, resisting my persuasive attempts to detain him. The man had a will of iron. I slept in till ten and then had a long shower, attempting to use as many of his toiletries as possible in the process: bath gel, face mask, moisturiser, the works. I finished up with a plentiful dab of "Eternity." Men's aftershaves are perfect in the morning; they help to wake you up. Then I rummaged round the kitchen for some coffee. There was no instant stuff, just a deeply impressive espresso machine dominating the counter. It was exactly like the kind of sculpture I was making years ago: silver levers and pulleys jutting out at angles from every inch of its surface. I toyed with the idea of trying to work out how it functioned and then gave up. I didn't think it would be an auspicious start to our affair for me to ring Sebastian at work explaining how I had just blown up his vastly expensive coffee machine. Besides, I couldn't find the sodding coffee.

Instead I left a pointed note telling him to provide some instant and left, closing the front door behind me. I was, not surprisingly, feeling rather smug. It was sunny. I put on sunglasses, rolled up my shirt sleeves, knotted my sweater around my waist and pretended I was somewhere on the Mediterranean. To aid the illusion, I picked up a halfway decent espresso and croissant from a little Italian bar. Strolling out again on a surge of high-voltage energy from the coffee, munching the croissant, I was suddenly surrounded by about thirty expensively dressed and accessorised little brats who had materialised out of nowhere, jabbering away in French and whacking my legs with the designer mini-rucksacks which their mothers had thoughtfully coordinated with their trainers.

"Fuck off," I said, trying to remember rude things in French. "*Merde*. *Vaffanculo*—no, that's Italian. Eric Cantona. Um . . ."

A teacher with her hair scraped austerely into a bun and one of the regulation droopy dresses brought up the end of the crocodile. She gave me a reproving stare, though she hadn't heard what I'd said; her eyes were focused on my croissant. Bad manners, eating in the street. I took a big bite. Flaky pastry scattered everywhere. She walked past me looking disdainful.

The children vanished mercifully into the distance, heading in the direction of the Natural History Museum. I pitied its employees, not to mention the dinosaurs. Shaking my head as if to clear away a hallucination, I headed for the van. Sebastian was damn lucky he was handsome, knew how to cook and was good in bed. I wouldn't come down to these badlands for anything less.

. . .

Duggie rang me at lunchtime, or what would have been lunchtime if I'd been hungry.

"Sam *darling*," he said in a rush, "just wanted to ask you how the session with Tony went. Were you happy with him?"

"No, actually I wasn't, Duggie. He's a monster. He was really rude about my nose."

"There's nothing wrong with your nose, sweetie! Pay no attention, that's just his way. We should be getting the contact sheets through soon. I'm sure they'll be lovely. He's really very good."

"Why bother to ring me, then?" I muttered into the phone.

"What?"

"Oh, nothing. How's Adrian?"

"He *has* to go," Duggie said passionately, his head doubtless wobbling uncontrollably; it always did when he was over-excited. "I don't care what Willie says, he's driving me mad, the horrible little turd. And his clothes are getting sillier and sillier. If I'd wanted someone in the gallery who looked like a sales assistant at *Uomo* Camp I'd have hired one. What?" He put his hand over the receiver for a moment, then came back on the line. "Sorry, sweetie, must dash. We've got some Americans in. Not before time."

"Tell them to buy a mobile," I said to a dead line, and then pulled a face. With the amount of commission Duggie took he'd have to sell at least five before I saw any profit.

I really ought to do some thinking about the sculptures for this exhibition Duggie was planning, but next year seemed far too far away for me to take the idea seriously and my brain was not in gear. I decided to recharge my batteries. As usual, this took the form of curling up on my battered old sofa with a copy of the *Guardian*, various trashy magazines and daytime television whirring away in the background. Later there would be *Oprah* and *Mork and Mindy*. I was as content as it is possible for a human being to be.

The afternoon shaded gradually into early evening, the skylights in the roof of my studio darkening gradually as if on pre-set dimmer switches. At seven, starving hungry, I tore myself briefly away from the television to make a foray to the local off-licence and Indian takeaway. Sebastian rang as I was forking down a mouthful of *mutter paneer*.

"Oh hello," I said and promptly choked on a pea. "Just eating dinner, 'scuse a second. . . ." I thumped myself unwieldily on the back and slugged down some beer to wash down the pea. "Aaah." I took a deep breath. "Better now."

Sebastian's self-protective instincts must have been telling him firmly to hang up now and forget he'd ever met me, but some other part of him prevailed. I just hoped it wasn't purely anatomical.

"I got your note," he said. "I'll show you how to work the coffee machine next time you come round."

"Hope I don't need a Physics A-level."

"I wondered if you were doing anything on Sunday night?" Sebastian said. He seemed already to have decided to deal with me by the simple expedient of ignoring most of what I said. Sensible man.

"Sunday night?" I said incredulously, drinking more beer. "You have the nerve to ring up a girl as sought-after as me on Saturday evening to ask if she's free on Sunday night? That's practically no notice at all! Who do you think you are?"

"So you're free?"

"Yup. What are we doing?"

"Well, there's the rub. No pun intended," he added hastily as I said simultaneously:

"As the actress said to the bishop."

"If you could just drag your mind up from the gutter for a moment—"

"Didn't notice you minding last night," I muttered.

"—I was going to say that I've just been invited out by Suki Fine for her and Belinda's twenty-fourth birthday. Sir Richard's taking all of us lot to dinner. I asked if I could bring you along, and she said of course."

"How *lovely*," I said in silken tones. I meant that more than he could know; this was the perfect opportunity for me to improve my acquaintance with most of the people who had been there when Bill had his heart attack. "All right, I'll come. As long as no one throws bread rolls at me. I hear you Sloaney types do that to work up an appetite."

After we hung up my hand was still hovering over the telephone. Finally, giving in to the impulse, I started to dial Tom's number. One of us had to make the effort. He was still living rent free in a basement in Belsize Park belonging to one of the many psychoanalysts with whom the area was littered. Having dumped her patients on to a colleague up the road and gone to some American university on sabbatical, she had for some mysterious reason thought it a fine idea to let an unsuccessful poet with a taste for Guinness and rock and roll look after her flat while she was away. Doubtless she was not immune to Tom's brand of cod-Irish charm. I just hoped he would not only throw away the pizza cartons and empty bottles, but also ideally hire some cleaning firm to come round with their best industrial-strength equipment before she returned. The garden was already a lost cause. Too many drinking acquaintances of Tom's had pissed in it when they were too boozed up to find the toilet. And I don't just mean the men.

The phone was answered by a prissy little voice which I had no difficulty identifying as belonging to Miss Anaemia 1997. She sounded so wet you could wring her out and hang her up to dry. I asked if I could speak to Tom. Since this was Tom's phone number, it was a natural enough request; there was no need for her to make the prospect sound as difficult as if I had asked for a quick word with the artist formerly known as Prince. After a while, however, Tom came on the phone.

"Tom? It's me."

"Who?"

I narrowed my eyes in anger. BA—Before Alice—neither of us had needed to say any more than this to be instantly recognised.

"It's Sam. Sam Jones. Remember me? The one who used to tell blonde jokes before she realised that she was digging a cynical sinkhole with her tongue and saw the error of her ways."

"Oh. Hi, Sam. Did you speak to Alice?"

"How else could I have told her that I wanted to talk to you? Sign language?"

"There's no need to be sarcastic, Sam," Tom said austerely.

"It's the *raison d'être* of my existence, Tom," I snapped. Even someone as insensitive as myself could see that this conversation was not exactly rollicking along merrily. "Look," I continued, "I was ringing so we could make up, OK? What's a spat or two among friends?"

Tom's voice softened slightly. "I'm glad you rang, Sammy," he said. "How are things?"

"Well, I'm shagging an investment banker called Sebastian who lives in South Kensington, for a start," I said nonchalantly. In the old days—sod it, a mere three weeks ago—Tom would immediately have started pumping me for details. It was a measure of how much Alice had already brainwashed him that he said in the grave tones of a born-again Christian:

"Well, I hope you're practising safe sex."

I removed the receiver from my ear and held it for a moment in front of my face, staring at it in disbelief. Then I headbutted it a couple of times. When I was feeling slightly calmer I put it to my mouth and said:

"I know how to do it, dickhead, I don't need to *practise*. What do you think I am, some character from *The Deer Hunter?*"

"You what?" The old Tom would have picked up the reference in a second. Alice was probably rotting his brain by making him watch late-night BBC2 documentaries on prison conditions in the Third World. Tom was very easily influenced.

"Russian roulette," I explained. "And while we're on the subject, I certainly hope you're not putting it to Alice without some clingfilm on your pork sword either."

There was the sound of breath being inhaled sharply. Then Tom said:

"Sam, I won't tolerate you talking in that manner about Alice—"

"You mean you haven't managed to slip her a few inches of the one-eyed trouser snake yet? You're losing your grip, Tom. Take her down the Bell, and get her so pissed on Guinness she doesn't know which end is up. That should extend the possibilities considerably."

"Alice doesn't drink, and nor do I these days," Tom said in what would have been a pious tone if his teeth hadn't audibly been clenched together.

"That's a shame. At least it'd give you two something to do in the evenings instead of playing hide-the-salami."

Tom slammed down the phone so hard he probably broke it. Another thing to replace before Dr. Whatsit got back from America. I did feel slightly guilty for a while. I must have drunk more beer than I had realised. So much for letting bygones be bygones; the only thing I'd managed to let was blood.

8

I got to Sebastian's flat reasonably on time Sunday night, wearing a new, violet linen frock bought only that afternoon at extraordinary expense for a garment that did not involve a great deal of material—if it had been a ballgown with five metres of fabric in the skirt I could have understood the price. I really was going to have to get another artistic commission fairly soon.

If I'd been more enterprising I would have arrived half an hour early to catch Sebastian in the shower. Still, when he opened the door I put one hand behind his neck and kissed him so thoroughly that we were both reeling in a satisfactory way by the time I let him go.

"I want to tie you up and cover you in whipped cream," I said.

"For Christ's sake, Sam, come inside!" he said, darting glances up and down the corridor in a hunted sort of way.

"You're right," I agreed, "there's nothing to tie you up to out there."

Even the roots of his hair were pink. I advanced on him. He was wearing a white linen suit and blue shirt out of which his neck rose strong and firm like a Greek column. There was something about Sebastian that prompted me to these poetic similes. I started unbuttoning his shirt.

"You can either feel me up or do a line of the coke I bought yesterday," he said. "We haven't got time for both."

"Drugs first, sex later," I said, promptly buttoning up his shirt again. "I'll make a cocktail while you do the business."

I made a Martini while Sebastian cut up the coke on one of the pale green tiles of the kitchen counter. The lines looked too pretty there to disturb, but I had one anyway.

"Mmph," I said, sniffing away. "Drink?" I handed him the Martini. "Do you know, if you grew your hair you'd look like Brad Pitt in *Interview with the Vampire*? I bet all the boys at school were in love with you."

"Sam, if you don't shut up I'm going to revert to type and give you six of the best."

"Promises, promises . . ." I taunted.

Sebastian was approaching me with a menacing gleam in his eyes.

"Don't touch me," I warned, "I don't want to have to hurt you. Ow! Bastard! Ow! I thought you said there wasn't time for both! If you rip that, Sebastian Shaw, I'll kill you. I just bought that. I don't care how long it takes me, I'll kill you and then I'll . . . hang on, I'll undo it myself—Oh. *Oh*—"

The rest of the conversation was untranscribable.

. . .

Despite the unscheduled delay and much fussing afterwards from Sebastian, who packed me downstairs and into a taxi almost before I'd had time to rearrange my clothing, when we finally arrived at the restaurant we were informed that our party was still in the bar.

"See?" I said sourly to him. "There was no need to get my knickers in a twist."

The party was drinking champagne, all six members of it: Suki Fine, her father, James Rattray-Potter, Minor and a woman of a certain age clad in beige silk whose grooming was so exquisite that she made even Suki Fine, elegant as she was, look slightly overdone. A little aloof from the group was a young man with a sardonic air wearing an immaculate suit and a stripy tie whose colours clashed too nastily for it not to be the insignia of some exclusive club.

"Sebastian!" bellowed Sir Richard. "And Sam! Very nice to see you again, m'dear." He shook Sebastian's hand in a manly sort of way, then patted mine while kissing me on the cheek—a sort of combination of the English and Continental styles of greeting.

"Let me introduce you to the gathering," he continued. "Right. M'daughter Susan you know, of course. Young Grenville here and what is it—Rattray-Potter—I imagine are also familiar. This is Geneviève Planchet, a very dear friend of mine, and her son Dominic. Names pronounced differently in Frog, of course. Don't suppose you speak it? Make Genny a happy woman. No? Oh well, there you go."

A waiter was offering me and Sebastian glasses of champagne. I wondered whether the Fines employed a full-time member of staff to perform this function for them wherever they went. Geneviève was saying something to Sebastian. I wasn't surprised she was French. There was a subtlety to the cut of her clothes and her jewellery that only one Englishwoman I had ever met had achieved.

Dominic Planchet shook my hand. Now I had had a chance to look at him, I was sure that he hadn't been at the reception for my mobile. Neither had his mother; I could cross them both off the list of people that Bill might have been accusing. Still, I was curious about him. The initial impression I had had was confirmed in spades; though only thirty, at most, the expression on his face was that of a Georgette Heyer hero, cynical and world-weary. To add to the resemblance, he was tall, dark and handsome, his thick black hair cut very short to his head. I would have to watch out for him curling his lip ironically. It was the favourite pastime of Georgette Heyer's heroes, when they weren't racing curricles to Brighton.

"You must be the artist," he said to me without a trace of French accent.

"That's right. I'm Sam Jones. Are you a friend of Suki's?"

"Practically from the cradle. My mother and Sir Richard have known each other for a very long time."

I wondered if the twist he gave to that piece of information was habitual or if I were supposed to deduce something from it.

"Are you a banker too?" I said politely.

"No, I'm an entrepreneur. I deal in property and so on. I have a couple of restaurants in Fulham."

"Like this one?" I gestured around us. The restaurant was extremely famous; I hadn't even been able to afford to walk down this Knightsbridge backstreet before. Outside we had run the gauntlet of a couple of dishevelled paparazzi who had looked disappointed when they realised that I was neither blonde nor a Wonderbra model.

"No, not quite this smart," Dominic was saying. "All-night hamburger joints for Sloane brats with more money than sense."

I might have warmed to Dominic Planchet if I had felt any equivalent temperature coming off him, but he was as cold as frostbite.

"How come you speak such good English?" I said flippantly.

On closer observation I could see that he wasn't actually handsome; his features were too strong, his jawline too defined. The close cut of his hair accentuated this rather than softening the effect. Perversely, this made him more attractive. I couldn't see any resemblance to his mother at all.

"Actually, I was brought up in England. My mother moved over here when I was three."

"Your father's still in France?"

"Yes. My parents are still married, technically," Dominic said, and to my delight his upper lip curled back slightly in approved romantic-hero style. "They're the kind of Catholics who don't believe in divorce but are perfectly happy to live in separate countries."

"What are you boring Sam about now, Dominic?" Suki Fine appeared at his elbow. Her blonde hair was piled up on top of her head; she was wearing a white silk trouser suit and looked ravishing. And she certainly did make a practice of breaking into conversations I was having with attractive men. Maybe it was just a coincidence. And maybe Suki's father wasn't slipping it to Dominic's mother.

"I was telling her about Geneviève and Alain's rather unorthodox set-up."

"That must be fascinating for the poor girl," Suki drawled, effortlessly casting me as a social inadequate who was incapable of extricating herself from a dull conversation. "Dominic, where is that bloody sister of mine? The table was booked for half an hour ago."

"Happy birthday, by the way," I offered. "You're twenty-four now, aren't you?"

"That's right. Even if Bells acts as if she's a good ten years younger sometimes," Suki said disdainfully.

I watched Suki as she spoke. It seemed to me that her concern for her sister's lateness went beyond the simple fact of good manners to her guests; she seemed edgy, unrelaxed, and her eyes kept flickering around the room as if looking out for her sister. But just then there was a commotion at the door and Belinda Fine finally surged into the bar, followed by Charles de Groot. Her sheer prettiness silenced everyone for a moment, giving her the cue to exclaim:

"Daddy! Suki! Sorry I'm so late, everyone. The traffic was ghastly."

"Traffic? You could practically have walked from Charles's flat," Suki said sharply. Now that Belinda had arrived, Suki would hardly look at her.

The requisite flunkey had already appeared with two more glasses of champagne, and was currently refilling mine. Despite my socialist principles I found this aspect of the evening very pleasant. I caught Sebastian's eye over Geneviève's impeccably groomed head. He grinned at me. Meanwhile Belinda was greeting everyone, drawing the centre of attention around her scanty body with long-practised ease. Like Suki, her long blonde-streaked hair was pinned up; she was wearing a white Lycra tube dress so snug-fitting that it showed every bump and curve, which in her case comprised two nipples—they must have been attached directly to her breastbone, because she seemed to have no bosom whatsoever—and two protruding hipbones. Though she did possess a bottom, it was the minimum required for her to be able to sit down without slicing herself to ribbons on her own pubic bone. If she weren't anorexic, the imitation she was giving was highly convincing.

"To us! To the twins!" Belinda said, raising her glass. We all followed suit.

"I say," remarked James Rattray-Potter, who had borne down on me again, "your bit of arts and crafts is going down a treat at the bank. Very good show. If I had space I'd get you to knock me up something for my bachelor pad. Though you could always pop by and have a look at the flat anyway. Never know your luck, eh?" He leered at me. "Sebastian's a lucky man, I must say." A sly expression slid across his fleshy face. "Dare say he's told you all about our little bet by now, eh?"

James brought out the worst in me.

"To put you in a pigsty and play Spot The Odd One Out with the farmer?" I suggested.

"Oh, ha ha. Very good." James's eyes narrowed slightly. "No, the one about you. Bet him he couldn't get you into bed. So what about it? He won it yet?"

A sudden move behind James's shoulder distracted my attention. I looked past him to see Sebastian standing there with a horrified expression on his face.

"Of course he told me," I said lightly. "We agreed to split the winnings. But tell me, James." I leant forward. "Did you specify that it actually had to be *bed,* or does the roof of his car count as well?"

James went the colour of a turkey's wattle and made strange gobbling noises. I smiled at him sweetly, finished my champagne and started to move away, Sebastian hot on my heels. Before he could speak to me, however, Sir Richard intercepted us.

"You mustn't try to keep this delightful girl all to yourself, Shaw. Not done. Right, everyone, let's head through. I'm as hungry as a wildebeest. Show us to the table, will you?" he said to the champagne waiter, placing a proprietorial hand on my arm.

On the assumption that Richard Fine was paying for the meal with the money his bank had wrested from deserving Third World economies, I ordered scallops (on a bed of wild rice) and lobster (half, with lemon mayonnaise) and sat back thoughtfully. I had Sir Richard on one side and Minor on the other; James Rattray-Potter was far enough away from me not to present a nuisance, and I amused myself by deliberately avoiding Sebastian, who was desperately trying to catch my eye. By the end of dinner I thought he was going to stand on his chair and start semaphoring at me.

"James is doing himself well," observed Simon Grenville—I couldn't call him Minor, it sounded so silly—as the former tucked in heartily to a brimming plate of brown, dripping offal.

"Isn't he revolting?" said Suki cheerfully. She was sitting on Simon's other side, nibbling at a plate of plain grilled chicken. At least she was deigning to eat it; I noticed that her twin sister contented herself with pushing forkfuls of food from one side of the plate to the other without ever raising them far enough to reach her mouth. "I do like having James around. He's so grateful to be included that he does whatever you tell him."

Across the table Geneviève was talking to Charles de Groot. Observing them, I realised that she was not a beautiful woman, not even pretty; like her clothing, her looks in themselves were neutral. The magic lay in what she had sculpted from the raw material. Geneviève Planchet was not at all my idea of a rich man's mistress; probably that was why she had been so successful at it.

"Looking at Genny?" Suki said, following the line of my gaze. "She practically brought us up, you know. Mummy died when we were five and Daddy met Genny a couple of years later. It's worked out very well for both of them. Daddy bought her the house next to ours. I think he thought he was being discreet."

"Will they ever get married?"

"Don't think so. Genny couldn't get a divorce, and they don't need to anyway. Dominic isn't Daddy's son, you know," Suki added airily. "People always wonder about that till they see a photo of Alain. Dominic's the spitting image of his papa."

It occurred to me suddenly that if this was supposed to be the Fine girls' birthday dinner, where were all their friends? Suki and Belinda seemed to treat the boys more as social acquaintances rather than close companions.

"Do you two not have any girl friends?" I asked Suki, rather too bluntly.

"Because there are none here, you mean?" Suki looked surprised. "Well, we do have *some* good friends . . . I had one at school, only she had an affair with my boyfriend. . . . I mean, we know *lots* of people we could have invited. We just didn't. . . . I expect because we've been twins we've never needed anyone else really close," she finished defensively.

Simon Grenville's face had gone quite blank. I had the feeling that he could have made some pithy comment on the subject had he wished, and decided to try to get him on his own, if possible, to ask him about his views on the Fine sisters and this set-up. Unexpectedly, however, I found myself feeling pity for Suki Fine. Boyfriends, even suitors, were all very well, but they came and went, and you needed someone to ring up and cry over when they were gone. Nor had I seen many signs of the vaunted understanding between Suki and her sister—this evening at any rate.

I looked over at Belinda. She was sitting on the other side of her father, chattering away to him, her eyes hectic and sparkling. She hadn't eaten anything worth mentioning and she had been to visit the toilet twice. No prizes for guessing what she was up to. I felt someone watching me and turned to see who it was. Charles de Groot's golden head ducked abruptly to his plate. I stared at it thoughtfully. Had he noticed my curiosity about his girlfriend's freneticism? Or had he been wondering if Bill had said anything to me before he died? No one had mentioned Bill's death. To them it might never have happened. So why did I have the feeling that at least one person around this table had something serious on their mind? I had no idea of what could be considered normal behaviour for any of these people, no way to judge who was acting out of character. My eyes lingered on Charles de Groot. He seemed tense; I could put this down to concern about Belinda, but there was still something about him, his manner, that rang warning bells. I disliked him without even knowing why.

I ordered strawberry tart for pudding but despite my best efforts I couldn't do it justice. Very disappointing. I would have to get my stomach in training—build up with some whipped cream here, some Gorgonzola there, crab-filled choux pastry or lobster Mornay with roast potatoes on a daily basis—till I was ready to tackle a three-course French meal, accompanied by the finest wines available to humanity, and clean my plate with nonchalance at the end of each course. Sir Richard Fine was breasting the finish line triumphantly to my right; a few more spoonfuls and his chocolate mousse with brandy syllabub would only be a distant memory.

Belinda had declined a dessert and was playing with her napkin, her fingers making quick, nervous movements, her eyes bright. This must be what Evelyn Waugh's heroines had looked like, their beauty stripped down to the bone, jittery and febrile. I darted a glance over at Charles de Groot. He was watching Belinda, and he looked strained.

"Well!" Belinda announced suddenly. "Charles, darling, I think it's time, don't you!" She clapped her hands. "Charles and I have something wonderful to tell you, everybody!" She jumped up from the table. Inconsequentially I thought that her white dress must be well lined; you couldn't see anything rude through it, even outlined against the light as she was. "We're going to get married!" she exclaimed. "Isn't that brilliant news!"

She stretched her hand across the table to Charles, who stood up to take it, looking even more uncomfortable than he had before.

"I meant to ask you first, sir," he said to Richard Fine, who was looking very taken aback.

"Oh, Bells has always been impulsive!" Suki said quickly. "It's not your fault, Charles. You'll have to get used to this kind of behaviour, you know."

"Isn't anyone going to congratulate us?" Belinda said pettishly. "Daddy?" She turned to her father and said in cooing tones: "Aren't you glad I'm so happy?"

Sir Richard melted. "Darling girl . . ." He stood up too and hugged her. Dominic called over a waiter and ordered some champagne. Geneviève was kissing Belinda now, but as she pulled back and smiled at her nearly-step-daughter I thought that both mother and son had the faces of poker players, their true emotions kept firmly beneath the surface. The champagne arrived, a magnum. James was shouting:

"Oi, let's get that poo opened, shall we? Kiss the bride, everyone!"

The diners who hadn't already been looking over at our table were doing so now. Belinda was in full exhibitionist mode, lapping up the attention. Beside me Simon Grenville, who was the opposite, was practically shrinking into his chair with what I assumed was embarrassment. And Suki was staring at Dominic so hard that it looked as if she were trying to communicate with him telepathically. Dominic, sitting back in his chair, smoking, legs crossed, eyes on the ceiling as if he wished this whole vulgar display would come to an end, seemed unaware of the fixity of Suki's gaze, but he might have been pretending not to notice her.

Sir Richard leaned over and said to me, nodding in their direction:

"Let's hope those two make up their minds to it next, eh, m'dear?"

So that's it, I thought, that's why she's looking at him: Suki's in love with Dominic. The waiter handed me a glass of champagne. I was becoming quite blasé about this kind of thing; you could see how easily rich people became spoilt. Dominic, still ignoring Suki, raised his glass to me, smiling slightly, his black eyes narrowed. He looked as if he were imagining my worst desires. If Suki really were in love with him it wasn't difficult to see why. I dragged my gaze away from him with an effort.

Charles had put a good face on the embarrassing position into which Belinda had thrown him; he was smoking a large cigar, laughing as he accepted Geneviève's congratulations on the engagement.

Belinda threw her champagne down her throat and replaced the glass on the table so unsteadily that it would have fallen if Dominic hadn't caught it in time.

"Steady, Bells," he said easily.

"I'm so happy!" she announced to the world, throwing her arms wildly into the air. "I'm just so *happy!*"

Even then I wondered how long it would last. I caught Dominic's eye for a moment and his expression left me in no doubt that he was thinking the same thing. But I didn't imagine that the engagement would be quite as short-lived as it actually was.

An unfortunate choice of words, under the circumstances.

9

After dinner we went on to a club in Kensington which was full of James Rattray-Potter clones called Toby and Jamie and Harry; big, with fleshy pink faces, their chins already descending to become jowls hanging down to the fleshy pink bodies spreading out under their suits. A handful of the girls were quite large, and bounced around being determinedly jolly in velvet headbands and pie-crust blouses, but most of them, unfairly enough, were prettier and thinner than the men. They had straight mousy hair streaked to blonde, like Belinda Fine's, with lemon juice and vodka, and wore the latest fashions rather self-consciously, knowing that by the time their husbands' jowls were well formed they would be living in the countryside wearing corduroys and Wellington boots, their time in London a distant memory.

The dancing was what one might expect from the leaving ball at an agricultural college in Cirencester, and there was no escape in the bar, which was fitted out as a sort of living room with chintzy sofas. Here the conversation was of art courses in Florence and cooking courses in Chelsea; the boys talked business and shooting and sprayed each other and their girlfriends with bottles of champagne, which they called poo for some arcane reason. I dodged a drunken Henry hosing down a squealing Sophie and my swerve took me right into Sebastian.

"I need to talk to you," he blurted out. "I wanted to explain—"

"About that bet with James? How much did you win, by the way? I want half of it."

He looked very embarrassed. "A bottle of champagne. But it wasn't like James said. All I said I'd do was go up and talk to you. I was staring at you—intimidated by your dress, actually—and James said: 'Bet you a bottle of bubbly you don't have the nerve to chat her up.' I wouldn't have summoned up the courage otherwise."

"What about the getting me into bed part?" I yelled. We could hardly hear each other; some young stockbrokers were pretending to ride the back of the sofa behind me, yelling: "Giddy-up, Dobbin!"

"Well, after I'd been talking to you for a while you went off and James charged up and said: 'All right, double or quits you can't get her knickers off.' I told him to rack off, of course. He was just stirring when he said we'd actually made a bet on it. He really is a slimy little creep. Sam, please understand, I didn't mean to—"

I waved my hand to dismiss these apologies; I had heard all I needed to hear. I headed across the dance floor towards James, who was looking distinctly the worse for wear.

"James!" I greeted him. "You owe us two bottles of champagne, I think."

James looked first baffled and then horrified. "What, you want them *now?*"

"A bet's a bet. Come on, stump up." Sebastian was entering into the spirit of the thing now, visibly relieved at my attitude.

It took a while to get the reluctant James to come across; as I had calculated, to buy a bottle of champagne in a club like this would cost an arm and a leg. Two would leave him limbless. Finally James produced his credit card and we fought our way to the bar. On the far side I could see Dominic, surrounded by sycophantic blondes and looking distinctly under-impressed by the experience. The total bill made me blink and James look physically ill. I swept up the two bottles and nodded at James. Belinda and Charles were necking on a sofa, Suki and Simon dancing in the next room. It was more than time to go.

"Thanks so much. We must do this more often. Coming, Sebastian?" I nodded towards the door.

"You mean you're not even going to drink it here?" James said, jaw dropping unattractively. "I don't call that playing the game, Shaw! At least give a chap a glass of bubbly!"

"Certainly not," Sebastian said, relieving me of the bottles in a gentlemanly sort of way. "We'd have to share them with all sorts of riffraff if we stayed."

The bouncers stared at us as we emerged, giggling, Sebastian with a bottle of champagne in each hand. The night was warm and almost sultry. An open-topped GTi drove past the club, full of party-goers in black tie and taffeta, shouting merrily.

"They'll be headed for one of Dominic's eateries," said Sebastian. "Hamburgers and beer at two o'clock down the Fulham Road and too drunk to notice how much they're spending. He's a smart boy, Dominic."

We started walking down the road. I said casually:

"What do you think of him, by the way?"

He shrugged. "Keeps himself to himself. He rather gives the impression of looking down on the rest of the world. He was always like that, even at school. But he's OK. Doing well for himself, too."

"Are he and Suki going to get married?"

"It'd make sense. He's well off, but not on the scale of the Fines. And he's very ambitious, our Dominic. He and Suki should tie the knot, if only for financial reasons—half Sir Richard's money in the end and a hefty dowry to be going on with. Dominic probably feels he's owed it. He assumed he was Richard's son for a while, you know. Richard's always treated him like one. He was pretty pissed off when he saw his father and realised he was his spitting image. Went off the rails for a while, apparently."

"So marrying Suki would be very neat."

"Geneviève's been rooting for it ever since she met Richard. The French are very practical about marriage, you know, especially the aristocratic ones. And Geneviève's as unsentimental as they come."

Walking along these quiet streets with their grand, lofty buildings, deserted apart from the occasional carful of drunken revellers, discussing the possible alliances of rich, titled people, Sebastian beside me in his linen suit with a bottle of champagne in each hand, I felt as if I were playing at being someone else for the night—a sort of alternative Cinderella. I should be prompting Sebastian to tell me more about the Fines and their entourage, but I felt as if I were on holiday for the night. I didn't want to think about Bill, or what he had said to me, or death in any shape or form, or in fact anything but my own selfish pleasure.

"Where are we going?" I said idly.

"To the park." He grinned at me. "You'll like it."

We were just passing the Royal College of Music; across the road was the broad flight of steps leading up to the terraces behind the Albert Hall, bathed in orange floodlights. We passed up the steps in the shadows beyond the pool of light. The night was so still that there wasn't a sound we didn't make ourselves. We rounded the Albert Hall and before us lay the wide, empty lanes of Kensington Gore, its thoroughfares now quite deserted, only the faint sound of a car in the distance, over towards Knightsbridge. Beyond the road was the bulk of the Albert Memorial, shrouded in tarpaulin for repairs like an unsuccessful Christo installation, and beyond it was the park, stretching away from us into the night. I turned my head to Sebastian and smiled. He hoisted one of the bottles under his arm and with his free hand took mine.

We ran across the road and Sebastian showed me where to vault over the low fence into Kensington Gardens. I took off my shoes and went barefoot on the grass, feeling more than ever like a character in a film. In companionable silence we skirted the Albert Memorial and started across the park. The waning moon cast a little light, and there were the streetlights too, running along the sides of the main pathways, white and eerily beautiful. Ahead the Serpentine gleamed, a silvery ribbon with delicate bridges arching over it. We reached a small stone pavilion raised a few steps above the ground; Sebastian leaped up them easily, his white suit glimmering in the moonlight. I followed and stumbled over something. It was a beer can. Looking closely I could see more scattered about among the piles of cigarette butts.

"We're not the first to come here tonight," I said.

"Little bastards." Sebastian kicked another can away from him crossly. "Boys from St. Paul's. Lots of them live in Kensington and use this place as a rendezvous. The girls too. Bunch of snobbish brats."

He was spreading out the napkins which had been wrapped around the champagne bottles for us to sit on. Then he popped out one of the corks between his thumbs, aiming for the pavilion roof. It hit and bounced back with such a ricochet that we both instinctively ducked. The champagne fizzed into my mouth and up my nose. I sneezed and drank some more.

"There's something about drinking this straight from the bottle," I said. "It goes right to your head."

Sebastian put the bottle down and took me in his arms.

"Am I forgiven?" he said.

"Of course! It's the kind of thing I'd do myself—come to think of it, I *have* actually done it myself."

"Have you really?"

"Mm."

"Did you win your bet?"

"Not telling."

I kissed him. If you happened to find yourself in the middle of Kensington Gardens at two o'clock on a balmy starry night with a handsome man in a white linen suit, there was really nothing else to be done. The clichéd romance of the whole situation was as inevitable as the moonlight. We fell back slowly on to the floor of the pavilion. I stretched myself along the length of his body, running my bare feet down his legs.

"So have you ever had sex here?" I whispered in his ear, describing its outline with my tongue. "With one of those snobbish little brats from St. Paul's?"

He groaned as I took my mouth away. "Not unless you count heavy petting."

"Which I don't."

I drew myself slowly up and down his body till we were both panting with excitement, all the while kissing him: deep, lingering kisses further lubricated by champagne. I trickled it into his open mouth and he licked the bubbles up with an eager tongue, eyes closed. The champagne made his lips seem moist and swollen, shining in the moonlight as if they had been glossed. Sitting astride him I drained the last drops from the bottle and looked down on him lustfully.

"God," I said, "you look good enough to eat."

His voice came out thickly, his hands already reaching high up my thighs, pulling back my dress, guiding me towards his mouth.

"You first," he mumbled.

. . .

Dawn was breaking by the time we walked back through the park, depositing the two empty bottles virtuously in a dustbin along the way, and picked up a solitary taxi cruising past the Serpentine Gallery. If you're going to make grand romantic gestures you might as well do it properly. I flopped back on to the seat of the taxi with a deep sigh. It was wonderful to sink into a yielding leather surface after the stone floor of the pavilion. Our clothes were crumpled dish rags; the dry-cleaner's round the corner from Sebastian's flat would be getting some business this morning.

"How lovely to sit down on a proper seat," I said hedonistically, yawning so thoroughly I thought for a moment I was going to split something.

Sebastian pulled me across him till I was resting on his lap. I resisted at first; the idea of curling up by myself in a corner of the seat had been appealing. But he was insistent and I was too tired to argue.

"I wish we were in a limousine with tinted windows," he whispered in my ear, his hand straying up my leg beneath my skirt.

"Jesus! Stop that. I'm tired." I slapped ineffectively at his hand, my body reacting despite my exhaustion. "Stop it, Sebastian, I really am tired. It's all right for you, you got some sleep."

"I thought you did too."

"Just dozing." I yawned again. "Nothing to boast about. I can't wait to get to bed and pass out properly."

Sebastian, ignoring this, slipped his fingers even further up my leg. The taxi rattled down Exhibition Road, museums looming up on either side.

"For God's sake," I hissed crossly, "you know what's up there by now! Can't you keep off it for ten minutes?"

"No." His long fingers navigated unerringly round the only obstacle and slid into me. I arched my back and gripped on to him.

"Want me to stop?" he whispered into my ear.

My eyes closed, half in tiredness and half in something else altogether.

"Bastard," I mumbled back. "I'll make you pay for this. . . ."

I held out as long as I could, but when the taxi swung into the street where Sebastian lived and bumped hard over a pothole, I yawned and came almost simultaneously. It was a personal first.

. . .

It was rather overwhelming being with Sebastian. Not only was the sex good but so was the conversation; it was what the Americans call a total environment. Being accustomed to a more formal separation of these elements—men for the former, friends for the latter—sometimes I found it necessary to come up for air. Doubtless that was very immature, but my character was formed by now and there was nothing I could do about it.

In the pursuit of oxygen, therefore, I rang up Janey twice. Once I got her answering-machine message and the second time I got Helen, the girlfriend. The former was infinitely preferable. After Helen had informed me that Janey would be much too busy filming to ring me back for ages, she asked me in a falsely solicitous voice how I was doing—she was an actress, for God's sake, surely she could at least have *tried* to sound sincere—and told me all about her own brilliant career.

I stared despondently at the kitchen wall after I'd hung up. On it was a picture painted by a friend at art school, like a frieze of exotic fruit in mismatched colours: green strawberries, mauve tomatoes, cobalt grapes, dangling from a single vine. It always made me wonder what they'd taste like. I had lost touch with the girl who'd painted it long ago; she had gone off to America and never written. Few of my old friends were around any longer and the two who were both had girlfriends to whom the sound of my voice was less welcome than that of Typhoid Mary. Gloomily I scanned the television schedules, but there was nothing on apart from the kind of seriously intellectual programmes Alice was doubtless constraining Tom to watch. Poor Tom: up till now his idea of TV with a message had been *Baywatch*.

There was nothing for it but to have a night in with my own company, a couple of videos, a six-pack and a takeaway pizza. The thought cheered me up considerably. On reflection I disconnected the phone too. If I was going to retreat into myself I would damn well do it properly.

10

Belinda and Charles's engagement party took place a mere ten days later, on the penthouse floor of the Mowbray Steiner building. This was a giant greenhouse without the plants, a huge glass dome which had been built to impress the hell out of the opposition. I could have spent the afternoon lying on the moss-green carpet watching the clouds scudding by above my head, but social convention, alas, forbade this. Still, the views across London were spectacular; it was early evening, the sun only just beginning to set, and most of the guests were outside on the roof terrace, gathered in groups leaning over the rail pointing out distant landmarks to one another. It was the first time I had ever looked down on the dome of St. Paul's rather than up.

I didn't know many people here and I didn't want to know most of the ones I did. It had quickly become obvious that the great disadvantage of being involved with Sebastian (apart from the previously mentioned sex/conversation axis) was having to socialise with his circle of friends. The only one of them I liked at all was Simon Grenville, and fortunately it was he and not James Rattray-Potter who came up to me as I stood leaning on the balcony, looking over the City, thinking about what Bill had said to me just before he died. The Lloyd's building, silver ducts twined around it like parasitical worms, shone dramatically in the sun, just as incongruous amongst its sedate grey stone companions from the aerial perspective. On the outside of the building its lifts slid up and down like gadgets on a child's toy worked by a lever at the back.

"Bloody frightening, those lifts," said Simon, following the direction of my gaze. "Been in them a couple of times and I wouldn't repeat the experience. You've got to have a strong stomach. People who work there generally avoid 'em like the plague."

It was six-thirty in the evening, the sun still bright enough to dazzle. Perhaps it was the reflection off the Lloyd's building. A light summer breeze caught my hair and tugged it across my eyes. I turned to look at Simon and my instinct told me at this moment that I could talk to him about part, at least, of what was on my mind. I found myself saying:

"Simon, can I ask you something? Does anyone ever mention Bill, the security guard who died?"

Simon looked very taken aback.

"Well, um—not really. I'm sorry, I know he was a friend of yours. Sebastian told me. He was a nice chap. But life goes on, I suppose." He raised his eyebrows. "Why do you ask?"

"Oh, as he was dying he said something to me that was very strange. He almost seemed to be accusing someone in the room."

"Accusing them of what? There isn't any doubt that he died of a heart attack, surely?"

"No, no, nothing like that. I don't know." I was scarcely going to tell Simon everything. "As if one of them had upset him enough to cause the attack, though."

Simon stared at me, hard. "I didn't really see who was there. I was too busy giving him CPR."

I took this as a question. "There was Sir Richard, Belinda and Suki, Charles, James, Sebastian—though I think he was actually to one side of Bill—Marcus Samson, and a couple of others I didn't recognise. They were more in the background, though."

"Right." Simon's voice was so flat, so deliberately lacking in inflection, that it sparked my curiosity.

"Simon—" I started, but we were interrupted by a voice behind us.

"Could I take your photograph, please?" it said insistently. Simon turned automatically, so I did too. The camera snapped away.

"Lovely," said the photographer, fiddling with a notepad. "It's the Hon. Simon Grenville, isn't it? And what's your name, miss?"

I pushed my hair back from my face again. "Sam Jones," I said. "Look, what's this for?" I had assumed that Belinda and Charles had hired a photographer to commemorate their engagement party; but if so, why was he asking for our names?

"*Tatler*," he said, looking surprised. "Nice pic, too. Thanks."

He started to move away. I caught him by the arm.

"Look, I don't want you to use that," I said urgently.

"Why ever not?" He stuffed his notepad back into the pocket of his jacket.

"I just don't," I said rather desperately. "It's not . . . it's not *me*."

He stared at me uncomprehendingly. "Well, that's the first time someone's asked me *not* to put them in," he said. "Usually they'll do anything for a photo. What's up? Your boyfriend doesn't know you're hanging out with the Honourable Simon?" He leered at us knowingly.

"No, it's not that—"

"What's all the fuss about, then? Great dress. Look good in the photo."

This frock was becoming the bane of my life. Panic rushing through me, I opened my mouth to protest further when Simon leaned forward, his voice reassuring.

"Don't worry, Sam, I'll have a word with Venetia. She's their diary editor. I'll make sure it doesn't go in."

The photographer had made his escape to another group of people, who were positively preening for the camera. I looked at Simon, still worried.

"I don't want you to think I'm making a fuss about nothing," I said plaintively, "but I'd lose all my street cred in one fell swoop. *Tatler*!" I shuddered. "I'd never hear the end of it."

"Any publicity is good publicity, no?" Then he saw my face. "Don't worry!" he said, laughing. "I'll talk to Venetia, though she'll think you're mad. All this lot scan the pages every month hoping to see themselves looking at their best and standing next to someone eligible."

"I expect you're very eligible, aren't you?" I said, leaning back against the balcony.

He shrugged. "I don't get the title, you know. My brother inherits that."

I decided to let this pass over my head. "Well, anyway. Look, what we were saying before, about Bill—"

Simon cut me off in such a way that I saw it was no good insisting.

"I can't help with your mystery, I'm afraid. It was probably nothing, you know."

I nodded, deciding to leave it for the moment. But I thought I would return to the subject at a later date. Something I had said, some name I had mentioned, had rung a bell with him. Putting that to one side, I drank some more champagne. Soon I would expect this everywhere I went: go down the pub and ask for a pint of champagne. At the wine bar down the road a bottle of Moët cost £40, and when we'd met Belinda and Charles there for a drink a few nights ago Charles had stumped up for a couple of bottles without even thinking about it. No, one had been pink champagne, because Belinda preferred it. That was

£45. I knew because I had checked the wine list. I didn't feel like Cinderella any more so much as a cultural anthropologist on assignment.

I told Simon something of this. He winced.

"I expect we do rather take it for granted," he said ruefully. "Or some of us do, anyway. I try to think about it a bit myself. This will sound pathetic to you, I'm sure, but I've been wondering about getting into ethical investments. It's taking hold now, that kind of thing."

"Even here?" I looked around us, with one glance comprehending the chinless hordes in their smart suits. And that was just the women.

He shook his head. "I'd have to move down the road. Still, that would scarcely be a hardship." He smiled at me. It was a very sweet smile. "I'm afraid we're all past praying for," he said, "thoroughly corrupted by privilege."

"And honours. Sir Richard'll be Lord Something in a few years, won't he? And I heard Marcus Samson was up for a knighthood."

"Really? I wonder who told you that," Simon said.

I shook my head, smiling. It didn't do to piss off a journalist. You never knew when you might need some information.

"Anyway," Simon continued when he saw he wasn't going to get any joy from me, "it's pretty much par for the course here, a K to go with your three Ferraris."

"Marcus Samson has three Ferraris? I don't believe it!"

Belinda and Charles de Groot passed us, his hair lit by a ray of sunlight to bright gold. She whispered something to him, reaching out and taking his hand. He clasped hers tightly for a moment and let it go, smiling at her.

"They look like something out of a Timotei advertisement," I observed as they walked away.

"Charles has been spending a fortune on bubbly, then?" Simon said, harking back to what I'd told him earlier.

"That's right. Why?"

There had been something about his tone that had rung a false note. He said too dryly:

"Oh, Charles throws money around in no uncertain fashion."

"Why shouldn't he?" I said, puzzled now. "Surely he must earn a fortune?"

Simon shrugged. "Only about £80,000." I let the "only" pass with considerable difficulty. "And to the other Eurotrash in equities he hangs round with that's pocket money—they have their family income to supplement their salaries, not to mention their own flats. Charles keeps up with them just on what he makes here. Makes you wonder."

I looked at him thoughtfully. Was he trying to hint at something?

"You seem to know a lot about what goes on round here," I prompted.

"People talk to me," he said lightly. "I like to listen."

"Do you get to do much talking about yourself in return?" I asked sympathetically, remembering that at the birthday dinner he had preferred to ask me questions rather than answer them, saying firmly that his life was much less interesting than mine. For some reason this attempt at sensitivity touched him on the quick. He went as pale as a sheet. Stammering something about getting a drink, he walked away. I stared after him in surprise. What on earth had I said to upset him?

I went inside the dome and bumped into Sebastian almost straight away. He put his arm round me affectionately.

"Sorry to abandon you," he said. "Something came up."

I shook my head. "It's not a problem. Look, I've just pissed off Simon and I don't know why."

"Have you? Don't worry about it. You probably misunderstood." He was practically patting me on the head.

I glared up at him. "Don't do the 'never mind, little woman' stuff with me, Sebastian."

I went over to the white-covered banks of tables to get myself some canapés. My stomach must have been accustoming itself to puff pastry; I put down three prawn and mushroom vol-au-vents without the least protest from the gastric area.

"Shit," Sebastian said, looking over my shoulder. "There's a client I've got to have a word with."

"A client?"

He looked at me as if I were an idiot. "If there weren't some clients here Richard couldn't bill this do to corporate entertainment, could he?"

He disappeared into the crowd. I looked around for someone I knew but could see no one, which was a relief; it meant I could get stuck into the canapés. I had been to the gym that morning, which meant that this evening I could eat what the hell I liked. Geneviève Planchet came up to me while I was demolishing some more vol-au-vents. I was about to ask her if what I was stuffing into my mouth were really called flying-in-the-winds in French when she said, without preamble:

"Richard was wondering if you've seen Charles and Belinda anywhere. He wants to make the announcement now."

The abruptness of this request surprised me; previously she had always had perfect manners. I stared at her for a moment, chewing unaesthetically and praying that I didn't have any flaky pastry attached to my lipstick. She was wearing a mint-green suit with a white silk blouse, and her tights were exactly the colour of her skin, so fine I could hardly tell she was wearing them: several of the women here had failed to assess correctly their personal hosiery shade and looked in consequence as if they were wearing prosthetic bandages on their legs. That was a mistake Geneviève would never have made. I bet she would know exactly what to wear even if she were about to be eaten by cannibals.

She seemed to realise that she had taken me aback and retrieved her mistake, saying with a little laugh:

"Do excuse me for sounding hurried! Only we can't find them anywhere."

I shrugged and swallowed my canapé, wondering briefly why all the words for upmarket snack food were French. Smart restaurants called them *amuse-gueules*, but I didn't see that catching on down the Harvester chain. "They'll emerge eventually. Young love and all that."

She gave me a look which showed me, clearly enough, what she thought of that statement. I remembered Sebastian's comment on her lack of sentimentality. "Well, I shall have to go and dig them out nonetheless," she said, dismissing that idea. "Richard is becoming restless."

She looked across the room. On the far side stood Richard Fine, frowning; catching her eye he pointed at his watch impatiently. Geneviève raised her shoulders eloquently and spread her hands wide. Excusing herself to me, she disappeared. I hardly noticed; my attention had been held by someone else in the throng of guests, someone who stood out by virtue of extreme scruffiness—the camouflage jacket, the sagging jeans: it could only be Tony Muldoon. He was talking to a tall, skinny girl who towered over him. Her hair was razored and she wore a cropped sweater which strained across even her narrow chest, leaving a good few inches of pale skin bare beneath it. Her skirt was a pelmet over her hips and her legs were almost as bone-thin as Belinda Fine's.

She was looking around her; being nearly six foot tall without the stiletto heels of her boots this was easy enough. Her gaze fell on me before I had time to hide, and she proceeded to forge a path towards me, which wasn't difficult. People couldn't clear out of the way fast enough when they got an eyeful of her outfit.

There was nowhere to run. I was backed up against the canapé table. Prudently I furnished myself with some more champagne and waited in resignation. I should have expected this. Baby turned up everywhere. She was like one of those mosquitoes that blithely ignores even the strongest repellent cream. Well, she worked in PR. What did I expect?

"Samantha *darling!*" she exclaimed, having finally arrived at the table. People she had left in her wake were staring after her with expressions of distaste. They missed the point: whatever the latest fashion was, punk revisited or librarian chic, Baby would wear it, no matter whether she were going to a garden party at Buckingham Palace or a Washington DC crack den.

She bent down to kiss me, her balance not of the steadiest. It registered that I was moving inexorably up Baby's scale of People Worth Knowing: from art school, where we had met and definitely not been friends, to here in the Mowbray Steiner penthouse, with my sculpture hanging in the front hall, was a progression substantial enough for her not only to kiss the air so near my cheeks that I could feel her breath on my face, but also to italicise the "darling" in her customary greeting.

"Please don't call me Samantha, Baby," I said between gritted teeth. I wondered if my new status would prevail enough for her to listen. If not I would start calling her Eleanor. I had learnt her real name through painstaking journalistic research—i.e., asking Tim, who was her cousin. "My name's Sam, OK?"

"Of course, darling! Whatever!" she said. "I've seen the contact sheets of Tony's. They've come out terribly well. You look fab. You must be excited."

"You what? Oh, the photographs." I cheered up at this. Nothing like hearing that flattering photographs of oneself are in circulation for raising the spirits. "You've taken out your navel ring," I said, noticing that Baby's shallow umbilicus boasted nothing more spectacular than a few clumps of fluff and a little red hole directly above it.

Baby stared at me blankly. "Well, of course!" she said. "That's *so* last year! God, *Amanda de Cadenet* has a navel ring! I've had my nipples done now."

"God!" I said involuntarily, my hands raising for a moment across my own bosoms as if to ward off any piercing implements that might be coming my way, like men in cinemas all crossing their legs simultaneously when some character on screen gets kicked in the balls. "Didn't it *hurt?*"

"Oh yes, lots," she said airily. *Il faut souffrir,* I assumed, *pour être percée*. "Much more than the tummy ring. Do you want to see?"

"No. Absolutely not," I said firmly, thinking Baby's nipple-piercing might have been more sensible than it at first appeared; at least this way she had doubled her bosom area. "Jesus, Baby, what'll you do when that gets out of date? Pierce your labia?"

"Yes—unless everyone does it." She added this with preternatural seriousness.

"I think you'll be all right there," I said reassuringly. "I don't see it catching on in the suburbs."

"Baby doll!" Belinda Fine exclaimed, hastening towards Baby with her arms outstretched. "Long time no see!"

The two mannequins hugged. I winced in sympathy for Baby at the thought of her nipple rings being thus compressed against her ribcage, but she bore it nobly. Belinda's shoulders were turned to me; she was wearing a halternecked Lycra dress with long sleeves and a cutaway back, and her sleek ponytail hung straight down the delicate knots of her backbone. It must feel delicious when she moved.

"I'm *so* glad you came," Belinda was saying. "It's *dire* here, all these stuffed shirts. Oh hello, Sam! Do you two know each other?"

"From art school," I said. It was sad to think that my stock had risen with Belinda Fine because of my acquaintance with Baby, but so, obviously, it had. "Geneviève was looking for you and Charles," I added. "Something about the announcement."

"I'm getting *married!*" Belinda said to Baby instantly. "Look!" She extended her left hand. On the fourth finger was the largest diamond I had ever seen. The diamond part was an assumption, but somehow I didn't think it was a cubic zirconia. She launched into a barrage of questions that was manic even for her. "Isn't it exciting? So have you seen Gabby recently? Is it true you're going out with Tony Muldoon? I loved those photos he did of those deserted warehouses for *The Face*, they were just so . . . so *empty!*"

"Oh God, I *know*," Baby said. "Really profound. But it's a big secret that we're together—it only happened at the weekend and he hasn't even told his girlfriend yet! You mustn't tell a *soul*."

"Oh, I *won't*," Belinda assured her, "I won't breathe a *word*."

"So where's your man?" Baby said. "I'm dying to see him."

"Oh, he'll be up in a second." Belinda's eyes flickered. She continued quickly: "You'll love him. He's so gorgeous. And he's a count, or whatever you call it in Dutch. A Graf, I think. I'm going to be a Griffon or something. It's all so exciting I can't even *think* about it."

Belinda must just have completed one of her visits to the toilet. She was talking faster than a speeding bullet and her eyes had that familiar glitter to them. The irises were so dark I couldn't see the pupils, but if they were anything approaching their normal size I was a banana. I excused myself and set a course through the crowd, meaning to pay a visit to the toilet myself. At least there I wouldn't have to talk to anyone. But before I reached it the lift came up and the doors opened. Inside were Sebastian, Joe and a middle-aged man in a grey suit. Their faces were so drained of colour that they might have been attacked by vampires on the way up.

Sebastian stepped out of the lift and walked over to Richard Fine, who was saying something to Dominic with such impatience that it almost seemed overdone. Tycoons were not used to being kept waiting by anyone, I assumed, let alone a prospective son-in-law without much money of his own. Sebastian drew him discreetly to one side, while Joe stationed himself in front of the lift doors. Meanwhile the middle-aged man had regained some colour. Green as a stagnant pond, he ducked into the toilets.

"Joe?" I said curiously. "What's happened?"

Joe started visibly when he saw me, his head jerking back.

"You'd better ask Mr. Shaw that, miss," he said in a rigidly official tone of voice.

"Sam," I corrected automatically. Ever since I had been going out with Sebastian, Joe had called me "miss," as if my social status had somehow been raised by association. "What the hell's up, Joe? Why are you looking at me like that?"

An expression of relief spread over Joe's face. I looked over my shoulder. Sir Richard Fine was looming up behind me, Sebastian escorting him. Dominic Planchet had remained where they had left him, smoking a cigarette with his habitual world-weary expression.

"Better see for myself," Richard Fine was saying. "I still can't believe—" He turned to Joe. "Look here, you stay where Mr. Shaw very sensibly put you, here by this lift. Right? There's a good chap. No one moves from this floor till we give the say-so."

Joe nodded, looking shaken.

"Isn't there a flight of stairs as well?" I asked. "Someone could go down that way." All three men stared at me in surprise, as if a pet animal had just piped up with a pertinent suggestion.

"She's right, y'know," Richard Fine said. "Where do they come up?"

"Over there, Sir Richard." Joe gestured down the side of the dome to a pair of heavy, fireproof swing doors, just as Simon Grenville came through them.

"Minor!" Sebastian called. "Stay where you are!" He dashed over to Simon. I couldn't hear what he was saying. So far none of the guests seemed to have realised that something out of the ordinary had happened. Simon retreated a few paces and put his back to the swing doors, looking very shaken.

"He'll stay there till we get back, sir," Sebastian reported.

"Good man. Right, let's take a look." He glanced at me. "Bring her along too, Shaw, if she wants. After all, it concerns her too, in a manner of speaking. You the possessor of a strong stomach, young woman?"

I nodded. My expression must have convinced him because he said abruptly:

"Right then. All aboard."

The lift doors closed behind us. I was dying to ask questions but something in the way Sebastian was looking at me made me keep my mouth shut. Besides, if I made my presence felt, Sir Richard would come the heavy. This is no place for women and children, Shaw, tell your girlfriend nicely to buzz off.

The lift doors opened. We were on the ground floor, the green and white marble squares of the atrium stretching away from us like a giant chessboard; but there was something huge and incongruous at the centre.

The sculpture was no longer suspended in the air; it had come down to earth with a bang. And there had been someone in its way. A pair of trousered legs ending in well-polished black shoes protruded with bizarre neatness from underneath the bulk of the sculpture. Floating Planet squatted on the body of its victim. Fallen, half smashed, it had the same sulky malevolence that I remembered from the Thing before I made it into a mobile. The top half still had its original shape, but the lower portion was smashed flat over the body as if it had been trying to blot him out of existence. Around them, the giant silver rings lay like a frame. The sight was so surreal that for a good few seconds I couldn't take it in; it was like a tableau, a staged work of art. It was easier to believe that the body, its face hidden, was a dressed-up shop dummy rather than flesh and blood.

Sir Richard cleared his throat.

"He dead, Shaw?"

"Yes, sir. I checked at once. There's no pulse."

"Who is it?" I said, though I had a pretty good idea.

They didn't answer immediately. Finally Sebastian said, as if the words had been dragged out of him:

"It's Charles de Groot, Sam."

The expression on his face as he looked at me had not changed; he was wary of me, aloof, almost mistrustful. Now that I understood it I was even more angry than I had been at the sight of my sculpture used like that to kill a man. I turned my back on him to look again at Floating Planet. For a moment I had an image of it shaking off its chains and plummeting in a kamikaze death fall on top of Charles de Groot as he walked across the centre of the atrium.

It wasn't so impossible to picture. At that moment the damn thing looked hostile enough to do anything.

11

"Of course it wasn't my bloody fault!" I said angrily, still further annoyed to hear the note of defensiveness in my voice when there was nothing I needed to defend. "I knew that straight away."

"How?"

I sighed. I was going to have to spell the whole thing out again.

"I put the chain on that mobile and hauled it up myself," I said, patiently enough. "There was a figure-of-eight hook on the balcony wall already, because of the chandelier that used to hang there, and I tested the hook first, to be sure. It's like a curtain tie-back, only bigger. You wind the chain around it in a figure-of-eight pattern and then loop it over the top of the hook."

"That was the only thing holding its weight?"

"The chain? Yes. There were about eight lighter ones to keep it steady, like spokes on a wheel. I fixed them round the balcony rail. But once the main chain went they'd have been pulled away in the fall. Look, I secured that chain myself." I was speaking more calmly now that a policeman was actually listening to me without the kind of bored expression that signified imperfectly controlled disbelief. "There was no way it could have snapped or come loose. Someone either filed through a link or unwound it from the hook. It wouldn't have taken that much strength."

I was pacing up and down the room, a bottle of beer in my hand. Hawkins, on the sofa, was listening intently.

"I've told them all this, anyway. Your lot, I mean. Not that they were really paying that much attention to me—they were too busy licking Sir Richard's posterior. But they'll see I'm right when they have a look at that chain. Either it'll have been filed through, or there just won't be anything to see. No marks on the chain and the hook still in the wall, no signs of it being dragged forward by the weight of the mobile. Which means that someone must have unwound the chain from the hook and let it go."

I took another slug of beer. It looked as if Hawkins was about to say something, but I carried on: I was in full flood now.

"Besides, the idea that the mobile just happened to fall on top of Charles and smash in his head is much too neat. Even if Charles had been beneath it when the chain gave way, he'd have heard it on its way down. There's no piped music or anything in the atrium, and it was Sunday, everyone was on the top floor. No one making any noise to distract him. Suppose that someone had loosened the chain, or filed through it, when they saw Charles coming. He'd have had plenty of time to hear the chain running along the balcony floor, look up, and see the mobile coming down—he'd easily have been able to jump to one side. At worst it would only have struck him a glancing blow. It's light as a feather, you know—"

"Yes, I wondered when we were coming to this—"

"—it looks huge and impressive, but it's just thin sheets of aluminium welded together. Chicken wire over the top and some hollow tubes in rings around it. That's why I could haul it up myself. It didn't weigh that much. Not like a chandelier; have you ever held one of those crystals? They're heavy little buggers, hundreds of them, all attached to a wrought-iron frame. That would have done a lot more damage. Look how crumpled up the mobile was by the impact: it smashed like an orange. A chandelier would still have been in one piece. More, if it hit him in the right place it could practically have taken his head off."

I perched on the arm of a chair. "The chandelier was held up by a whole system of plates and winches—have you ever seen *The War of the Roses*? But it wasn't worth using that for Floating Planet, because it weighed so little, and besides, the point was to have it hanging there almost looking as if it were floating in space. I'd arranged for someone I know to design a much smaller winch for it, which would hardly show, and we were going to install it in a month or so. But Mowbray's didn't want to wait that long. Hence the chain. It wasn't ideal—look at what happened, it was too easy to unfasten for anyone who might be walking by—but it would have done for a few weeks in normal circumstances. David Stronge approved it."

"On his own head be it."

"Very funny. Look, I've thought of something else, just now. Why *would* Charles have been crossing the atrium? The way his body was facing, he was heading for the reception room or that big conference room, and there's nothing in either one of those to interest him. No, I think someone smashed him over the head and then had the brilliant idea of dragging him into the atrium and dropping Floating Planet on top of him to make it look as if my sculpture did it. Work Of Art Goes Haywire. Distressed Creatress Says: It Had A Mind Of Its Own From The Start, There Was No Telling It Anything." I practically spat on the floor in fury. "Bollocks."

I finished my beer and wiped off my lips. "*God*, I'm pissed off," I said forcefully. "All day yesterday everyone was staring at me like a pariah, thinking I was the kind of stupid little twat that couldn't hang up her own sculpture without it crashing down on someone's head less than a month later. And not just anyone, mind—the son-in-law elect of the chairman of the bank at his own engagement party. Nice one, Sam.

Talk about a social faux pas. Sebastian was very kind to me after he got over the shock. That was the worst part of all—speaking from a purely selfish perspective—the ones who were *sorry* for me. They'll eat their words."

"Who's Sebastian?"

"Never mind."

"You're staring at that bottle as if you wanted to carve up someone's face with it."

"I bloody do. I want to bottle whoever tried to make me look like an incompetent, if not worse. All I need right now is a manslaughter charge." I glared at him. "And don't say anything clever about my lurid past or it'll be the worse for you."

He was holding up his hands. "Leave me out of it, OK?" His blue eyes were clear and steady. "Look, now you've got that out of your system, come and sit down here a moment. There's something you should know."

I perched on the edge of the armchair. "What is it? The autopsy results? Bet they rushed that one through fast enough with Sir Richard Fine and Mowbray Steiner on their backs."

He scowled at me. More than once Hawkins and I had got into arguments about the police; he would rarely even admit that they could be leaned on by people of influence. "Finished with the party political broadcast?" he said with heavy sarcasm.

"Christ, Hawkins! That was my sculpture! You saw me making it, you know how long it took me! Just tell me what the hell happened to it!"

He took a breath. "You were right in a way," he said. "It wasn't the sculpture that killed him."

"I knew it!" I crowed triumphantly.

"Did you ever have any doubt?" he said curiously. "Not once?"

I shook my head. "No way. Never. Go on." I was leaning forward impatiently.

"Sometimes, Sam, your sheer blind self-confidence—no, *stubbornness*—"

"Hawkins!"

"All right. The sculpture didn't kill him because he was dead already." He held up his hand to stop the words I was about to say. "But you were wrong about that part of it. You'll never guess this one. Mr. Charles de Groot, or not Mr., they tell me he had some obscure title or other—well, anyway, our Charles was a bit of a junkie. How'd you like that? Enough pure heroin in his bloodstream to kill a horse."

Despite the jocular tone Hawkins was looking at me hard. He must have seen that my surprise was genuine.

"My God," I said slowly. Charles de Groot, the golden boy, the blond bombshell, a smackhead. "You can't tell about anyone these days, can you?"

"You didn't know." It was a statement. "OK, next question: do you know where he was getting it from?"

"Come off it, Hawkins. I wouldn't tell you if I did."

And I wasn't going to tell him what Bill had said to me, either. Though I had my suspicions, they remained only that; it was all too nebulous. I needed something more concrete before I could discuss it with him. Hawkins knew I was touchy about the subject of giving information to the police. Still, he made the mistake of saying:

"Look, Sam, I happen to have put in a good word for you to Brand, OK?"

"If that's the inspector who gave me a hard time yesterday afternoon he can put your good word up his arse and set fire to it," I snapped. "You should be damn careful of coming in here and pumping me for information. You know it gets my back up."

"It's not my fault you can be irrational sometimes about the police—"

I exploded, all the pent-up fury of the past thirty-six hours pumping through my system like adrenaline.

"Oh, right! The police who plant drugs or nick people's stash or beat up suspects in the happy certainty that even if the bloke dies they'll never get done for it! I know someone who got framed for rioting during the poll tax demo. Two of your lot lied to the magistrate and he went down for twelve months. And what about charging striking miners on horseback—ever heard of Peterloo, Hawkins? Don't get me started, OK? Just don't get me started." I took a deep breath. "I'm not saying you're like that," I continued. "But I'm still not telling you anything I don't want to, no matter how many good words you put in for me, not till I've had a think about it first. All right?"

I opened another beer.

"You're looking at me like you want to storm out again," I said irrelevantly. "Your eyes have gone that special concentrated blue they only go when you're angry."

"Or having sex."

"How d'you know that?"

"You told me. And anyway 'special concentrated blue' sounds like something out of a washing-powder advertisement."

"OK, so I wasn't expressing myself to my usual elevated metaphorical standard. Sorry about that. They are, though. Your eyes, I mean. Are you still pissed off?"

"No, I'm debating whether or not to kiss you senseless."

"I think that would be a bad idea at the moment."

"Why? Are you infectious?"

"Not unless you count the cynicism. Look, could we get back to the subject under discussion? Can you tell whether this was a one-off, or Charles shot up regularly? I mean, if they didn't find any marks on him apart from that one, it could be that someone injected him with extra-pure deliberately."

As I had hoped, this distracted Hawkins.

"No, he was a user," he said straight away. "Nice clear set of old track marks."

"He couldn't have done it that much, though," I objected. "Probably a weekend user. De-stress from the strains of the job."

He nodded. "That's what Brand's assuming. The body wasn't riddled with them; just a few on the arms, mostly not that recent. He didn't shoot up every day or anything like that."

"Was it just smack they found?" I said curiously, having had some time to ponder this.

His gaze sharpened. "Why do you say that?"

"Look," I assured him, "I don't know anything at all about that lot's drug habits. I really don't. Take that on faith. I was just guessing that it might have been a speedball—you know, a bit of charlie mixed in. It seems more likely that at his own engagement party, just before the big announcement, he might have sneaked off to do one of those rather than just smack. No matter how much self-control he had—and I'd say quite a lot—you'd have to be a maniac to want to knock yourself out before something like that, with photographers from *Tatler* and all your set watching you. A speedball at least'd have picked him up a bit."

"Well, you're right. I bow to your superior knowledge. That's what he thought he was doing. They found baby laxative in him too. Someone must have sold him it as cocaine."

"Or given him the whole thing ready made. Otherwise he'd have realised what it was if he had any nous at all."

I stared ahead of me.

"If someone wanted to kill him," I said slowly, "and they were an economic sort of person, they wouldn't bother giving him any charlie in it, would they? Be wasted, seeing as he'd overdose straight away on the smack. They'd bung in the baby laxative instead to save money."

"Is that what you think? That it was murder?"

I looked up at the Thing, remembering Floating Planet as it had been in its prime. It was making me angry all over again. Hawkins followed the line of my gaze and promptly handed me another bottle of beer in the hope, I presumed, of neutralising my bad temper with alcohol. Wise man.

"I don't know. Why go through all the bother of dropping my sculpture on his head, in that case? The only reason I can think of is that it wasn't planned—he overdosed by accident and the dealer found him, panicked because he or she was still holding, and decided to distract the police till they could get rid of their stash. You'd have searched everyone there if you'd known that there were drugs involved, wouldn't you?"

Hawkins nodded.

"Though, mind you, he or she could just have flushed it down the loo. . . . It was lucky for them that Joe wasn't at his desk at the time," I said casually. "Otherwise they'd just have had to push Charles down a staircase instead."

"Come off it, Sam," Hawkins said. "I admire your loyalty but we know damn well that your friend Joe was having a snooze in front of the telly in the back room. He's already told us. And he said that you knew about it."

"I expect I do look very suspicious," I admitted. "No wonder he gave me such a funny look yesterday. One: it was my sculpture. Two: I knew that Joe popped down the corridor to watch the telly whenever he had a chance. I expect he thought that everyone was safe upstairs for another hour—"

"Why did he go all the way down the corridor to watch the TV?" Hawkins interrupted. "It was a portable. Why didn't he just set it up in the control room? There'd be much less risk. If anyone came by he could just switch it off and pretend that he'd been watching the security cameras."

"The video screens interfere with the reception," I explained. "My God, the security cameras!" I turned to him excitedly. "The videos!"

Hawkins was shaking his head. "Someone wiped all the tapes," he said. "Easy enough to do—like on a normal video recorder."

"Oh dear," I said cheerfully. "And Joe was showing me how it worked just the other day. I must be the prime suspect—if you really believe that I'd do something like that to my own sculpture." I drank some more beer. "It must have been someone who worked in the bank, don't you think? Anyone from outside wouldn't have run the risk—for all they knew Joe might have come back any second. Whereas if you knew him, you could just pop down the corridor a little way and check that he was snoring in front of the telly. It wouldn't take long to drag Charles's body across the hall—oh, hang on, where were they coming from?"

"Brand's working on the theory that he was shooting up in the downstairs toilet, the one just off the hall. It's right next to the stairs, very discreet. Everyone else was gathered at the top of the building—no one'd even know he was there, let alone what he was doing."

"Apart from the person who gave him the stuff."

This brought me right back to where we'd started. Hawkins stared at me appealingly.

"They're working on the assumption that it was murder, Sam," he said. "And it's impossible to get much out of the bank employees. Sir Richard wants everything hushed up and they know it. Brand can't give them too hard a time—Sir Richard, or rather the bank, contributes a healthy whack to the Tories on a regular basis."

"Must make him one of the few left who does." Still, I took his point. Pressing Belinda to tell who her fiancé's dealer had been would be a doomed enterprise—she'd be screaming for Daddy if you even looked at her sideways.

"I'm not saying I'll do anything," I said firmly.

"Whoever it was smashed your sculpture to a pulp," Hawkins pointed out with his usual tact. "Is it a write-off?"

"I don't know!" I snapped. "It's still locked up in the bank. They wouldn't let me look at it."

"I'll ask when it'll be OK for you to go and check it out. No strings," he added quickly. "It doesn't put you under any obligation."

"You're damn right it doesn't."

"I expect this Sebastian bloke wouldn't know anything about Charles's habits," Hawkins said over-casually. "He's the one who found the body, I take it? Sebastian Shaw. Up-and-coming young man. Escorting a client out deferentially when confronted by an unpleasant sight in the hall. Behaved very properly: checked that unpleasant sight was no longer breathing and kept everyone else from trampling round the area. Even prevented said client from scarpering, which I bet he would've done if given half a chance."

"You don't miss a trick, do you, Hawkins?"

"Very kind to you, I think you said he was earlier."

"He knows how to treat a girl," I said coldly. "His idea of courtship is a world away from yours. Sebastian is a gentleman."

"Sounds bloody boring to me," Hawkins muttered.

"Not necessarily," I said smugly.

12

After Hawkins left I sat thinking for a while. Then I rang the Fine house. Suki answered. She sounded tired, but not shattered. Nor was she cold to me when I told her who I was, which I found interesting considering that practically everyone yesterday had automatically assumed that it was my carelessness which had put an early end to Charles de Groot. Apart from the murderer, of course.

"I just thought I'd ring to see if Belinda was all right," I said.

"That's really kind of you, Sam. She's terribly shaken, of course, but it could be worse. The doctor came yesterday and gave her a sedative to calm her down. She's in bed at the moment." Suki hesitated, then said: "You wouldn't like to come round, would you? I can't leave her in this state, and it would be nice to have some company. Of course, if you're busy. . . ."

"No, no," I said hastily, thinking once again how lonely these two girls must be. Didn't they have any friends they could get to come over? "Can I bring anything? Do you need any shopping done?"

Suki sounded absolutely amazed at the naïveté of this suggestion. "God, no. I mean, I can order stuff in if I need it. We've got accounts everywhere. But thanks anyway," she added as an afterthought.

"I'll be round in half an hour at the most."

This gave me a few minutes to put on some casual wear that I thought would be acceptable to Suki. There was no way I would get a Sloane princess to relax and confide in me if I looked like Tank Girl, even without the bazooka. I donned some black jodhpur-type leggings, my forest green silk shirt and a nearly-matching green suede jacket with fake chinchilla collar. Suki wasn't to know that the last two had been bought second-hand. My black patent ankle boots were posh, anyway. Pied à Terre. Before leaving the house I even remembered to peel the SALE sticker painstakingly off the soles. I'd been meaning to do that for ages.

I wasn't trying to look Sloane—a faint hope that would have been—simply not to scare her off by appearing too alternative. It seemed to have worked; when she opened the front door she didn't recoil visibly and say "I'm sorry, we don't believe in giving to charity" before slamming it in my face.

The Fine family mansion was even more impressive than I had been expecting: a huge white edifice in a quiet square just behind the King's Road. I didn't even want to speculate about how much it had cost. Then there was the immaculate state of its maintenance to factor into the bill; it looked as if, like the Forth Bridge, no sooner had the workmen finished tarting up one end of it than they started again with the other. I parked my van on the capacious driveway out front, next to the latest Toyota jeep, which didn't have even a speck of mud to mar its matt mauve finish. The closest it had been to the country was Hyde Park. Suki had the Honda convertible, so this would be Belinda's; I considered it ludicrous to have a jeep in town, unless you were such a bad parallel parker that you needed to be high up above the fray to see what you were doing.

The entrance hall was painted yolk yellow and hung with eighteenth-century prints of ducks. Suki led me into a kitchen which was practically the size of my entire studio, its walls stippled in various shades of yellow, its décor country-kitchen-meets-restaurant chic. The curtains were chintzy, the floor was of Tuscan handmade tiles and the rigorously functional steel fittings looked as if they had been bought wholesale from the Conran Shop. Through the French windows at the far end I could see a garden the size of Lord's cricket ground, only even better maintained. I made admiring noises.

"Do you like it?" Suki said brightly. "Oh, I'm so glad. Would you like to see round the house?"

What could I say? We spent the next twenty minutes tramping up and down ochre-carpeted stairs and in and out of about seventeen bedrooms plus a matching number of en-suite bathrooms (interrupting one of the Forth Bridge workers with her arm down a toilet: "Oh, I'm sorry to disturb you, Mrs. Hermesetas, I was just showing a friend round the house"). I bet Mrs. Hermesetas heard us coming and shoved her fag down the loo just in time. She had looked strangely distracted. There was Suki's suite of rooms to be endured (these done predominantly in yellow: "my favourite colour, it's so cheerful"), Belinda's suite, excluding the bedroom where the invalid lay (though I assumed that this was pale pink, in keeping with her living room and bathroom), and Sir Richard's (a masculine dark green with mahogany furniture), let alone the rest of the house ("we really use most of the ground floor for entertaining"). By the time we were back in the kitchen I felt as if I'd done the equivalent time on a StairMaster.

I said as much to Suki as we sat round the rustic kitchen table sipping Lapsang Souchong from pale yellow bone china with a gold border. (There is such a thing as over-coordination.) She looked surprised.

"Oh, it's not really *that* big, you know! Three of us live here, after all."

"Of course," I said. "I'd forgotten that."

"Do you like the way it's done?"

"Oh, yes." But I could see that something more was expected. Trying to imagine what *Country Life* would say, I took the plunge: "It's a nice balance between rustic and modern, if you know what I mean. Elegant and restrained but also really cosy." I shot a glance at her. She was rapt. "I love the use of chintz," I added in a final burst. "It just sums the place up for me."

Was that overdone? Apparently not.

"That's *exactly* what I was trying to achieve!" Suki looked radiant.

"Oh, you did it yourself?"

"Why?" Suki looked instantly, unpleasantly suspicious, her blue eyes becoming slits. "Who did you think had done the interior decoration?"

"Well, um, I don't know. . . ." I stammered. Actually I had imagined it to be one of those Chelsea firms with triple-barrelled names, but clearly I couldn't tell her that.

"Did Geneviève tell you she decorated the house?" Suki said in the same hostile tone of voice.

I didn't need to say anything to keep her talking, just look uncomfortable.

"God, I *knew* it! That's why I never got my interior design firm off the ground—I'm sure Geneviève went round telling everyone she did this house. Which is pretty bloody rich, when I even did all the paint finishes myself—I took a course, you know, I did that Etruscan green *faux* marble in Daddy's bathroom—"

"The veining was perfect," I put in sycophantically.

"You use feathers," Suki confided. "I'll show you if you like. Anyway, *I* did it, *not* Genny. God, I hate her! So she told you she did the house?"

"Up to a point." I thought I was safe on this one—it was unlikely that Suki had ever read *Scoop*.

Suki was still fuming.

"I've never liked her. Oh, it's no secret," she said venomously. "We're civilised in public but we haven't got a decent word to say for one another. They say she muscled in on Daddy almost as soon as Mummy died. Her own husband wasn't rich enough for her."

"Dominic's father?"

She nodded. "Terribly posh but no money at all—he's a second son, you see. He's a sweetie, Alain. I really like him. Genny was a fool to leave him for Daddy, I've always thought so. But she likes her creature comforts."

I thought the venom with which Suki Fine spat this out was rather overdone. She was sitting more than prettily herself.

"Didn't you tell me that your father bought her the house next door?" I said.

She nodded, indicating the garden with her head. "It backs on to ours. There's a connecting door through the garden. Daddy usually goes through to Genny, rather than the other way round. I think he thought he was protecting us from knowing about it till we were old enough. Convenient, isn't it?"

The sheer spite with which she said this left me speechless; but she seemed not to expect an answer.

"Shall we go up and see Bells?" she said, changing the subject. "She might be awake by now. The doctor said so, anyway."

We trooped back up the stairs and into the rose-carpeted zone that signified Belinda's territory, through a sitting room stocked with huge pink squashy sofas. There were no books, I noticed disapprovingly, just a giant TV screen with shelves of videos ranked on either side. Entering the bedroom, I blinked. I couldn't help it. The bed was hung with pink silk curtains suspended from a sort of canopy on the ceiling, the dressing table ditto. Ruches and swags of the same material formed valances round the furniture, spilling on to the cream carpet. The right-hand wall of the room was nothing but ivory fitted cupboards painted with climbing roses, courtesy, I assumed, of Suki. Had she made this room for her sister? It was like a little girl's fantasy come to life.

Meanwhile Belinda lay like Sleeping Beauty in the bed, her long blonde hair spread out over the pillows. She had thrown the covers partially aside; it was a warm day, or maybe she just wanted to reveal her peach silk pyjamas, trimmed with lace which had probably been hand-tatted to order by French nuns. Her face was even paler than usual. There were delicate mauve shadows under her eyes. How clever of her; they went with the room. The only discordant note was her stertorous breathing. In a man one would have called it snoring, but princesses neither snored nor perspired.

"She's still asleep," Suki said, keeping her voice down. I gave her marks for observation. "I expect I'd better not wake her."

I wasn't going to miss this golden opportunity.

"Is that the garden gate?" I asked, glancing towards the window. "I thought I heard something bang."

As I had hoped, Suki went immediately to look into the garden to check if Geneviève was invading her territory. Since this necessitated her leaning over all the taffeta pillows and fluffy toys with which the window seat was clustered, it gave me just enough time to slide up the silk sleeve of Briar Rose's pyjamas and look at her arm.

Around the crook of the elbow were clustered several neat little puncture marks, each with its own small, dark bruise around it. Somehow I didn't think this was the doctor's work. I shoved the sleeve of Belinda's pyjamas back down just as Suki turned around. There wasn't time to draw my hand back so I pretended to be taking her pulse.

"It's quite slow, but perfectly normal for the state she's in," I said nonchalantly. "Was there anyone there?"

"No, you must have heard a branch in the wind or something." Suki was looking at me. "Do you know about pulses and things?"

I didn't imagine she meant how to cook lentils.

"I used to teach weights in a gym," I answered, letting Belinda's hand fall to the coverlet. "You have to do a course in basic medical stuff, what to do if someone's having a seizure, all that kind of thing." I stood up.

"Oh, really?" Suki led the way downstairs. "Which gym?"

The Chalk Farm Gym and Leisure Centre: council run, near Camden Town.

"Trust me," I said gently. "You won't have heard of it."

. . .

I stayed with Suki for another hour, chatting away over more Lapsang. Since we had practically nothing in common this would have been difficult if I hadn't been on a fishing expedition. Suki instructed me at length on the best way of making tea, displaying once again her weakness for telling people how to do things. Finally I managed, by dint of talking about steroid use in gyms, to bring the conversation round to drugs in general. It was clear that Suki had not yet heard how Charles de Groot had died—officially, anyway—or she would surely have mentioned it. Instead she said, as if seizing the opportunity:

"I've been so worried about Bells, I can't tell you. Ever since school—well, even before that, if I'm being honest—she's been terribly uncontrollable. She dropped out at sixteen, you know. Well, we both did, but I went on to do all my courses."

Suki used this word with total seriousness, as if she were talking about advanced philosophy seminars or intensive Latin and Greek summer schools. Her list seemed unusually comprehensive: she had "done" cordon bleu, art appreciation (the Italian masters), paint finishes, interior decoration ("that was terribly serious, we even had an *architect* come in to lecture"), picture restoration and dressmaking. I may have left out a few.

"Getting Bells into this secretarial course was a miracle," Suki was saying. "The only way Daddy could make her was to say he'd sort out a job for her on *Mode* if she finished it. She should enjoy that, don't you think? She loves fashion."

"I met Baby Thompson at the engagement party," I offered. "She works in PR, fashion mostly. Belinda seemed to know her quite well."

Suki furrowed her porcelain brow. "Oh, *Eleanor!*" she said finally. "We were at school with her, you know. She didn't start calling herself Baby till later. It's silly, isn't it? I mean, it doesn't exactly suit her."

Since this was what I had always thought myself, a wave of sympathy for Suki flooded through my veins. Belinda Fine would be familiar with a not dissimilar sensation.

"I think she's quite into drugs," I said, happily traducing Baby's fair name in the service of information-gathering. Though maybe it wasn't slanderous: if someone told Baby it was the latest thing to mainline smack she'd do it like a shot. As it were. Anyway, it worked. Suki grimaced.

"Everyone smokes nowadays, don't they? I mean, *I* have, and everyone I know does. And stuff to keep you going at parties," she added euphemistically. "But not—you know, not . . ."

"The hard stuff?" I said, choosing my words carefully, not wanting to shock her.

Suki nodded so vigorously I thought the tortoiseshell hairclip was going to pop off her head.

"I hold Charles completely responsible," she said. "Bells didn't tell me so, but I could guess. I'm sure she never did that kind of thing before she knew him. You know. I don't want to say it." She mimed injecting herself. I looked suitably horrified.

"I want to talk to Felix—that's our doctor—about it, maybe get her into a clinic or something. They've got all these cures nowadays. Felix will know just the place. Now Charles is dead at least there won't be any more temptation, will there?" She looked at me rather shyly. "I'm so glad you came round," she said. "It's such a relief to have someone to talk to. I've been really worried about Bells. It's so nice of you to listen to me witter on. You will come back again, won't you?"

"Yes, of course I will," I said reassuringly. You bet I would. I had a lot more things I wanted to ask her about—her and Belinda, when Sleeping Beauty had finally woken up. Belinda was really the one to talk to; apart from all the other considerations, she was even less discreet than Baby. Suki would scare off much more easily.

It was ludicrous, but for a moment, looking at Suki, I felt hypocritical, guilty for trying to lead her to confide in me: despite the expensive furnishings with which she was surrounded and the equally expensive clothes draping her well-maintained body, she looked as sad and vulnerable as a lonely waif, an illustration for *The Little Match Girl*.

Then my sense of proportion cut in. Whose fault was it but her own if she didn't have any friends?

13

Hawkins gave me the all clear next day to go into Mowbray Steiner and check the damage done to Floating Planet: Inspector Brand, or one of his attendant lords, had apparently rung the high-ups at the bank to inform them that I was to be allowed visiting rights. When I turned up, Joe practically pressed me to his bosom. Now that gossip had got round as to how Charles had really died I was so squeaky clean you could have used me for a washing-up liquid advertisement. It took me a while to detach myself from a fulsome flood of speech about how he had never thought for a moment that I had been careless fixing up the mobile, and enquire as to where my poor battered sculpture was currently residing.

"In the main reception room, Sammy," Joe said at once. "Only I don't have the key." He tapped the side of his nose with his index finger. "All very hush-hush, eh? Mr. Stronge told me to ring up to him when you came in. He'll come down and open it up for you."

"Oh God, does it have to be him?"

"Afraid so. Sir Richard said Mr. Stronge should have the key on account of he wasn't here on Sunday and has a clean bill of health, if you know what I mean."

David Stronge appeared almost as soon as Joe had buzzed him.

"Samantha my *dear!*" he exclaimed. Luckily it was only midday and he was still relatively sober. The dandruff, however, was unabated. "Long time no see!" He embraced me and led me protectively across the hall, towards the reception room. "I hope you won't be too distressed to see your work damaged like this. I do understand the feelings an artist has for his work—or of course in this case her, and a charming her at that—what was I saying?"

But by this time he had managed to find the right key and open the door. I assumed Floating Planet had been moved in here because the double doors allowed just enough space for it to enter. Even so they must have had to tilt it on its side. It squatted in the middle of the room, looking like a monstrous, ill-tempered, shiny alien which might at any moment shoot death rays in our direction. David Stronge looked distinctly taken aback. Unfortunately he recovered almost at once.

"Can I get you a drink from the bar?" he suggested. "It must be an appalling shock for you."

He was already heading in that direction.

"No thank you," I said, "it's much too early. I'd like my cheque, though."

"Cheque?" He looked baffled.

"The second half of the payment for the sculpture. As agreed, on installation."

An expression of deep cunning spread like mould over his jowly face.

"Well now, perhaps we could discuss that over dinner tonight. After all, the sculpture is not now currently installed, is it?"

"Which isn't my fault. As the police have proved." I was sick of all this messing around. "I thought you, or rather Sir Richard, were purchasing the mobile as a token of support for young British artists, right? Well, I don't think he'd appreciate it much to see an article in the *Herald* outlining how his young British artist has been refused half the money she was promised, on the grounds that Mowbray Steiner couldn't look after her artwork for more than three weeks without dropping it on someone's head. Think he'd like that? If you're not sure, we could go and ask him together. Now."

David Stronge had gone a fetching shade of mauve. It clashed with his tie.

"Oh, that won't be necessary," he fluted, his normally orotund tones raised an octave in anxiety.

"You bet it won't, as long as I get my cheque within ten minutes." I smiled at him unpleasantly. "I hope that doesn't inconvenience you?"

"No, not at all. I'll just have to go and authorise the payment, but I'm sure that won't be a problem. . . . You'll wait here?" he said, obviously nervous that I would decide to pop up and beard Sir Richard in his den.

"For ten minutes I will."

I looked at my watch pointedly. David Stronge gibbered out of the door in an advanced state of terror and suggestibility. Maybe when he came back I could make him get down on all fours and present the cheque to me between his teeth for an encore. On present form that shouldn't be too hard. I decided to model myself on Joan Collins playing Alexis Colby more often. No more Ms. Nice Person.

And then I started examining the sad carcass of Floating Planet, and all exhilaration left me, replaced at once by anger. The mobile wasn't beyond hope; the top half had survived practically unscathed and the bottom part of the panels could be beaten back into shape without too much difficulty. Ditto for the chicken wire. But it wasn't the work involved that frustrated me, it was the misery of having hung it, pristine and perfect, only a few weeks ago, and now having to contemplate the prospect of disassembling it, taking it home and painstakingly going through the whole process again. One of the most difficult parts of making anything was knowing by instinct when it was done.

Finding the right moment to stop, because any further tinkering would be counter-productive, was a skill in itself. Once I had finally, reluctantly, finished a sculpture, once I had let it go, I never wanted to have to think about it again.

I would have to repair Floating Planet as quickly as possible, I decided; if I allowed any time to think about what I was doing I would only confuse myself. Just put it back the way it had been, and ban myself from any temptations to try improvements that could be made now that I had seen what it looked like suspended in the air. . . .

"Sam?" It was David Stronge, hovering at the door, holding a cheque out in front of him nervously as if it were an entrance ticket.

"Oh, right. Thanks," I said, ungraciously taking it from his hand and checking the sum. My bank manager would be a happy woman, albeit only till the clothes bills started kicking in. "I've finished," I announced. "You can lock up again. The police will let me know when I can take it away for repairs."

I left the room without looking back. It didn't help much: I could feel Floating Planet glaring at me for deserting it in this condition, even temporarily. David Stronge locked the door officiously behind me.

"I'll say goodbye, then, David," I said firmly, shaking his hand in a hearty, masculine sort of way.

"So you're not free tonight?" he said. He was a tryer, I had to give him that.

"Nope. And now excuse me, won't you? I must go to the toilet."

As I pushed open the door, I appreciated why Inspector Brand had made the assumption that Charles had come in here to shoot up; as always, the corridor and the toilets themselves were empty. To drag someone down the hall and across the atrium would be the work of a moment; all the floors were either tiled or marble, no carpet to catch at the body. I stared at myself in the mirror and ruffled up my hair a bit, giving David Stronge time to disappear. He wasn't hanging around outside the toilet door; as I reached the atrium I peeked my head out surreptitously, but he was nowhere to be seen. What a relief.

Someone had just come out of one of the lifts and was crossing towards the door. It was Simon Grenville. He stopped at Joe's desk.

"Oh, Joe, I'm just going out for . . . for lunch. I don't know how long I'll be. All right?" There was a nervousness in his voice, out of all proportion to this simple statement, which caught my attention. Then he cast a hurried glance back over his shoulder. Instinctively I found myself ducking into the corridor for a few seconds, and when I came out into the atrium he had already gone. I said to Joe curiously:

"People don't usually have to check in and out with you, do they?"

"Nah, they tell Susie upstairs. She's the one who takes messages. Don't know what Mr. Grenville was on about, but it doesn't matter to me. I just say yes, sir, no, sir, three bags full, sir—"

But I was already pushing my way through the revolving doors so hard that they spun round behind me like a Catherine wheel. Following someone clad in a navy-blue suit in the City at lunchtime was a task to strain even the most expert stalker. Thank God for the ethereal fairness of Simon's hair. I caught a glimpse of what looked like him disappearing to the left up Broadgate. There wasn't any time to waste; I dived into the crowd and after the apparition, hoping that I was following the right man.

We rounded the corner on to Liverpool Street in tandem, the horde of bankers, insurance agents and secretaries through whom I was pushing my way providing me with adequate cover, though the man who might be Simon never looked behind him. I didn't expect him to. The furtive glance back into the atrium had been more like a reflex than a genuine fear of having someone on his trail. It wasn't till he turned and dived down the stairs leading to Liverpool Street station that I caught a glimpse of his face and knew that I was following the right person. Relaxing, I let the crowd bear me down with them.

The new development of the station was a maze of walkways, shops, pubs, fast-food joints and stalls selling everything from silk underwear to fruit and flowers. I kept my head down, conscious that in this environment, with everyone dressed for business, I stuck out in my jeans and cropped T-shirt as much as Suki Fine would have done walking through Camden Market in her pink Chanel. Also, ducking my head helped me to avoid keeping my eyes fixed on Simon's back, an easy temptation if you're following someone, and a dangerous one too; after a while people sense that they're being watched, especially if they were as jittery as Simon was at this moment.

Luckily for me he was heading towards the tube station. Having a Travelcard, I could afford to hang back, giving him a comfortable margin of space in which to buy his ticket from the automatic machine and feed it through the gate. I strolled up to the same gate and pushed in my ticket. The wretched machine spat it back at me contemptuously. Impatiently I tried again, with the same result. Attempting to keep calm, I straightened the ticket out and fed it in once more with a couple of curses. Finally the machine deigned to let me through. I gave it a kick to teach it some manners.

Simon's head was disappearing ahead of me down the stairs. I shot after it. The station corridors were not as heaving with people as the concourse had been, but there were still more than enough bodies to cover me as I hurried through, looking around me for his straw-coloured head. At last we reached the Circle Line platform; the train was just arriving. For a moment I couldn't see Simon and panicked, but then, as the doors opened, I saw a fair head further down the platform and dashed down the train, managing to jump into the carriage next to his just as the doors were closing.

I stood in the swaying tube carriage, holding on to the rail above my head, leaning against the glass panel and keeping an eye on Simon, seated halfway down the next carriage and now looking deep in thought. What the hell I was doing I really didn't know; after all, he might just be going out to do some lunchtime errands, and if he spotted me dogging his movements the embarrassment factor alone would be enormous. All I had to go on were the alarm bells that had rung on hearing the furtiveness with which he had spoken to Joe, not to mention the way he had looked back nervously before leaving the bank. It wasn't much. But I hadn't had anything planned for the rest of the day. And it was stopping me from thoughts about my poor, sad, bruised sculpture.

Farringdon station clicked by. At King's Cross Simon's head was still in the clouds; it was a good ten seconds after the doors had opened that he looked up casually, clocked where he was and jumped up to leave the train. Cursing him, I pushed through the mob of annoyed people trying to board and stood for a moment on the platform, looking around me. Simon was already at the far end, feeding his ticket through the gate.

We walked at a fast pace through the station concourse. I wondered if he were heading up to the outside world, maybe to catch a mainline train at the rail station, but no, he dived purposefully down another set of steps, put his ticket through yet another machine and trotted over to the Northern Line escalator. I followed him on to it and immediately felt exposed. If he happened to glance back up the escalator he'd see me at once. I bent over as if to tie a shoelace, effectively hiding myself behind the back of the girl in front of me. Only I was wearing my patent leather ankle boots, which didn't have any shoelaces. After a while I started fiddling with the elastic instead. People who passed me, walking down, stared curiously at my feet. It seemed an interminable descent.

Simon chose the northbound direction of the Northern Line, which headed towards Camden Town, my usual stamping ground. That simplified matters considerably. If he did see me I would just tell the truth—mostly: I'd been to the bank to see my sculpture and now I was going to Sainsbury's to lay in some fast-food supplies. And what a surprise to see you here, Simon! Where are you off to? This isn't your normal neck of the woods.

But despite that, Simon seemed to know his way very well. This was obviously a journey he had made often; he didn't need to look around him except to check the destination board, which informed us that the first train was going to Edgware and would arrive in two minutes. They ticked by slowly. I hung back to see whether Simon would take this train or whether he wanted the next one, which served the Mill Hill branch of the line. But he got on. I emerged from the alcove in which I'd been standing and slipped unobtrusively into the next carriage, again stationing myself by the window where I could see him but not be seen. Euston, Camden Town, Chalk Farm came and went, the passengers thinning out noticeably with every stop. And then, as the train was pulling into Belsize Park station, Simon stood up.

My heart sank. Ten minutes ago I'd been cursing whoever invented escalators, and now I took it all back. Belsize Park station was so deeply sunk under Haverstock Hill that it wasn't practical to build an escalator there—it had lifts instead. This gave me a stark choice: get in the same lift with Simon and bluff out the moment of recognition, maybe even offering to walk with him to his destination, or wait for the next one to come, thus running the risk of losing him altogether. Sprinting up the stairs was out of the question; it would take too long. There were hundreds of the bloody things. Even if I made it to the top of the shaft in time I'd be too winded to do anything but sink to the ground panting.

Instinct warned me against the more brazen option, but in any case the decision was made for me. Only a handful of people had alighted and I had to fall back behind them to avoid Simon noticing me. By the time I had arrived at the entrance to the lifts he was already inside one and airborne. I crossed my fingers and prayed that the other one was working today; if I had to wait for Simon's lift to let him out, load itself with human cargo and chug back down the shaft again he'd be long gone when I finally saw daylight. The indicator for the second lift was lit, denoting that it was on its way down to us, but anyone who's ever travelled by London Transport, let alone on the Northern Line, knows precisely how much of a guarantee that was.

But just then the lift doors clanked open. I fell into them, histrionic with relief. The journey seemed to take forever. At ground level there was no one to check the tickets, which always annoys me, but it was one-thirty on a sunny afternoon and the inspector was doubtless down the road sitting outside a pub with his shirtsleeves rolled up, his bald patch peeling. Bastard.

I ran outside and looked around me frantically. For what seemed an age I didn't see Simon. All the cafés and pubs had arranged their tables outside and the trees were thick along the wide pavements, casting deceptive shadows over passers-by; every second person seemed to have golden hair, or maybe that was just the reflection of the sun through the leaves. But finally, across the other side of Haverstock Hill and proceeding in a downhill direction, I saw his blessed navy suit. It couldn't help standing out in these self-consciously artistic parts—we were nearly in Hampstead, after all, and the only suits one chanced across round here were unstructured Comme des Garçons or cheaper copies of same, definitely not office wear in navy pinstripe. Simon was turning right off the main road into a side street called Belsize Grove.

I threw myself across the road at the traffic lights, not waiting for the signal, waving apologetically at the honking drivers, and jogged lightly down the hill past the post office and the delicatessen and the greengrocer's to the junction with Belsize Grove. I sidled just a little way around the corner. Simon was walking along the far pavement, and as I watched he swung left into Primrose Gardens. I nipped up to the corner and stopped again, repeating the sidling procedure. This was beginning to feel like that training for runners when you sprint, jog and walk at random intervals. I think they call it fartlek but you don't have to tell people that while you're doing it.

Halfway down Primrose Gardens Simon stopped for a moment, checked his watch, and then went up some steps to a front door painted dark orange. He rang a bell, spoke into an intercom and was buzzed in. It looked as if he'd been expected. I hung around on the corner for a while, thinking that perhaps he was picking something up (drugs, perhaps? Hawkins would love that) and would be back out straight away. But ten minutes passed and he was still in there, though a woman had come out shortly after he entered. She had walked away from me down the street, giving me no opportunity to see her face. I decided that she needn't necessarily be connected with Simon; judging by the number of buzzers at the front door the house was divided into flats.

I looked at the time and revised my options. I couldn't risk going up to the door, and I couldn't stay on this corner much longer. Primrose Gardens was a deeply pretty little street with a large oval of grass in the middle furnished with trees, benches and a tiny children's playground like a miniature park, around which the narrow road divided and met again at the far end, like a river around an island. The houses encircling it were high and narrow, cars jammed down both sides of the road in a tight fit more strained than a builder's jeans over his behind.

It was time to make a move. Casually I strolled down the street and turned into the gardens. Mercifully, being summer, the trees and bushes were dense with sheltering foliage. I picked a bench with its back to the house in question and sat down. It was quiet here, even though we were so close to the main road; when anyone came out of the flats behind me I would hear.

Another ten minutes had passed, and no one had come in or out of the house. I was getting bored and was checking my watch too often, which made the time seem even longer. I'd never have the patience to do this kind of thing for a living. I had also realised that in my dash down the hill I hadn't checked out the greengrocer's to see if the young-Robert-Mitchum lookalike was still working there. Probably for the best; if I'd spotted him at the pace I was going I'd have tripped over a paving stone and gone flying. And it gave me something to look forward to on the way back.

I started reciting all the dirty limericks I could think of, which kept me going for a while. Then I heard someone coming up the street. I leaned forward and squinted through the bushes.

"Tom?" I said in disbelief. "What are you doing here?"

Tom stopped in his tracks, looking as surprised to see me as I was to see him.

"I live in the next street!" he said. "What are *you* doing here—communing with nature?"

"Not exactly." I was delighted to see Tom, and not only because his presence would provide me with what in spy novels is called cover. Chance meetings are always good when you've been quarrelling; they save face because neither of you has had to humble yourself by making the arrangements. I patted the bench. "Are you in a hurry? Come and sit down."

"Why are you whispering?" said Tom suspiciously. "I can hardly hear you."

But he walked through the gate into the tiny park and stood looking around him.

"Pretty in here, isn't it? I just came out to get the paper."

"Where's Alice?" I said, building bridges.

Tom darted me a deeply untrusting look. "She's at work."

"Oh really? What does she do?"

"She's a social worker."

I kept my face straight. No one could say I wasn't doing my best. I was dying to ask him whether they'd made the beast with two backs yet but I restrained myself nobly. Then I noticed that Tom was wearing a new sweater. For years I'd never seen him in anything but a dirty old white Aran or a dirty old navy ditto: now he was modelling a lumpy, handmade-looking jumper in various sludgy shades of brown and green with strange bobbly bits hanging off at random. I knew perfectly well who was responsible for this atrocity, but I was too cunning to denounce it to his face. Instead I said with subtle guile:

"Aren't you hot in that sweater?"

He smirked proudly. "I like to wear it. Alice bought it for me," he said. "Some woman in Wales makes them from goat's hair. They all come out different, apparently. It's nice, isn't it?"

"Mm." Things were even more serious than I had realised. Tom was sinking into a morass of hippiedom. From here it was only a short step to handmade leather sandals.

A door banged behind me. I looked round quickly but it wasn't Simon's. Tom hadn't noticed; he was looking down happily at his jumper. His beer belly seemed to have shrunk somewhat. I rather missed it.

"I really hope you and Alice can get on, Sam," he was saying seriously. "You've got so much in common."

What, for Christ's sake, apart from our sex? I wondered.

"Alice really cares about people," Tom continued. "She's so tenderhearted."

Since according to Tom I had all the softness and womanly sympathy of Catherine the Great halfway through a major tantrum, I failed to see why he thought I resembled her. Besides, if she cared about him so much, she wouldn't let him out of the door looking like that. Small children might throw stones at him.

"How's your work going?" I said, interrupting this paean before I heard that Alice was shortly due for canonization. A smile broke over the parts of his face that weren't already looking soppy.

"Wonderful!" he said. "I've started a sonnet sequence. There's nothing like being in love, Sam. You should try it." He looked at me sympathetically. "The true communication that comes from two people meeting with their minds, their souls—"

"What about the bodies?" I muttered. "They met yet?"

But Tom didn't hear, fortunately enough.

"Look, we're going along to a sort of club on Sunday," he offered by way of an olive branch. "Some people Alice knows run it. Why don't you come with us? It's in Highbury."

"What's it called?"

"Chill Out. It's supposed to be very relaxing. It starts at four and we'll be there right from the beginning. Alice promised to help set out the mattresses."

I stared at him blankly.

"*Right*," I said.

"It's in that converted church down behind the Toyota garage. You will come, won't you?"

For a moment a flash of the old Tom peeked through, and I wondered if he were really asking for some support at this dire-sounding event without having the nerve to come out and say so.

"Of course I will," I said, and was rewarded with a hug. Up close the sweater was as scratchy as a hair shirt—Tom was doing penance for being with Alice.

"I must be off now, Sammy," he said. "I'm halfway through a sonnet and I feel it coming on again. See you on Sunday, OK?"

He loped off. I stared after him, my mind revolving rescue plans, having completely forgotten about Simon Grenville and his mysterious appointment. Behind me a door closed. I peered cautiously through a bush. Simon was coming slowly down the steps, allowing me to have a good look at his face. It was no longer preoccupied, but released, washed clean of worry, as if he had had some excellent news; he looked happier than I'd ever seen him. I looked at my watch. He'd been in there for just under an hour.

He went back up Primrose Gardens in the direction that he'd come. I toyed with the idea of following him and discarded it. My instinct said that he was heading back to work; this trip would have taken him over two hours from start to finish, and his surreptitiousness on leaving the bank indicated that he hadn't covered his tracks by pretending he had to see a client. He'd need to be back at his desk as soon as he could. I preferred to wait and see who else came out of that house.

Another woman rang the bell and was admitted shortly after Simon had disappeared; I hadn't seen which buzzer he had pressed so I didn't know if she were visiting the same person. Crossing the street, I went up the steps and looked at the names on the four buzzers: B. Macpherson, Dr. Daniel Goldman, Alan and Jody Lloyd, Henry Smith. I didn't recognise any of the names. With Simon gone I could afford to be less furtive. Withdrawing to a bench that faced the house, I twiddled my thumbs and stared at the sky.

After another half-hour the orange front door opened and an extremely handsome young man came out, dressed in a cut-off T-shirt which showed off a gym-sculpted torso and a tight pair of jeans that did the same for his equally well-packed lower body. Full of energy, he slammed the door behind him and bounced down the stairs, a sports bag slung over one shoulder. His bright eyes passed over me indifferently as he latched the gate shut and headed down the street.

I watched him go with considerable interest, and not just for the fine display of gluteus maximus he provided as he walked away. He looked like the kind of man who was about as interested in girls as Alice would be in the latest issue of *Vogue*. And spending a lunch break with him would make anyone leave smiling.

It was prurient in the extreme, but I would have given a lot to know if it was he who had put that look of relaxed contentment on to Simon Grenville's face.

14

Sebastian's body and mine were doing less meeting these days, at least in any significant sense. And that wasn't to leave time for our minds to encounter on a higher plane, either; Sebastian was deeply stressed, being occupied with putting together a large and complicated bid on behalf of the client who'd been at the engagement party. He spent most of the pitifully small amount of free time left over in bed, asleep. I began to see how he earned his salary.

If I had been a nurturing sort of person I would have cooked him dinner and mopped his brow. As it was, I went round to his flat every so often to help him eat a wide selection of gourmet takeaways. The sheer variety of high-quality food that people were prepared to deliver to your door—providing you lived in the right postal district—dumbfounded me. It wasn't cheap, but then nor was the limit on Sebastian's credit card.

I didn't tell him about how I had followed Simon, though I did cast out a couple of tentative feelers about the latter's sex life. Sebastian repudiated the idea that Simon might be gay on the grounds that at school he had never seemed interested in that kind of thing, but since, at the kind of school that Sebastian attended, most of those who *were* interested in that kind of thing proceeded to spend the rest of their lives firmly denying any homosexual tendencies, I wasn't sure how much this reasoning proved.

I was mainly waiting for an opportunity to talk to the Fine sisters—Belinda in particular—and soon enough it came, at Charles's funeral, which took place a few days later. It was such a smart affair I expected to see the photographer from *Tatler* snapping everyone as they entered the churchyard: there had obviously been a run on chic black hats at Harvey Nichols. I had a Twenties black straw and ostrich feather confection pinned to the side of my head, purchased three years ago. This was the first time I'd worn it. I never threw any item of clothing away; sooner or later the right moment for it always turned up.

The atmosphere was naturally subdued, though I attributed that to good manners rather than grief. Charles apparently had no close family, just some cousins in Holland who didn't come over for the funeral, so Belinda was not required to console grieving relatives. She wore an enormous black picture hat and a long, narrow black dress, resembling the mistress of a tycoon paying her last respects to his coffin. The similarity between the twin sisters was accentuated by the formality of their clothes. They might have been clones.

Sir Richard had a paternal arm around Belinda for most of the service, Suki on her other side, though it didn't seem to me that Belinda needed much support, moral or physical. I hadn't seen her conscious since her engagement party, and either they had shot her so full of tranquillizers that she didn't know which end of her was up, or she had little difficulty in controlling any outbursts of grief for Charles. Occasionally she dabbed at her eyes with a black-edged handkerchief, but that seemed more for effect than necessity. Dominic, as always, had positioned himself slightly back from the family group, his black suit and darkly brooding eyes giving him a touch of Heathcliff. He was probably just wondering how long it would be before he could have a cigarette, but somehow his face always seemed to settle into these Gothic hero expressions.

The service was eerily perfect, down to the expensive wreaths of flowers and the cortège of black limousines for the Fines. Geneviève greeted everyone and circulated discreetly, receiving condolences and murmuring in return what were doubtless just the correct conventional responses. I hadn't known that etiquette required there be a hostess at a funeral, but it was a neat choice of role for Geneviève, since Suki was attached as possessively to her father's arm as his other was to Belinda. Geneviève, instead of engaging in competition with Suki for her place next to Sir Richard, was withdrawing herself smoothly and in the process behaving in a way that probably annoyed Suki even further. How well she was handling the situation, I reflected, watching her move around the various clusters of people, her manner dignified and restrained but with a faint shade of detachment which indicated clearly that one understood that nobody was truly mourning Charles de Groot. There was something inhuman about Geneviève's ability to cope with difficult situations. I didn't trust it.

After the lowering of the coffin, Sebastian and I went over to pay our respects and were promptly subsumed into coming back for drinks at the Fine house. No one used the word "wake." Maybe it was considered vulgar.

I was interested to note that, apart from the family doctor and his wife, we were the only guests. That was the Fine pattern: plenty of acquaintances but no close friends. Dominic and Sebastian talked about the cricket in lowered voices while Suki swept Belinda and me into the garden. Birds hummed in the trees and the rich smell of roses hung in the air like a perfume. Belinda perched on a little table under the apple tree and pulled off her hat, her gaze directed idly to the garden wall in the distance and the Planchets' large white house beyond it.

"God, it's hot," she said. "I'm glad I didn't buy that other hat, Sukes.

It would have been much too heavy." She twirled the huge straw cartwheel casually on one finger.

"How do you feel?" I said.

She looked at me blankly. "Oh, all right." Then, seeing my expression, she seemed to realise that more elaboration was required.

"You know," she said rather vaguely, "the more I think about it all, the more it just seems like a dream—Charles, the whole thing . . . it all seemed to happen so *fast* . . . I mean, of course I miss him, but I still find it hard to believe. . . ."

"How long had you been together?"

"Oh, not long," she said blithely. "We had fun, of course, and he was so handsome, but I never felt I really knew him, if you know what I mean. I woke up yesterday and I just thought, well, who *was* he? Who was that person?" She pouted wistfully. "It would have been fun to have been married, though. I've really done everything else. I'd have been a Griffon—Grafin, whatever. And I was having such a lovely time planning my dress—"

She looked infinitely sadder about the loss of the dress than she had watching Charles's coffin lowered into the ground. Dr. Jones diagnosed a bad case of skewed priorities.

"Suki?" Sir Richard called from inside the house. "Come here a minute, will you, m'dear? Some problem about the flowers."

"Do you want something to drink when I come back, Bells?" Suki said solicitously.

"God no, I'm fine thanks, darling."

"Well, if you're sure—"

"Oh, don't *fuss!*" Belinda said, but with such a charming smile that the words lost some of their power to hurt.

"Suki!" Sir Richard bellowed. Suki turned on her heel and went inside.

"She can be an old mother hen to me sometimes," Belinda confided. "I'm the younger twin, you know. I was a bit thin and sickly when I was little and apparently Sukes used to nurse me. It gets a bit much sometimes, her doing the older sister bit." She yawned widely. "God, those tranks Felix gave me really hit the spot. I feel all woozy."

Felix was a suave, silver-haired man with a blonde wife twenty years younger than himself. Like the funeral itself, he seemed too perfectly the stereotype of the society doctor to be real.

"Pumped me up with lots of stuff for the funeral," Belinda said. "To distract my mind from other things." She winked at me conspiratorially. "Naughty things. They want to clean me up, him and Suki. Such a bore."

I had no idea whether Belinda had got to the stage of dependency on junk or whether it was still an occasional indulgence. With Charles dead she would be short of a supplier, but how much would that matter to her?

"Do you—" I really couldn't think of a tactful way to put this. "Do you actually *need* it?" was the best I could do.

She was quite unoffended. "Oh no, not like that. It's fun, that's all."

This indifference to the subject emboldened me to press on. "Because now Charles is dead—Suki said he was getting it for you. . . ."

"Poor Charles," Belinda said casually. "I dare say I'm the only person sorry that he's dead."

"People didn't get on with him?"

She laughed. "You could say that."

"Why was that?"

But Belinda was off on another tack now. She was hardly aware of my presence, merely using what I said as cues off which to bounce her own wandering thoughts. Belinda Fine was the most solipsistic person I had ever met; other people to her were just projections to be switched on and off at whim—even, or maybe especially, Suki, who worried about her so much. She stretched out her arms, the narrow sleeves of her dress billowing out into trumpets over her slender hands, and examined her nails for a moment.

"I wonder if I'll get Charles's money?" she said meditatively. "If we'd been married I would. Not that it really matters."

"I didn't know he had any money."

"Not really. Nothing serious, I mean. But his bank account was pretty comfortable. Charles had his ways and means, you know."

"Do you mean he dealt drugs?" I said bluntly.

There didn't seem much point tiptoeing around her in this state, and indeed Belinda just widened her blue eyes to saucers and shook her head. It was a tiny movement and instead of a denial it could have meant that I shouldn't ask that kind of question. A movement at the French windows caught my eye; Suki was coming back.

"Where *did* he get his money from?" I said, feeling that I had nothing left to lose. Suki was walking towards us across the grass. Belinda focused on her instead of me and I thought that I had lost her attention, but just as Suki reached us she said, putting on a reproving voice:

"You shouldn't ask about other people's secrets," and started laughing. She put her finger to her lips. "Sssh! Sssh! Secrets!"

Annoyance rose in me like a sharp retort, but was silenced by quite another sensation. I looked at Suki. She was watching Belinda giggle away, half-doped on tranquillizers and God knew what else, and the expression on her face was unreadable. There was something unhealthy about the degree of Belinda's fixation with herself; to call it self-obsession would scarcely be an exaggeration.

I wondered if that were what Suki were thinking, if she were frightened for Belinda—or even of her. Because someone for whom the world only existed as a reflection of herself could be capable of doing anything if what she saw in the mirror didn't please her: anything at all.

. . .

Geneviève Planchet approached me as soon as I came back through the French windows.

"How is she?" she said, looking delicately concerned. Without seeming deliberation she turned slightly to one side, enclosing our conversation in a little niche of privacy away from the main body of the room. I admired her technique.

"She's in a rather funny mood," I said cautiously, "but that could be due to the tranquillizers."

"The what? Oh!" She frowned. "You thought I meant Belinda." Again there came that faint rise and fall of her shoulders, hardly pronounced enough to be called a shrug. "Belinda . . . goes her own way. Actually, I was talking about Suki. I'm rather worried about her. She's practically been dedicating herself to Belinda for the last week. She takes too much on herself."

This was so at variance with what Suki Fine herself had told me about Geneviève that I didn't know what to say. The oddest part was that I had believed Suki then, and I believed Geneviève now; I thought her concern for Suki genuine enough, even more so because she obviously didn't feel the need to pretend affection for Suki's wayward sister.

"Would you say she looked under strain?" Geneviève asked me.

"Well, yes," I said.

Geneviève clicked her tongue disapprovingly. Turning her head, she signalled Sir Richard, who came obediently across to us.

"Richard, I'm worried about Suki," she said without preamble. "She needs a break. She's doing nothing but nurse Belinda."

Richard Fine looked rather baffled.

"That's all very well, Genny, but what can I do about it? Eh? Suki's a grown woman."

"Maybe she needs her own flat," Geneviève said. "Belinda too."

"Offered them flats of their own years ago!" Sir Richard said. "Belinda said it'd be too much bother and Suki said she wanted to stay here. Said I needed someone to run the house. And I must admit, she's damn good at it. She did this whole place up herself, you know," he said to me. "Picked out everything. Damn good eye that girl's got."

I looked at Geneviève. She was nodding in agreement. I couldn't help remembering Suki's furious belief that Geneviève had tried to take the credit herself for the interior decoration. If this family's stories couldn't tally on even the most unimportant details, what would happen when something truly serious was at stake?

"Still," Geneviève was saying, "I can't help feeling that something should be done. . . ."

"Marry her off to Dominic," Sir Richard said. "Can't think why they didn't do it years ago. Set 'em up across the way and everyone's happy. Tell him to get his skates on, m'dear."

Geneviève shot a glance across the room at Dominic, who was lolling in an armchair, smoking a cigarette, looking completely at ease.

"It would be good for him as well," she commented. "A little responsibility."

The faint trace of French accent, the roll she gave to her *r*'s, was very charming. She said suddenly to me:

"But we're being so rude, Sam, just talking about our own concerns. I'm so sorry. We should be asking how your sculpture is."

I pulled a face. "I can repair it," I said. "It'll take a while, but it'll be as good as new. I'm just a little reluctant to have to think about it all over again."

"We'll foot the bill," Sir Richard said at once. "Get an estimate together and give it to me as soon as you want. No need to skimp." He made a sort of harrumphing noise. "Very embarrassing for the bank, y'know, something like that happening. Sooner it's back up there and we can all get on with things the better. Put it behind us."

"But what about the police investigation?" I said. "Surely they're still—"

Sir Richard interrupted me, and his tone of voice left me in no doubt how little he welcomed that kind of question.

"As far as I'm concerned," he said, "that young man was no good and my daughter had a lucky escape. End of story. Unlucky it involved your sculpture, of course, m'dear," he added as an afterthought. "But it'll all come out in the wash, eh?"

"You obviously had no idea that Charles was using drugs," I said innocently.

"No idea at all. Absolutely appalling!" he boomed, his face setting hard as a stone wall. "Quite apart from the engagement, that sort of thing is definitely not on. If I catch any employee of mine up to that sort of thing, he'll be out on his arse before he's had time to count to ten!"

Sebastian had come up to our little group in time to hear the last exchange. For a moment he looked so comically guilty that I had a hard time not bursting out laughing. Seeing him, Sir Richard relaxed slightly. Sebastian was clearly a favourite of his.

"Well," he said, "that's quite enough on this subject. What's the latest on the cricket, Shaw?"

15

That night I dreamed about Belinda Fine. She was sitting in the garden, wearing her black hat, though now it had a veil draped over it, behind which I could see her face only dimly. Through the shadowy black mesh her eyes burnt blue as gas flames and the expression in them was cunning and mad. Pressing her finger to her lips, she whispered to me: "Secrets! Sssh! Secrets!" and then started giggling. The giggles grew more and more deranged, their rhythm regular and loud, till finally with a start my eyes opened and I realised that the noise was the ringing of my alarm.

The dream was like a sign that the step I had been debating all yesterday evening was the right one to make. I didn't really want to do it, but there seemed little choice; I had no other possibilities to follow up that were as strong as this one. I went downstairs and rang the bank.

Simon took my call, but he sounded unusually guarded. I asked if he were free for lunch, saying that I wanted to talk about Charles, and he said too quickly that he was very busy at the moment. I suggested a drink after work and got the same response. In fact, he said, he didn't know when he would be free. He sounded as if he were about to hang up. I was as welcome as a rack of lamb at a vegetarian dinner. I wondered if this were the influence of Richard Fine's diktat: doubtless he had let it be known to the employees of the bank, as he had to me, that now Charles was buried the mystery of his death should follow the same fate.

Unwillingly I said: "I know about Primrose Gardens, Simon," and then cursed under my breath. It had come out much more bluntly than I'd intended.

The response was dead silence.

"Simon?" I said tentatively. His name fell into space and disappeared. There was nothing else I could think of to say. I expected to hear the small severing click that would tell me he had put the phone down on me.

But finally he spoke, and his voice sounded infinitely tired, almost that of an old man.

"Do you know a pub called The Queen's Head, behind Farringdon station? I'll meet you there at one."

Now he did hang up. I put the phone down, disgusted with myself, feeling like a cheap blackmailer. Behind the black veil, I seemed to see Belinda Fine's eyes laughing at me.

* * *

The pub was in a backwater of narrow streets, its dirty frontage promising little and its equally grimy interior delivering less. Simon was already there, in a back booth whose occupants couldn't be seen till you were halfway down the length of the pub. It was a good place to meet someone you didn't want to be seen with. He looked as weary as he had sounded on the telephone, his shoulders slumped, the corners of his mouth drawn down. With a flash of guilt I remembered his expression as he had left the house in Primrose Gardens, the access of hope and energy, of happiness in being alive, that had shone from him. The contrast between then and now was due to me. I didn't enjoy the reflection.

Sliding into the seat across from him, I said at once, before he could speak:

"I don't want you to misunderstand me. What I said on the phone was just to make you agree to see me, but it finishes here and now. I'm not Charles de Groot."

Something flickered in his eyes, though his features didn't move. He still looked drained, like a bottle when the wine has been poured off and nothing but the sediment remains. I pushed ahead. Nothing I said now could make it worse. Perhaps it was only self-justification that led me to hope that talking to me about it would help him.

"Charles was blackmailing you, wasn't he?" I said.

Simon looked up. He nodded slowly. "I thought that you meant—that you were going to—"

He met my eyes for the first time and read in them some message that relieved his anxiety: his body began to relax, the lines of tension clearing from his face.

"How did you guess?" he said.

"About Charles? Something Belinda said. I knew that there was some kind of blackmail going on at the bank, and what she said pointed directly to Charles. Then I remembered a comment you'd made once about his income. I thought at the time you were giving me a hint."

"Yes, that was foolish of me. I regretted it straight afterwards. It was just that he maintained such a perfect façade. Sometimes I couldn't resist cracking it just a little bit. Stupid, though."

The atmosphere had already changed. It was like the end of a debriefing, when for the first time spy and questioner can let themselves relax; the information is in circulation, the pressure of carrying it alone has been lifted. As if to signal this, Simon lit up a cigarette, offering me the pack. I shook my head.

"Charles asked me to meet him here about a year ago," he began. "I expect I must have had some idea even then, because I didn't ask him why. I just came. He showed me some photographs he had taken of me coming out of Dan's. Not that they proved anything in themselves, but they were like a symbol. He knew that. Just to see them was enough for me."

He looked up at me. "I know it's absurd to feel guilty about it. I don't really. Or I don't think I do. But I must do, mustn't I, or I'd have told him to go hang himself instead of agreeing to pay what he wanted?" He took a long drag at the cigarette. "It's something you absolutely don't do—where I come from, in any case. I'd probably lose my job. They'd think I was unstable. It's ridiculous, isn't it? Dan's been the best thing that ever happened to me. He's helped me work out who I really am. And for that I'd get the sack."

He sighed. "I couldn't really believe that you were going to carry on where Charles left off. It was the shock. I thought it was all behind me, that I was safe now."

"How did he actually manage it?"

"Oh, that was very smooth," Simon said. "He'd worked it all out in advance. He had a document for me to sign to say he'd loaned me a sum of money, on which I was supposedly paying interest. To be renegotiated after five years. Direct debit into his account at Coutts. Nothing underhand about the appearances, anyway."

I whistled. "How much were you paying him?"

He hesitated. "About £5,000 a year."

"My God. Simon, you do realise that he was pulling this on other people too."

"Oh, he was." Simon stubbed out his cigarette. "No doubt about it."

"One of them was Bill."

"Bill? You mean the security guard who had the heart attack?"

I nodded. "When he was dying he was trying to say something to me. He was looking at Charles. It must have been him."

Simon was staring at me. "What exactly did he say?"

"To me he said: 'I can't do it any more, even if he tells them.' And then to Charles he said: 'I won't,' and something that sounded like 'bloodsucker.'"

Ignoring the latter part of this, Simon repeated thoughtfully: "So he said 'do it'?"

I looked at him with increasing respect; he had seized on the most interesting point raised by Bill's words.

"Right. 'Do it,' not 'pay him.' It's impossible to imagine Charles wanting money from Bill—that would be chicken feed to him. But the opportunities presented by having the security guard in your pocket are tremendous. He could snoop round the bank when few people were there and get Bill to buzz him if anyone was on their way up. Bill patrolled at night, and the rest of the time he was watching the video screens. He could even switch them off if Charles wanted to go into somewhere he shouldn't, pretending that they'd malfunctioned. The possibilities are endless."

"And what do you think Charles had on Bill?"

"I don't know. Probably something small and sad that might not even have mattered to anyone but Bill himself. Charles gave Bill a note that evening, threatening him if he didn't cooperate any more. He pushed him too far."

Simon was nodding slowly.

"So, do you know who else Charles was blackmailing?" I persisted.

"No," he said flatly.

"I don't believe you."

"Why are you this concerned about it anyway?" Simon was angry now. Maybe he was remembering how I had made him meet me here. "What business is it of yours if a scummy little blackmailer gets put out of his misery by one of the people he was bleeding dry? You've just said that he caused Bill's heart attack! Charles was a piece of shit! Why do you care how he died?"

"Whoever did it used my sculpture," I retorted sharply. "Everyone seems happy enough to forget that. Richard Fine basically told me yesterday to put a figure on the damage and send him the bill—and don't tell me that wasn't an attempt to keep me from kicking up a fuss. I could have been in serious trouble, do you realise? I'd have been the perfect scapegoat! If they'd taken just a little more trouble to fake it up I could have been facing a manslaughter charge! And I still might be if I didn't—"

"If you didn't what?"

"Never mind." This was not the moment to boast about my unorthodox connection on the police force. I fixed him with my best penetrating stare and insisted:

"I won't tell anyone. I certainly won't tell the police. But you've got to tell me who else Charles was blackmailing."

Simon looked away. After a while he said uncomfortably: "It's not that I don't believe you. But you're putting me in a very difficult situation . . . I can't tell you that."

"But you know." I had already got more than I had expected. I might as well go for broke. "All right. What about telling me *how* you know?"

It was the second time in our acquaintance that something I had said had made him run for cover. He slid out of the booth and headed for the door as urgently as if I really had been meaning to take up where Charles had left off.

* * *

I didn't go after him. There would have been no point. Instead I sat for a while in the booth, thinking. Simon had left behind the pack of cigarettes in his hurry and I smoked one, not enjoying it, because I never did, but using the slow rhythm—inhale, exhale, inhale, exhale, tap off ash—to clear my thoughts. I seemed to have reached another dead end, but at least it was a stage further on; though I felt like a car juddering ahead, stalling, starting into life, and stalling again, I was definitely moving forward, slow as the progress might be.

I considered my options. I couldn't see how to get any more information out of Simon without threatening him, and I wasn't going to do that. Perhaps I should try talking to Belinda Fine again. I shied away from that idea. I didn't want the Fines to know how deeply I was interested in Charles's murder, and she was more than capable of announcing it to the world over dinner. I might already have pushed it too far with her.

I didn't even question why I wanted to find out who had murdered Charles. Whoever had dropped my sculpture on his head at best hadn't cared whether or not I would be held responsible for the disaster, at worst had hoped to drag me into it. That got my blood boiling. And once I get the bit between my teeth I won't let go till I've chewed it into pieces. Hawkins once compared me to a bulldog; that was how he got me into bed in the first place—sweet-talking me.

The cigarette was finished. I stubbed it out and stood up, walking to the door past the line of booths in which a motley collection of lunchtime drinkers were working their way to the bottom of pint glasses. Outside the sun was bright and I put on my dark glasses. Why I contrived regularly to find myself in the City or its environs at the lunchtime rush hour I had no idea. Incompetence, perhaps. Even these backstreets between Farringdon and Clerkenwell were bulging with office workers and sandwich bars. Well, at least it was convenient for my next destination. I headed towards the offices of the *Herald*, mulling over a way to find out who else Charles de Groot had been blackmailing.

There was no point asking Hawkins. If I told him why, he might do it, or rather pass the information to Brand; but I didn't want to expose Simon to that kind of scrutiny, let alone any other victims Charles might have had. And I'd have to smarm up to Hawkins just for a copy of the names, which I had no intention of doing. Nor did I mean to try that ploy on Tim; I didn't make promises I wouldn't keep. But I thought I might have some other form of currency he'd find almost as tempting. Maybe even more so.

. . .

The *Herald* was almost entirely open plan, spread over one floor of a huge office building; only the editor rated an office to himself. It being lunchtime, the place was practically deserted; most computers were on their stand-by screensaver programs, displaying silly sayings in neon colours which scurried randomly across the screen, or lawns which cut their own grass on automatic pilot. Tim, however, was at his computer, in his shirtsleeves, tapping away at the keys without much enthusiasm. As soon as he saw me he swung round on his chair.

"Sam! How are you?" Unfolding himself, he stood up and kissed me. "I thought that moron on the desk must have got the name wrong. What have I done to deserve a visit?"

I sat down at the next work station, currently unoccupied. Its owner had one of those ergonomic padded stools on which you half-sit, half-kneel. It felt distinctly strange. Across the computer screen scudded flying toasters pursuing slices of bread. I double-took and stared at it harder. They were definitely flying toasters, their wings silver and padded like the ones worn by fat cherubs in frescoes.

"Actually, it's about work," I said, wanting to disillusion him swiftly.

He grimaced. "Well, I didn't really think it was for the pleasure of my company. All right then. Whose work are we talking about here, yours or mine?"

"Both, hopefully."

"Oh really? How long will it take?" His tone was growing steadily more professional, more distant. "Because I've got to file this piece by two-thirty, three at the outside."

"Ten minutes. Fifteen at the most."

"OK, go ahead."

"What, here?" I said incredulously.

"Best place right now—it's nice and empty. Most people'll be out for another half-hour at least. If I take you to a pub anywhere round here it'll be infested with journos."

Sitting down, he straddled his chair and settled his chin on top of it in a Christine Keeler pose. The chair was high and cushioned, but Tim was tall enough to avoid looking silly.

"Fire away," he said, all business. We might just have met. I was impressed by this Clark Kent–like transformation: from admirer to news hound in half a minute, and no need to pop into a telephone booth. Ironically I found Tim much more attractive in his hardened work mode than as an admiring swain. My perversity was unbounded.

"It's sort of a tit for tat," I said. "I'm going to tell you something, and in return, if you can, I'd like you to get some information for me."

"With the usual provisos," he said.

I had no idea what he meant, but judging by his expression there was clearly no point in arguing. Instead I gave him a brief résumé of the events at Charles and Belinda's engagement party. He whistled slowly.

"It's a bit tabloid for us, but then my editor's been bollocksing us about the circulation ever since I can remember. This might be just what he's looking for. Nice highbrow list of characters as well."

"They were taking photos at the party for *Tatler,*" I suggested. "You might be able to get copies."

He nodded. "I did hear about this, but it didn't make much of a stir. Mowbray's PR people probably sat on it as much as possible. There's a way of making a story sound so infinitely boring that no one wants to touch it. But once you know it was the engagement party—fiancé crushed to death by falling sculpture—now that I like."

"Wait. I haven't told you the best bit. He didn't die because my sculpture fell on him. Someone dropped it, to cover up the fact that he was already dead. Overdosed on smack."

Tim unlaced himself from the back of the chair, swung it round to face his desk and started scribbling.

"This is brilliant—as long as no one sues us. Have to check that out. Be a great feature for the Saturday edition."

"Why Saturday?"

"More space. Maybe put it in the second section, get a two-page spread, lots of nice photos. . . . You don't happen to know who the investigating officer is?"

I gave him Brand's name.

"What about you? I can use you, can't I? Talented young sculptress, first big commission—"

"Second."

"Never mind, first sounds better. Do you have any photos of the sculpture, or you, or both?"

"Try my agent. He should have them. But for God's sake don't say you have any connection with me whatsoever when you're talking to people at the bank. Say you heard about it through Anne-Marie or someone. That Jordan girl."

"Understood. Though of course the City desk'll kill me for scooping them on this. What's your agent called?"

I gave him Duggie's name, reflecting that I should drop into the gallery and see the photographs myself. It would provide a welcome distraction. Tim went on scribbling for a minute, then said over his shoulder:

"OK, Sam, what's the pay-off?"

"You have to promise me that it's strictly confidential."

"Is it to do with this?"

I nodded.

"So I might be able to use it later?"

"Sure," I said. I could speculate till the cows came home; it didn't commit me to anything.

"All right, I promise."

By now a few people were filtering back to work. Keeping my voice down, I told him that I wanted Charles's bank records.

"For the last three years, say. The main thing I need is the records of the direct debits coming into his account, which is at Coutts, but I don't know the branch or the account number. I need the names of the people making the deposits, and the amounts. I thought you'd know some computer boffin who could pull those out for you," I added hopefully.

"What are these for?" Tim said at once, sniffing out a new trail. "Was he dealing? Mind you, you don't usually pay for your drugs on direct debit."

"I can't tell you now. But do you know someone who could do that?"

He looked at me for a long hard moment. Then he stood up, picking up his jacket from the side of his desk.

"Come on," he said. "We're going for a walk."

. . .

He took me to a telephone booth on Mount Pleasant and made me wait away from it while he rang someone. The conversation lasted about five minutes, during which Tim looked impatient and kept making interjections which the person he was talking to seemed to ignore. After this he hung up, came over to me and said:

"OK. He'll have the printouts with me tomorrow morning. I'll get them biked over to you. I'll charge his fee to the story, bury it somewhere in expenses."

"You mean he's not sending it by e-mail?" I said in surprise.

"This bloke hacks into other people's computers for a living. He knows how easy it is; he won't use his to transmit illegal stuff more than he absolutely has to. Especially to a journalist." He grinned. "He's probably right. Anyway, he insists I ring him from a payphone. That's why I picked this one—he knows I'm not ringing from the office because he can hear all the traffic going past."

I made a note to myself: project for the future, get to know Tim's contact for myself. Anyone who could come up with that sort of information was worth their weight in gold.

16

The next morning I dropped into the gallery to have a look at the photographs. Adrian fawned over me as I came in—though perhaps that's not the right word, implying as it does something small and soft with huge appealing eyes, preferably not dressed in a tight shiny orange shirt with exaggeratedly wide lapels and a pair of white linen hipster trousers. Adrian looked about as appealing as a mass murder in the Jean Paul Gaultier boutique. Duggie was out, fortunately, since I wasn't in the mood for talking—or being talked at. Adrian spread out the contact sheets on Duggie's desk and hovered over my shoulder, cooing at me, till I shooed him away.

Tony Muldoon turned out to be a very good photographer indeed. He had lined me up so that everything was in place; my nose looked as straight as a ruler. It was an idealised version of myself, how I would look if I were genuinely photogenic. I purred for a while in egotistical self-satisfaction.

Then, dragging myself away finally from the images of a perfect me, I turned to the shots of the mobile. They were just as good. Floating Planet soared in the background like a comet. He had caught the light on its chain so it shimmered, dissolved, the sculpture seeming to float in mid-air, a magical effect. I noticed that in a couple of photographs he had taken on the balcony the hook around which the chain was wound also appeared, showing how firmly it was secured. That might be useful.

I stuck a Post-It note on the top sheet for Duggie, indicating the numbers of the photographs I liked, and went home less happy than I would have hoped. Having seen "Floating Planet" as glorified by Tony Muldoon I was twitchy now for the police to release it to me for repairs. To that end I rang Hawkins when I got back to the studio, but he wasn't at the station. I left a message for him to call me back.

Tim's promised bike messenger hadn't yet materialised. I started pacing up and down the studio, trying to resist the urge to call him: there wasn't any point. If Tim said he'd send me a copy as soon as it arrived he meant it.

An hour later the messenger arrived, bearing a large manila envelope. I signed for it, thanked him and practically slammed the door in his face, ripping the envelope open. Inside was a compliments slip from Tim and a computer printout. Five names, in alphabetical order, with a list of figures following each one. My eyes raced over them. Then I went over to the kitchen table, spread out the list and read it again:

Simon Grenville
Patricia Makamoto
James Rattray-Potter
Henrik Claes Smith
Nicola Walters

The absence of Bill's name from the list of direct debits tied in neatly with my theory that Charles had been blackmailing him not for money but for the advantages of his position at the bank. I loaded up the percolator and set out a coffee mug, my brain racing with ideas. Ideally, to crosscheck I would need a list of the guests who had been at the engagement party. Hawkins could probably get that for me. Or I could get him to check out the names. Another thought struck me; I went over to the sofa and picked up the telephone, dialling Sebastian's direct line. He answered abruptly, hard at work.

"It's Sam," I said.

"Hello, you!" His voice lightened. "Look, I can't really talk, I'm up to my eyes in it right now."

"That's fine. I just wanted to ask you something."

"Fire away."

"The security passes that you all use to get into the bank—they work for the main door, out of normal hours, and for some internal doors as well, right? Can everyone just come in and out as they please?"

"No, we all have different levels of clearance. There's something called a Chinese wall within the bank, for instance, so that the trading floor and the investment people can't communicate information to each other, to avoid insider trading. Well, that's the idea, anyway. And if you need to work late or at weekends, you say so and get special clearance. Mine expires at midnight usually, but I've got it extended because of this bid we're working on. There's always a night guard on duty, because we have a 24-hour typing pool, and the cleaners come in. Someone has to be there to let them in and out, apart from the security side."

I homed in on what really interested me. "Would a director automatically have 24-hour access?"

"He might. I don't know. Depends on whether his job needed it."

"And who did you have to see to get special clearance?"

"David," Sebastian said.

"David Stronge?"

"Yup. I told you before, that's how David justifies his existence here—he does all the fiddly administrative crap no one else can be bothered with. Look, darling, I've really got to go. God knows why you wanted to know something like that. You can tell me some other time. See you Saturday night, I hope. I'll ring you tomorrow."

He hung up. The percolator was boiling. I poured out my coffee and thought about the information Sebastian had given me. After I'd finished the coffee I was jittery from caffeine and speculation; deciding that if I stayed around here, waiting for Hawkins to return my call, I would start twitching up the walls, I changed and went off to the gym, leaving a message on the answering machine to say what time I would be back. Three hours later, refreshed, showered, exercised, tension released and with two plastic Sainsbury's bags in tow containing foodstuffs which on the whole were virtuous, I returned to find that Hawkins still hadn't rung, the bastard. Tim had, however. I called him back.

"It's going well," he said with a kind of controlled excitement. "The editor's over the moon. He can't even complain if the bank kicks up a fuss—he's been moaning about the City coverage being too bland for the last couple of years."

"You didn't use my name when you talked to him, did you?" I said anxiously.

"No, don't worry. Tip-off from a reliable source. And now Jordan's gone into convulsions. Said she had some story she was working on and I've ruined it."

My brow creased. "To do with Mowbray Steiner?"

"I assume so, but she's closed up tighter than a clam—won't tell me what it was about. Threw a major wobbly this afternoon and now she's disappeared to sulk somewhere."

"What about Anne-Marie? Does she know what the story was?"

"Apparently not. I mean, they might be keeping their cards close to their chest, but I think A-M would tell me what was going on."

"I bet she would," I said dryly. "I wish I knew what Jordan was looking into."

"I warned her that if it was anything that could get in the way of the story she should tell me now," Tim said. "This is going in the Saturday edition, lead story in the second section—it's got to be bigger than anything she has on. If she sabotages it she's in real trouble."

"When is it running? Next Saturday?"

"That's right."

It occurred to me that I should definitely put my invoice in for repairs to Floating Planet as soon as possible; I'd want the cheque cleared before the shit hit the fan. I try to think of everything.

...

Hawkins finally rang me next morning. He sounded as impatient as usual ("I can't keep bothering with this kind of thing, you know, I've got cases piling up on my desk three feet high"). When I asked him to check if Patricia Makamoto, Nicola Walters or Henrik Claes Smith were at the party when it happened he nearly blew a gasket. But he wrote the names down.

"I'll do what I can. God, you're a bloody nuisance. Got to run. Ring you back when I can."

"Hang on! There's one more thing. Your lot searched his flat and his desk at work, right? His car? Did they find anything odd?"

"If you mean drugs, no. Nothing to indicate he was dealing, none of the usual paraphernalia."

"No, I meant . . . paperwork of some sort. Loans he'd made to people—"

"*Loans?* I don't think so. I'll ask. Look, I've really got to go, OK?"

All the men I knew seemed much too occupied with their busy, important jobs even to have a chat. I sulked for a while. Then I turned on the television, consoling myself with the reflection that if they were so bloody busy they wouldn't be able to enjoy the sybaritic pleasure of watching afternoon TV. Serve them right for being so sodding adult. I settled myself on the sofa and surrendered to self-indulgence.

. . .

I hadn't forgotten my appointment with Tom on Sunday, though I couldn't say that I was looking forward to it. Sebastian had been too busy to see me the night before, so I had gone to bed reasonably early, rising at ten and climbing up to the roof of my studio to clean out the skylights. I hadn't attacked them for about six months and they were once again filthy with pigeon shit and general London refuse. The weather was so lovely at the moment it seemed a shame not to be able to see it above my head.

I hauled a bucket of hot water up on a rope and scrubbed off the debris, spraying the glass afterwards with ecological insect repellent. Janey, who suffered from pigeon infestation herself, had had this recommended to her by her landlord. I didn't know if it would work, but at least it made me feel that I was taking steps. The sun beat down on my head, the water was warm and foamy on my hands; I rolled up the sleeves of my T-shirt over my shoulders, body-builder style, and squinted happily into the sun. There was something perversely satisfying about just how dirty the water was getting.

Across the roof plodded Fat Shirley, the cat who belonged to the night watchman of the warehouse that adjoined mine. Doubtless she considered herself to be on the prowl, though I didn't think the pigeons even bothered to fly away when they saw her coming. No domestic cat, even one who watched its weight and worked out regularly doing step exercises up and down the chimney pots, would take on a London pigeon. They were an excellent example of how the survival of the fittest worked in practice—oversized, diseased rats with wings. They weren't eating human flesh yet, as far as I knew, but that was the best that could be said for them.

Fat Shirley's stomach swung majestically from side to side of her undercarriage, and as I picked her up it spread itself out like butter coating my hands. She started purring, a long slow rumble like a heating system turning itself on. I stroked her for a while behind her ears, feeding the rumble, and then put her down; she stretched out on the roof and went to sleep at once, drugged by the heat. When I moved the bucket the clink woke her up and she opened one eye in surprise, stared at me in an offended way for a moment and shut it again.

The third skylight finished, I emptied the bucket over the back of the studio and, leaving Shirley still fast asleep, lowered myself back down through the skylight directly above my sleeping platform, the bucket swinging over my arm like Camden Market's answer to the Kelly handbag. I was sunwarmed and happy, flooded with virtue and UV rays. It was early yet to meet Tom, but I felt like going out; I pulled on a miniskirt and a tight little T-shirt, my hot-pink sandals with stacked heels and a pair of John Lennon sunglasses and sallied out to cruise through Islington.

...

I got off the bus at Highbury Corner just after four-thirty. I had been shopping in Islington: the vinyl bag hanging over my shoulder contained two CDs and a second-hand black Fifties cocktail frock which hadn't been there when I started out this morning. I made a resolution to get that invoice to Richard Fine tomorrow—who knew when my next sale would be? The church was only a few minutes' walk away. I found the entrance round the side. No bouncers, just a boy sporting a tie-dyed T-shirt, flared jeans and non-existent pupils. I said I was here to meet Tom and Alice and help with the setting up. His eyes glazed. I spoke to him firmly: I might have turned up here to see Tom out of friendship, but the impulse went only so far. I certainly wasn't going to pay £7 for the privilege. Finally he let me in free and stamped my hand with a flower design. Well, I hadn't been expecting a skull and crossbones.

Inside was a long, echoing tiled corridor which made me think at once of an old-fashioned school; all it was missing were the rows of hooks down one side and a bench below them to put your gym shoes on. Oh yes, and the smell. At the far end, a pair of double doors opened into a huge, gymnasium-sized room with a balcony running round three sides. I blinked, my eyes adjusting to the semi-darkness. The skylights had been blacked out with paper. Well, it made a change from pigeon shit. Strings of coloured lights glowed round the balcony, but the main illumination came from an enormous sheet of material hung on the fourth wall of the room, on to which were being projected a hallucinatory series of trippy images: endless geometric patterns in bright colours blending together, spirals spinning round, trying to eat their own tails, dizzily feeding off each other in a random series whose only rule was constant change.

On the floor were what looked like hundreds of mattresses pushed together to form a giant lying area on which quite a few people were already stretched out. Round the edges of the room were arranged dilapidated sofas, some of them occupied. Dreamy, ambient music flooded the hall at low volume, like a tide washing in. I wandered around the mattress formation, looking for Tom or Alice and feeling rather out of place; this wasn't really my scene. The clientele were a mixture of New Age types and ravers coming down after the night before. Though the latter were cleaner than the former they all wore loose clothes and sensible footwear, trainers or sandals—and by the latter I didn't mean hot-pink high heels.

At the far end of the mattress room was a door which led to another institutional corridor and a staircase. I picked the corridor first. At the far end was a large room, lit by daylight, which had been set up as a café stocked with plastic tables and chairs as institutional in feeling as the corridors, offering food baked in large tins and cut into stodgy wedges full of muesli or lentils. I thought not. Backing out politely with a smile at the apron-clad, dreadlocked chef, I went back down the draughty corridor and up the stairs. Halfway up was a sign indicating that I was going in the right direction for the bar. It was manna to the eyes. I quickened my pace and arrived at the top. To my right was another large room with more plastic chairs and tables, posters on the walls and a trestle table at the far end. It looked like the canteen of an impoverished youth club. This must be the bar. Thank God. I was dying for a beer.

"Sam! Over here!" Tom was waving to me from a table by the window. He was wearing the sludgy sweater. I supposed it was inevitable. Alice, next to him and frailer-looking than ever, a butterfly tossed on the cruel winds of life, had on a sort of batik bag with gathers across the bust. Donatella Versace, eat your heart out. I pulled up a chair and sat down. The other person at the table was introduced to me as Saul. His long dark hair was pulled back into a ponytail and his T-shirt advertised some band I'd never heard of whose name was entirely composed of numbers.

"Found it all right, then?" Tom said, an idiot question he'd never have asked if he hadn't been nervous. Being on my best behaviour, I smiled sweetly instead of being sarcastic and said that the club looked very interesting, which was one of those useful, Humpty-Dumpty words that means just what you want it to mean.

"Have you seen the stalls yet?" Alice said enthusiastically.

"No, just the café downstairs."

"Oh, we must show you round, mustn't we, Tom?"

"Why don't you take her to see them?" Tom suggested, jumping at the opportunity for Alice and I to Get To Know One Another.

"I want a drink first," I said firmly. If I was going to be dragged round a kind of New Agey school fête, having a can of lager in my hand would help to dull the horror.

"Of course. Tea or juice?" Alice said enthusiastically.

I stared at her blankly. "Well, I was rather hoping for—"

"There are lots of energy drinks, too," Tom interrupted.

"—a *beer,*" I finished with a certain emphasis.

"Oh, they don't sell any *alcohol* on the premises," Alice informed me, her smile vanishing. She had placed the same stress upon the word "alcohol" that I might have given to "child porn."

"None at all?" It came out as a bleat. I caught Saul's eye; he was looking, it seemed to me, distinctly sympathetic.

"The E-heads are coming down and the hippies don't fancy it," he said laconically.

"Bet there's enough puff here to knock out an army," I muttered.

Alice was on her feet. "Shall we go?" she said.

Ungraciously I got up, leaving my bag with the boys, and followed her out on to the landing and through a door to the balcony. It had been partitioned off into stalls, leaving a few feet free on the rail side for people to circulate. The darkness descended again till my eyes accustomed themselves to it. Some stalls sold all manner of glow-in-the-dark paraphernalia for clubbing: lighters, badges, jewellery painted with UV paint in fluorescent mauve, citron, orange and lime. Others offered T-shirts, palm reading, hair weaving and bootlegged tapes of concerts. The only one out of the ordinary was empty apart from a wide raised bench covered with a white cloth on which you could lie while being given a holistic massage.

I looked down over the balcony. The mattresses were full now, most people lying full length or propped against each other, smoking joints; the haze hung over the area like a mushroom cloud. In the Seventies this set-up would have been an orgy; I was reminded of that film with Clint Eastwood, *Coogan's Bluff*. There's a famous scene in a club the size of a football pitch, everyone dressed to kill—mainly in crochet—drugged up to their eyeballs and rolling over the floor with everyone else. But we were in the Nineties now and we didn't do that kind of thing; we took drugs that made us love our neighbours but not want to do it with them.

The music was louder up here, its endless winding rhythms like the images projected on the screen, turning over each other in an incessant free fall of sound and motion that could go on seamlessly forever, an acid trip where time stretched out like soft toffee in the hands. Alice was saying something to me, pointing at a stall which sold very similar sweaters to the one Tom was wearing, but we were up against the speakers and I couldn't hear her. Still, it snapped me out of the reverie. Gesturing that we should walk away from the noise, she led me out on to the landing and said earnestly:

"That's the woman who made Tom's jumper. It's all natural goat fibres, you know. And she brews the dyes herself from seaweed. I could get her to make you one if you wanted."

Was this a peace offering, or was she cunningly trying to sabotage my entire look? I froze to the spot.

"They're lovely," I said carefully, "but it's just too hot to be thinking about sweaters at the moment. Maybe in the autumn?"

And if you're still with Tom by then, I was thinking, he'll be lost to me anyway, so I can tell you exactly what I think of your suggestion to dress me in something dyed with kelp.

We went back into the so-called bar. Tom and Saul were still at the table, heads together. Alice went off to get some herbal brew and I rejoined the boys. They were drinking orange squash from paper cups. Saul poured another and pushed it in my direction. To be polite I took a sip. Then I took a bigger one to confirm the initial finding: there was a more-than-decent ration of vodka in it. I looked up at them. Tom looked sheepish and Saul winked at me.

"Tom's been telling me that you're a bit of an amateur detective," he said.

I rolled my eyes and drank some more vodka cocktail.

"You don't want to listen to this piss-artist," I said.

"Talking of which, don't tell Alice," Tom said anxiously. "She won't be able to smell it on my breath."

"What if she drinks some?"

He shook his head. "It's got too many additives for her to touch it."

"You seem to have worked it all out." My spirits rose. There was some small corner of Tom that Alice hadn't managed to corrupt.

"Saul's really been wanting to meet you," he said, changing the subject. "He only came along today because I told him you'd be here."

Saul shot a keep-your-big-mouth-shut look at Tom. My spirits rose still further; had this attractive young man been admiring me from afar? I favoured Saul with an encouraging smile.

"Yeah, this isn't really my kind of thing," he said, looking embarrassed and making a gesture which encompassed the room. "But look, is it true what Tom's been telling me about you? That you found out who killed a friend of yours who was being blackmailed about some letters?"

I shrugged, uncomfortable now. This wasn't the approach I had been expecting; I had been hoping for fulsome compliments on my art or my beauty. Or why not both? "There's probably a grain of truth floating around there somewhere. But I'm an artist," I added firmly. "I make sculptures. Mobiles. I've just done one for an investment bank."

"Yeah, Mowbray Steiner. I heard about that." Saul's stare hadn't left my face all the time we'd been talking, as if he was trying to read me. My curiosity was stirred. I returned his gaze, reading concern in his eyes. He was serious. He had a nice face, strong without being handsome; his steady brown eyes looked trustworthy.

"Wasn't that where that guy got killed?" he said. "Are you looking into it?"

"I might be. Someone dropped my sculpture on top of him to confuse the issue. I wouldn't mind catching the bastard who did that."

"I've heard the guy who got the chop was a nasty piece of work," he said.

"Really? Where'd you hear that?" I said with sharpened interest.

"Saul works at a print shop in the City," Tom volunteered.

"One of those 24-hour ones where everything gets passed through an iron grille?" Sebastian had told me about them.

"These banks are security mad," Saul said. "Can't blame 'em. We're putting out documents about buying and selling companies worth millions of pounds."

His tone was casual, but his eyes had left mine for the first time.

"But who told you about the guy who got killed?" I persisted.

"Just gossip. A lot of that going round."

He looked as if he were going to ask me something else, but then Alice rejoined the table and suggested we all go downstairs, and the moment was lost. It took about half an hour before we found a space on a mattress—hippies these New Agers might be, but sharing worldly goods was one commandment they weren't following. Finally some of them left and we scurried eagerly on to the vacant mattress, despite the fact that they had left a rather farmyardy smell in their wake. Probably all wearing sweaters made of organic goat.

The music was the perfect soundtrack to the images on the screen, pleasant if you didn't listen to it directly but just let it float through you. Tom and Saul rolled up and we worked our way through the rest of the orange squash bottle, getting steadily more stoned and tipsy until the projections before us, by now strange computer-generated fantasies where little silver figures ran and jumped and split themselves down the middle in post-apocalyptic landscapes, began to make sense to me and I wasn't in a state to question anyone about anything more complicated than what time the last tube left from Highbury and Islington.

17

I was awoken at ten the next morning by the phone which, since I hadn't switched on the answering machine, rang incessantly, shrilling at me like a scratched recording of a below-par coloratura till I grumbled myself into my kimono and down the ladder to answer it. I made a resolution to buy an extension for the fifteenth time. Now, though, I had some money to do it with. There were no excuses.

On the line was a woman I didn't know. She sounded nervous but resolute.

"Could I—is that Sam Jones?" she said.

"Yes." I pulled the kimono around me and tied the belt.

"I wanted to talk to you—someone gave me your name—about the death at Mowbray's. I understand you're trying to find out what happened."

"You know my name but I don't know yours."

"Oh. I'm— My name's Nicola White."

That was the worst attempt at a pseudonym I'd ever heard. But perhaps she didn't know I had a list with her name on it. I said nothing, not wanting to scare her off. After a moment she said:

"Could I come round and see you?"

"When?"

"In an hour?"

I felt my eyebrows raising all by themselves.

"Fine," I said. "I'll put the coffee on."

I waited till I heard her hang up; then I clicked the button down, freeing the line, and rang Hawkins' number. He wasn't there but he had left a message for me with WPC Gilbert. They bounced me through to her.

"Is that Miss Jones?" she said dubiously. "I'll just read out the notes he gave me, verbatim. I think that'll be best."

"Fire away."

"Um . . . well, it goes like this: 'Nicola Walters is on the list of the bank staff but wasn't at the party. Makamoto and Claes Smith don't ring any bells. And Brand didn't find anything like you asked about. Nothing funny. Nothing that looked like loan repayments. Just the usual—letters, bank statements.'" WPC Gilbert paused. "I hope that makes sense," she said rather grudgingly.

"Almost too much. Thanks. Oh, I've just thought of something—could you put me through to Inspector Brand?"

I wasn't vouchsafed a conversation with the man himself, but someone else who answered, curtly, "Incident Room," and upon hearing my request to take Floating Planet home for repairs put one hand over the receiver and then proceeded to yell so loudly he might as well not have bothered with the first stage of the process.

"Sir, it's that sculptress woman, friend of DI Hawkins. Wants to know if she can take her thingy, mobile, back to hers to do it up again."

There was a pause and then he unplugged his hand, saying to me:

"Yeah, the inspector says that's all right. Seeing as it's not the murder weapon. We've got all we need on it."

I started to thank him but he had already put down the phone, so I did the same, staring at the wall. About now Nicola Walters would be booking a taxi or ducking out to the underground, pleading a client meeting.

I made another short phone call and then it was time to get changed. I didn't think I'd impress Nicola mightily in a kimono. Not having a deerstalker and pipe to hand, it'd better be the black trousers and green silk shirt combo that had gone down well enough with Suki Fine to make her confide in me. I wasn't necessarily attributing this success entirely to my outfit, but you can never underestimate the value of appearances.

Nicola Walters had taken a taxi. I heard it pull up outside and wondered if she'd charged it to the bank. She was medium height, with clear brown eyes, a squarish jaw and straight dark hair in a short, business-like blunt cut, her suit nondescript but as unobjectionable as the haircut. I had passed hundreds like her in the streets outside the bank at lunchtime, heading for the gym or the health-conscious sandwich bar. The only thing about her that didn't project quiet efficiency was her state of mind. She put out her hand smartly enough to shake mine, meeting my eyes in the approved, we-can-do-business manner, but the fingers weren't as steady as they should have been and her eyes were as confident as a failed con artist's.

"Come in," I said, leading the way over to the sofa. She hardly took in her surroundings, which was unusual for a first-time visitor; not a look up at the Thing or down at the power tools in the middle of the floor. She was strung up as tightly as an over-tuned piano. She sat down, or rather perched, on the edge of the sofa, automatically positioning herself so that her skirt wouldn't ride up, her feet placed close together, fingers clasped in her lap. I took the armchair and waited. It was up to her to talk. I bet she'd been rehearsing a speech in the taxi.

"I came to you because . . ." she started before her voice seemed to lose its way. Wrenching it back on course, she continued: "Because I heard that you might be able to help me with a problem I have. I've been told that you have dealt with this kind of thing successfully before."

"What kind of thing?" I said. "Blackmail?"

She stared at me. Her lips moved but nothing came out.

"You weren't the only one," I said. "Charles had his hooks into quite a few people."

She swallowed. "Could I hire you?" she said, reaching for her bag. "I can give you an advance right now. . . ."

"Hire me to do what?"

Her eyes flickered. "Get them back . . . his notes. . . ."

"Look." I leaned forward, softening my voice. "Nicola. I'm curious about what happened to Charles de Groot because I have a personal interest. But I'm not a private detective, and if your brother told you I was he got hold of the wrong end of the stick."

Goodness, I was pleased with myself. She was tough; she absorbed the shock well. Her brown eyes widened slightly and her calf muscles tightened up, but that was all I could see. I assumed she was used to unpleasant surprises. After all, she was paid serious money to take serious risks.

"Don't blame Saul," I said, trying not to sound too smug. "He didn't give anything away." Apart from using the word "blackmail." I had wondered about it at the time and as soon as Nicola had rung me I had checked with Tom on the hunch that there would be some connection between them. It explained why Saul had been so keen to meet me. That would teach me to imagine myself as irresistible. "I put two and two together after you called and asked a friend what Saul's surname was. I already knew you weren't called White, and that you worked at the bank. Besides, you two look very like each other. I might have guessed anyway. You got him to check up on me, right? See if I was the sort of person who could be trusted?"

"Actually, it was Saul's idea. He's known Tom for ages, and Tom had told him about you already. Someone killed a friend of yours and you went after him. He died, didn't he?"

"I don't talk about that. Ever."

My voice was so harsh it shocked me, let alone Nicola Walters, who moved back on the sofa instinctively, lifting her hands in reflex as if to ward me off.

"I'm sorry," she said. "I didn't mean to offend you." Her eyes were fixed on my face in the way her brother's had been yesterday, as earnestly as a nineteenth-century physiognomist deducing my character from the bumps on my forehead or the set of my eyes. Finally she continued:

"I think I can have faith in you. I'm going to tell you everything. Saul told me he'd heard you could be trusted." She paused for a moment as if gathering her notes together. "I'm not pleading for sympathy," she said, "but I'm only the third woman ever to do my job at Mowbray's. I'm on the trading floor, as you probably know, and it's been hell getting there. Only about a quarter of the new recruits are female, and most of them drop out. They make you do all the worst, most boring, menial jobs, and the working hours are impossible, especially if you want to have a relationship. Boyfriends won't put up with the same nonsense as girlfriends will and they resent you earning more money than them. I've had to fight and manoeuvre to get promoted to my current job, and I know it's still just tokenism. I'll never be head of dealing. Only about ten percent of assistant directors, even, are women, and they're all Oxbridge types. I'm not. I've worked hard to get this accent."

It was a good speech. This must have been what she was preparing in the taxi. But it wasn't that easy to sympathise, on the grounds of sisterly solidarity, with a woman who was shoving stocks in and out of pension funds and creaming a percentage off the top for her trouble; to find a less socially useful job you'd have had to start sieving through government quangos. I didn't say anything, just looked at her. She had an admirable ability to sit still and concentrate everything into what she was saying.

"Anyway," she said, and I could see how she'd got where she was; there was a determination in her manner that couldn't help but impress, the same determination that had doubtless helped her lose the faint Essex accent with which her brother spoke, replacing it with the Received Pronunciation which would be more acceptable to her employers. "You probably don't give a damn about all that. But I wanted to explain why I did it. I'm under terrific pressure to achieve, even more so—much more so—than the men. They have infinitely more leeway, more room to make mistakes, than I do: if I slip up the whole floor knows about it and I'm sure they gloat at me. I needed to get some kind of edge to balance up the score."

"Don't tell me," I said. "You got Saul to pass you information he saw in the print shop."

It had been a wild guess, but clearly today was one of my good days.

"How did you know?" she said quickly. "You must have Charles's file."

"File?" I said as swiftly. "What file?"

She let out a long sigh, the last defence down. "It's all in there—the loan agreement I signed, and the list he'd made, a printout, linking deals the investment side of the bank was putting together and trades I'd made at the same time. Each one might have been a coincidence, but when you put them all together—well, it wasn't conclusive, but when you factored in my brother in the print shop, it would have got me sacked."

"And prosecuted?"

"No. Not quite enough evidence. Anyway, they hush that kind of thing up as a matter of principle. But my career'd have been finished. Washed up at twenty-five. And then there's Saul."

She looked directly at me with those eyes I remembered from yesterday, her brother's eyes, the ones I'd thought were trustworthy.

"He didn't want to. It was my idea—I made him, banged on at him for months before he'd tell me anything. I got him to stick to Mowbray's stuff, mostly, because I thought that if anyone did find out they'd think someone in M and A—that's mergers and acquisitions—had been passing me information, they wouldn't link it with Saul. I was trying to protect him. I know that sounds pathetic but it's true."

The set of her knees under the skirt was as neat as ever, her hands still. I could see that she was used to meetings, to the necessity of making her case, convincing stubborn bosses to see matters her way. She wasn't much good at hiding things but when they were out in the open she'd sell them to you and look you straight in the eye while she was doing it.

"Did you kill Charles de Groot?" I asked, almost conversationally.

"No. I wasn't even there." The answer came promptly, but not so fast as to be suspicious. She'd passed that test. Such as it was.

"Does your security pass let you in on the weekend?"

"No. You can check that out if you want to."

"Who do you think killed Charles?"

"I don't know. I really don't. But it must have been someone else he was blackmailing."

"How do you know he was putting the screws on anyone else?"

"Firstly because you told me so just now. Secondly because it was such a neat arrangement he had set up—a document saying he'd lent me the money, a direct debit agreement—that he must have done it before. And thirdly because he must have been watching me. I mean, I hardly knew him. He wouldn't tell me how he'd found out Saul was my brother, but he'd tracked back through the computer and put together a list of big trades I'd made, just on the off chance, to see if it would correlate with what corporate finance had been doing at the time. That's a lot of work, but he was prepared to do it. He must already have known what rich pickings he could get from people with the right information."

I nodded slowly. "Fair enough. Do you have any idea who else he was blackmailing? I'm not asking you to accuse anyone," I added, "just unmuddy the waters a bit."

She looked away for a moment. "This is awful," she said. "I'm prepared to tell you this because I don't like him."

"James Rattray-Potter," I said, swinging the advantage back to me. "That was easy."

"Have I told you *anything* you didn't know already?" Nicola said involuntarily. "Do you know who killed Charles?"

"Could we stick to James for a moment? Why did you think Charles was blackmailing him?"

"Nothing much. The way I saw him looking at Charles a couple of times, across a room. As if he could have killed him—I just meant that as an expression," she said quickly. "And I once heard Charles say something to him about his girlfriend. James's girlfriend, I mean. It was odd, as if it had a deeper meaning. Teasing, but not in a friendly way—more like he was twisting a knife in a wound. It wouldn't have meant anything if I hadn't been wondering about them already."

"Was this recent? I didn't think James had a girlfriend."

"A couple of months ago."

"What exactly did he say?"

Nicola creased her brow with the effort of remembering. "Well, we were in Dornford's, the wine bar down from the bank, on a Friday. Everyone was still very high from work. These two traders had had a punch-up that morning. One of them had blocked the other's car in the parking lot. Everyone was laughing about it, and Charles said to James something like: 'One to tell your girlfriend about, eh?' I was just bringing back the drinks and I happened to be right behind them—he was speaking very quietly—otherwise I wouldn't have heard anything."

I pulled a face. It meant nothing to me.

"What are you going to do?" said Nicola. "I mean, do you know where Charles's file is?" She fixed me with that making-a-deal stare again. "I meant it about paying you. I will, if you find it. To thank you."

"If I find it, you can have it—what he had on you, anyway. No charge."

"I'd rather," she said strongly.

"I wouldn't."

Our eyes met and locked.

"We'll see," she said, unwilling to relinquish the point. She looked at her watch. "I'm sorry, but do you mind if I use your phone to ring for a taxi? My mobile's on the blink."

...

I distracted myself from what Nicola Walters had told me by making out my invoice for repairs to Floating Planet. It was good and large; I employed the time-honoured technique of thinking of a number and then doubling it. Instinct told me not to stint. Then I rang Sebastian and informed him that (a) I was still alive, (b) that I would be going into Mowbray's that evening to collect the mobile and (c) that I was therefore available for dinner afterwards should he be able to remember what I looked like.

"I really am working very hard," he said defensively. "I'm sorry. I'll definitely make dinner tonight. Buzz up to me when you come in."

"A small test first, however. What colour are my eyes?"

"Brown."

"Hair?"

"Brown. Curly. Sam—"

"Any distinguishing marks?"

"I can't answer that over the telephone. I'm booking the restaurant right now, OK? Satisfied?"

"You could just take me home and tear my clothes off."

There was a pause. Then he said carefully: "I'll certainly take that matter into consideration."

"Someone walking past your desk?"

"Yes, that's absolutely correct."

"Will you get the whipped cream or will I?"

"I look forward to discussing that with you at the appropriate time. It's an interesting suggestion but I'm currently unable to give it the attention it deserves."

I blew a raspberry into the phone and hung up.

. . .

I reached the bank late that afternoon, parking my van up on the pavement in front of it. I'd charge any fines I got to the bank. Joe was at his desk, reading the paper. He looked pleased to see me. That wouldn't last, and not just because I got him to help me wrestle the sculpture out through the main doors and into the back of the van, where, thanks to whoever had dropped it on its bottom and squashed it flat, it just fitted. I should have been grateful to them, but somehow I wasn't.

Joe went to put the kettle on while I drove the van down the alley and into the car park. The guard there knew me well enough by now, but, being a petty jobsworth, objected to my leaving the van there until I suggested he ring Sir Richard Fine's office. Then he reluctantly reached out his hand for the keys. For him this was as major a climbdown as a sherpa-less descent from Everest.

I got back in to find Joe in the kitchenette making the tea. Just then the phone rang on Joe's desk and he fairly shot down the corridor to answer it, obviously nervous that people would think he was napping again.

"It's Mr. Shaw, Sammy," he said. "Wanting to know if you're here yet."

I went over to the phone.

"Sam?" Sebastian said. "Do you need a hand with the removals?"

"No, thanks. Joe and I have done it already."

"I'll be another half an hour or so."

"That's OK. I've got something to drop off to Sir Richard."

"Oh really?" His voice sharpened with interest.

"Nothing of interest to anyone apart from me. I'll see you down here when you're ready, then."

Joe was talking to a bike messenger with thin Lycra-covered shanks who had just come in to collect a package. I went up in the lift to the second floor where, behind the main reception desk, sat Susie, pretty, fair-haired, big-eyed Susie, the proud possessor of more curls than she had brains. It was all she could do to sit behind the desk without falling off her chair. She was busy running her tresses through her manicured fingers and flapping her blue-mascaraed eyelashes at James Rattray-Potter, who was propped against the desk in a suave, man-of-the-world pose, ankles crossed. He was a generic Mills and Boon hero to Dominic Planchet's Mr. Darcy, but I could see that his brand of florid good looks would appeal to secretaries and girls who lacked confidence.

"Oh, hello, Miss Jones," Susie fluted. "I'm so glad you've come to rescue me. Mr. Rattray-Potter here's being very naughty."

James nodded at me rather abruptly and leant over the desk, muttering something in Susie's ear. She giggled, her cheeks a pretty shade of pink, and said in a half-whisper:

"I really couldn't say . . . well, maybe . . . all right, Friday it is, then."

James mumbled something else, looked at his watch and headed off down the corridor. Susie giggled again and kept going till I said politely:

"Would you mind ringing Sir Richard Fine's office and telling them I'm here to drop off an invoice?"

"All right, then." She picked up the receiver and started tapping out the extension number with the tip of a pen, to save her nails. "He's a one, isn't he? Mr. Rattray-Potter, I mean. Been on at me for ages to go out with him. Won't take no for an answer— Oh, hello, is that Phillipa? Miss Jones here in reception to see Sir Richard. . . . All right, I'll send her along. . . ." She put the phone down. "Cheeky, isn't he?"

For a moment I thought she meant Sir Richard. The mind boggled.

. . .

When I reached the director's suite of rooms Phillipa, Richard Fine's secretary, told me to go through into his office. Homely and efficient, she was the exact opposite to Susie; I consoled myself with the thought that the latter might get to sit in reception and flirt with all comers but Phillipa probably earned three times Susie's salary. There was some justice in the world.

Sir Richard Fine stood up to greet me as I walked in. His desk was in proportion to himself, a giant lump of mahogany, one of those old partners' desks made a century ago for two people to work at and now a statement of not only his achievement, but the sheer size of the office he could command. The huge plate-glass windows behind him showed both the City and the skies above it, cloudless and Wedgwood blue, to full advantage. I expected that he was used to the view but if I had an office like that I'd have spent the first week here doing nothing but sitting by the window, watching the world pass by.

"Sam, m'dear!" he said, coming round the desk to kiss my cheek. "What can I do you for?" His manner was even more jolly-old-tar than usual; I had been expecting the opposite in business hours, and I wondered why he was making a special effort to be jovial with me.

"Actually, I just came to drop off my invoice for repairs to the sculpture. I didn't mean to disturb you." I was rather embarrassed, having envisioned leaving it with Phillipa and sliding discreetly away down the lushly carpeted corridors. "You suggested after the funeral that I—"

"Absolutely!" He waved his hand to indicate that I needed to say nothing else. "Where is it?"

I produced the invoice from my bag. Sir Richard was already buzzing through to Phillipa.

"Bring me the chequebook, will you, Phil, old girl? Chop chop."

He uncapped the lid of his fountain pen. Phillipa entered the office, placed the chequebook on his desk, and withdrew.

"What's the damage? Whoops—unfortunate phrase, eh? Let's have a look."

He unfolded the invoice. I cringed, remembering just how much I'd bumped it up, but Sir Richard didn't even blink. I thought wistfully that I could have doubled it again. He wrote out the cheque, signed it with a flourish, blew on it and handed it to me.

"Thank you," I said demurely.

"Not at all, not at all! Hopefully we can put this whole affair to rest now."

"Have the police let you know anything?" I ventured.

His face promptly went a light shade of purple.

"Don't know their arse from their elbow. Wanted to search the entire place, can you believe it? Soon put a stop to that. Think of the business they'd have disrupted. Ridiculous idea. All that happened is that he stuffed himself full of that rubbish and conked out. Then whoever was with him got the jitters and tried to make it look like an accident. Bloody stupid of him, too."

"So you're not worried that this might be connected with the bank?"

"Not at all. Not at all. More likely the load of riffraff hanging round that day, friends of his and Belinda's. Hope she'll have more sense than to see them now. It'll be one of them. You see that punk girl? Six feet tall and about as much flesh on her as a starving African?"

I thought this was a tad unfair on Baby, considering that Belinda herself looked as if you could break her arms by pinching them.

"Anyway, enough about that, eh? Look forward to happier times." He was walking me to the door. "We'll see you on Sunday, I hope? We're taking a boat and going down the Thames for Marcus's birthday. All work and no play, y'know? Let's hope the weather holds. Shaw'll tell you about it. That's a young man going places." He patted me on the hand. "Look forward to seeing you there. And the sculpture, of course, back in place. Very striking piece of work. Don't worry your pretty head about this any more, m'dear. Water under the bridge."

I found myself in Phillipa's antechamber, slightly dazed but with a cheque in my pocket for a satisfyingly large sum of money. Dinner was on me tonight. Strolling back to reception I couldn't help but wonder what Sir Richard's mood would be like on Sunday once the *Herald*'s feature had come out; his face would be the colour of a Victoria plum.

Oh well, today was Monday: by the weekend my cheque would have cleared. One must try to keep things in perspective. I just hoped there was no way he could trace back to my connection with Tim. Otherwise my lifeless corpse would probably be found floating down the river on Sunday evening after the river cruise, an Ophelia in polluted waters.

18

I hadn't been into this bar for a while, and in my absence they had redecorated it so completely that if it weren't for the familiar positioning of the counter and the staircase I would have thought I'd walked into the wrong place through the right door, like some trippy episode of *The Avengers*. I had always fancied myself as Emma Peel.

Last year it had been pastel and wrought iron, the tea-in-the-garden look. Now it was scarlet walls and black tables whose paint finish was as shiny as lacquer: opium in the boudoir. An image transformation as shocking as Kylie Minogue's from girl-next-door to trash princess, though rather more plausible.

Still, the clientele were happily the same, a selection of the prettiest and least heterosexual boys in London, most of whom had longer eyelashes and better legs than I did. There were some girls as well, both gay and straight; a couple of years ago a beautiful blonde tried to pick me up here and whenever I came back I wondered if I'd ever see her again. I was too sober to succumb; but in my defence I plead that it had been mid-afternoon.

They were playing the Pet Shop Boys, which was always a good sign. I have a theory that Neil Tennant is the bastard grandson of Cole Porter. Janey was already there, settled on one of the high stools by the window, her capacious satchel on another, reserving it. When she saw me she lifted it off and dropped it to the ground; it fell heavily, being as usual stuffed full of scripts, her bulging Filofax, and God knew what else. As long as Janey lugged that around with her all day she wouldn't need to do upper body work at the gym.

"Hiya," I said, kissing her. "What're you drinking?"

"White wine."

I looked around me. "I thought Helen was coming too."

Janey's blue eyes stayed wide as ever but her mouth pursed up expressively.

"She went downstairs when we came in to see if any people she knew were here. That was twenty minutes ago."

"Right."

I headed off to the bar and ordered our drinks from the indeterminately sexed, exquisite piece of nature posing behind it, reflecting that Helen never lost an opportunity to network. She was plugged into the media-friendly grapevine tighter than an eighteen-hour girdle.

She had still not appeared when I brought back our drinks, for which I was grateful and Janey less so. She was right to be worried. Helen had doubtless located a hack from a magazine programme or someone who wrote episodes of TV soaps and was at this moment leaning forward, greenish eyes narrowed on her target, promising God only knew what for a brief mention on air or a part written with her in mind. I managed to distract Janey successfully with the information that I was currently involved with a merchant banker.

"I don't *believe* it!" she said, all thoughts of Helen forgotten. Staring at me, she automatically adjusted a couple of gauzy scarves which were working their way free and sliding floorwards. Janey's style of dress hardly changed with the seasons; in summer the pale floating layers were silk or cotton, rather than wool, but the scarves and necklaces, the bracelets and earrings, were there always. "What *do* you see in him?"

"He's very good in bed," I said apologetically. "And he's terribly handsome, even if he does wear suits—proper suits, I mean, not baggy black Japanese ones. We go out to dinner at smart restaurants and take taxis back. He's got a BMW. It's like a window on another world."

I could draw Janey this kind of thumbnail sketch without being misunderstood; she knew me too well to assume that my motives would be purely mercenary.

"Film star?" she said incisively.

"Brad Pitt in *Interview with the Vampire*. Only short hair."

"Bed rating?"

"Oh, 8½."

Janey dismissed these high scores with a wave of her hand. "That's all very well," she said fretfully, "but what do you actually *talk* about?"

"Not much at the moment. He's busy putting together some probably deeply unsound takeover bid."

Janey pulled a disapproving face. "I don't know why you can't get together with Tim. He's so sweet, and you have so much in common. You'd be very good for each other."

"Exactly."

"Oh well," Janey sighed, "I'm in no position to give relationship advice, God knows." She looked wistfully towards the head of the staircase, from which Helen gave as yet no sign of emerging, and moved on to her second glass of white wine. "I take it this man works at the bank that bought your sculpture. You don't suspect him of anything nefarious, do you?"

"Nope. But he was the catalyst, in a way—if I hadn't been seeing him I'd never have been there when it happened."

And if I hadn't been wearing my dress, I reflected, James wouldn't have bet Sebastian to ask me out, without which he wouldn't have summoned up the nerve to do it. So should I blame the shop where I'd bought the dress, or the designer? Or both?

"It's the most extraordinary thing," Janey was saying. "Such a spectacular way to die."

"Exactly," I said. "It would take a very particular kind of person to kill someone that way."

"What do you mean?"

I wrinkled up my nose. "The two parts of it don't really go together," I said. "Slipping Charles an overdose was very cunning, and difficult to trace back to the source. No one's found out where Charles got his drugs from. He was as discreet in that as everything else—it's a dead end. But then dragging him out into the middle of the hall and dropping my mobile on top of him couldn't have been more risky. Using my sculpture was such a flamboyant thing to do. It doesn't quite make sense to me. Yet."

"*Yet*," Janey echoed. She let out a sigh. "There's no point telling you to be careful, is there? How could someone as nosy as you keep from poking round a murder if it happens on your doorstep?"

"It's not nosiness," I retorted. "It's metaphysical curiosity."

Janey's sarcastic reply was masked by the return of Helen, clad in a long, tight black dress, who pecked me on the cheek with her thin beak-like lips. She had narrow little features which photographed well, all planes and angles and pale green calculating eyes.

"Who did you find to talk to?" Janey said.

"Oh, just the usual dyke pack, no one special. Chattering away about their analysts."

Helen had been in therapy for years. The sole effect it had had was to make her even more selfish than she had been before.

"I told them how fabulous mine was and they all got on my case about seeing a man," Helen was continuing. "But I really feel that it's helping me resolve some primal conflicts. Seeing a woman could be too womb-like, too cosy, too much of a retreat into single-sex issues. I told him that and he was terribly understanding."

As far as Helen was concerned, the process of transference meant that she did her best to give her analyst a crush on her, rather than the other way round. I bet she stretched out full length on the couch to give him a good look at her assets. Such as they were.

"How did your processed-cheese commercial go?" I asked. There was no point even trying to make the question seem ingenuous; Helen was too sharp.

She glared at me. "Oh, wonderful," she said airily. "Like a free holiday. We were up in Scotland. They put us up in a great hotel, four star, à la carte, everything."

"Was it one of those brands of cheese that come in foil-wrapped triangles?" I said, refusing to let her off so easily. "Did you have to open them in front of the camera? I always find the little red strip tears off too soon and you have to peel the foil off with your fingernails instead."

Now it was Janey glaring at me.

"Helen's got a very exciting audition coming up," she said firmly. "The BBC are planning an adaptation of *Crime and Punishment*."

I flicked through my mind for the possible parts Helen might be up for, regretfully discarding the automatic response: "Typecasting, Helen—you'll make the perfect unsuccessful prostitute." Instead I said meekly, under Janey's basilisk stare: "That sounds fabulous, good luck," and was rewarded with the transformation of the stare into a beautiful smile.

Why were all my friends going out with frightful women? I was obviously suffering under some sort of curse.

. . .

"All my friends are going out with frightful women," I said gloomily to Sebastian that evening. He was distracted, however, being busy squeezing some tobacco out of a Silk Cut without breaking the paper, and didn't answer. When the tobacco on the mirror was a neat little heap he started sucking the neat little heap of cocaine next to it up into the cigarette by way of replacement. We had already done a couple of lines each and were feeling no pain.

"How's work going?" I said in an attempt to play the sensitive girlfriend.

"Don't ask."

"Oh, well, I won't then." It had been a bad idea anyway; I could only do sensitive so long before exploding.

As usual, we were hanging out at Sebastian's flat, which suited me only too well. Apart from the much higher level of creature comforts (not only were there infinitely more labour-saving electrical appliances here, for instance, but they actually *worked*) it freed me from the worry that Hawkins would turn up unexpectedly and cause an embarrassing, Feydeauesque situation to arise. Not that there were many doors in my studio to dash in and out of.

The sitting-room windows were open to the night and a light, warm breeze blew over us. This was not as sensual as it sounded; Sebastian had taken a shower as soon as we had got back and had repulsed my various attempts to join him, claiming mental and physical exhaustion. We'd see about that later on. He couldn't expect to lounge around clad in nothing but a scanty pair of silk undies, flaunting a set of abdominals so flat you could balance a beer can on them, and remain unmolested for long.

"What's all this about a boat trip down the Thames on Sunday?" I inquired, averting my gaze from his thighs. This was not the moment to seduce him. I should let him get his strength up first. Sebastian removed the filter of the Silk Cut and substituted it with a pre-rolled cardboard roach, his movements precise and experienced. It was like watching a presenter on *Blue Peter* assemble a project, only omitting the washing-up liquid bottle with its top cut off and the inside of the toilet skin. By now *Blue Peter* was making such an effort to be trendy it probably showed kids how to roll up.

Sebastian lit the cigarette and took a deep inhalation. "Oh, fuck. You don't want to come, do you?"

He passed it to me. I did the same. A rush started inside my head. "Why? Have you invited someone else?"

"I wouldn't submit any innocent female to at least three hours cooped up on a small boat with a load of traders getting apocalyptically drunk. God knows what might happen."

"But I'm not innocent," I pointed out, taking another drag. The top of my head was opening up nicely. I handed back the cigarette.

"You have a point there."

"Sir Richard mentioned it to me," I said in the Fine sisters' clipped accent. "He seems to be expecting us."

"Oh, he is, is he? Damn." Sebastian offered the stubby end of the cigarette back to me. I took a last puff and stubbed it out, a wonderful dizziness spreading through my limbs. Through the haze I said:

"He said you were a young man going places."

"Did he?" Sebastian, who had been slumped on the sofa, sat up straight. "What did he say?"

"That."

"Oh." Sebastian looked pleased with himself. I drank some beer to balance myself out, adding:

"In the direction of the local Job Centre, I assume."

"Very fucking funny. Well," he said, opening another bottle of beer and lolling back against the cushions, "I expect we'll go then."

"Good."

"Why are you so keen on it?"

"I thought it might be interesting. Everyone will be there, from what he was saying. . . . Do you know that he's decided that Charles's death has nothing to do with the bank?"

"He's certainly put the word out that it's not a suitable topic of conversation."

"I hear that Charles was a rather unsavoury piece of work."

"Well, unless someone else injected him full of heroin, which seems unlikely, I think we can take that for granted."

"No, it wasn't to do with drugs. Something else entirely."

Sebastian turned to look at me. "What are you talking about, Sam?"

"I don't really know. Just that I heard he had some very dodgy sources of income."

Sebastian gave me a long, steady gaze. "I wouldn't be surprised," he said. "I never liked him much. But who have you been talking to?"

I shrugged. "People."

"Be careful, Sam."

"What do you mean?"

Sebastian drank some beer. "Someone killed Charles, after all. Or was desperate enough to cover up his death."

"Who do you think it was?"

"I don't know. And my boss doesn't want to know either. So I'm not going to think about it."

Now he wouldn't look at me.

"Is it true that some papers of Charles's have gone missing?" I said.

"What kind of papers? Work stuff? Look, what exactly are you talking about?"

"If I knew I'd tell you," I said mendaciously.

Sebastian turned to face me.

"Look, Sam, I don't know what you're up to, but leave this alone, all right? Leave the police to do their job."

"That's all very well for you to say. It wasn't your sculpture," I pointed out. "Do you know something you're not saying?"

His grey-blue eyes looked straight into mine, his fringe falling sideways over his forehead.

"No, I don't," he said firmly. It was an impressive display of sincerity, not to mention fringe. So why was it my instinct that throughout this conversation I hadn't been the only one telling lies? I returned his gaze.

"Well, that's that," I said. "End of discussion."

"I hope so," he said.

"Tell me," I said, remembering something, "does James have a girlfriend?"

Sebastian snorted. "You must be joking. He's busy sowing his wild oats in as many temporary secretaries as possible."

"He was chatting up Susie the other day."

"Well, there you go. Girls like that love James, God knows why. Weren't you saying something before about your friends' girlfriends?"

"The most noxious females imaginable."

"You've never introduced me to any of your friends," Sebastian observed in a studiedly casual tone of voice.

I stared at him. "Do you *want* to meet them?"

"Well . . ." He drank some beer. "You know mine . . . I mean, I know I'm not exactly the sort of man you normally go out with, but I'm quite capable of holding a conversation with arty types, you know. Even if I do work in a bank."

"Is that a coded appeal for me to throw a dinner party at which you'll be introduced to carefully selected members of my coterie, thus putting our liaison on what, in the 1990s, passes for a regular footing?" I said, hoping that by phrasing it in this way he would feel forced to laugh off the idea. Instead he jumped at it. Big tactical error on my part.

"We could have the dinner here," he said eagerly. "When I have a bit more time on my hands, of course. I could do that tuna I made the first time you came round, with the black bean salsa."

My imagination boggled at the idea of Tom and Alice, Janey and Helen sitting round Sebastian's antique dining table, making polite conversation. Alice probably didn't eat anything but seaweed and raw grains, Helen would flirt with Sebastian, thus distressing Janey, Tom, unable to drink under Alice's reproving eye, would become crabbier and crabbier as the evening wore on, and I, oppressed by the horrendous respectability of the whole set-up, would either have a nervous breakdown or keep popping into the toilet to do drugs.

"I don't think it's such a good idea," I said diplomatically.

"Why not?"

"I just don't do things like that. My friends would think I'd gone mad. Besides, all their girlfriends are horrendous. I told you. It would be the Dinner Party From Hell."

Sebastian pouted. His persistence with such an unsuitable idea was beginning to worry me. Still, he did look cute. I leant over and kissed him on his out-thrust lips, partly because I wanted to but partly also to distract him from the topic under discussion. He yielded for a moment, but then pushed me away.

"What is it?" I said.

He mumbled something I didn't catch. I wasn't going to let him get away so easily. I kissed him again, nibbling on his lips, teasing him with little licks and bites until he parted them with a sigh, letting me into his mouth. I knelt above him on the sofa, his head sinking back into the cushions, eyes closed, his endless lashes brushing his cheeks delicately, his lips pink and swollen, beautiful and, in his near-nakedness, almost pornographic at the same time. If we can just keep it like this, I thought, taking his head in my hands and kissing him, slow, syrupy kisses, trailing them down to his neck, his bare chest, the lines of muscle on his abdomen. He groaned above me and stretched out his legs, his position one of total abandonment, hands outflung by his side.

His skin was as smooth as a child's, stretched like pale satin over his long muscles, only the lightest of down on his thighs, and as I stroked them I had the sense of caressing a sculpture, veined like marble. I wouldn't let him move; I took what I wanted and pressed back his hands when he tried to pull me up to kiss me, feeling drunk on the sense of power this conferred and on his beauty, and when he cried out, his hands clutching the edge of the sofa, their knuckles white with the pressure, and then released, it was as if I had won a victory.

Afterwards he told me that he thought he was in love with me.

19

I was becoming increasingly puzzled over the fact that the police had failed to find, either in Charles's flat or his desk at work, any evidence whatsoever of his extracurricular financial activities. Though I assumed that Charles had been too clever to leave anything incriminating about the place—such as the printout he had shown to Nicola Walters or the photograph of Simon—it was hard to believe that he wouldn't have kept their signed direct debit forms, at least, with the rest of his papers. After all, he had gone to considerable trouble to make the payments seem like legitimate transactions. It would make sense to have stowed the blackmail evidence away in some bank vault, but why go to that trouble for the innocent-looking paperwork? It was merely a guess, but I wondered whether someone else—one of his victims?—had laid their hands on the file Charles had mentioned before the police had been able to do so.

That didn't necessarily indicate someone who had been in the bank when Charles was killed. If whoever it was had known that he would be attending his engagement party that evening, they might well have used that opportunity to search his flat.

I preferred the idea of the papers being at his home, since I had absolutely no chance at all of examining whatever Charles might have left behind at work. Before last night I had had the vague idea of asking Sebastian if he could rifle through anything remaining of Charles's possessions at the bank, but his attitude had made it abundantly clear that I had as much hope of this as Michael Jackson did of recovering from the rare skin disease that had not only turned him white but given him Julie Andrews's nose.

So it was the flat or nothing. It was worth a try, though some base cunning would be needed to gain entry. I put on my blue linen suit, which was as snug as ever; I made a resolution to go to the gym more often. Adding a pair of black high heels, a pearl choker and about three times the amount of make-up that I usually wore, I put my hair up in a chignon and checked myself out in the full-length mirror. It was extraordinary what effects you could achieve by putting together items of clothing which you'd never normally dream of combining. I looked even more like a lady who lunched than Suki Fine did.

. . .

I took care to park the van a healthy distance away from the block of apartments in which Charles had lived; it didn't quite go with the image I was presenting. I have an extremely sophisticated sense of what's appropriate. I had been assuming that an address as upmarket as his would have a caretaker or a hall porter included in the package, and so it did. As soon as the heavy glass and wrought-iron door clanked shut behind me, a figure ensconced behind a mahogany desk at the far end of the hall said with the utmost deference:

"Can I help you, madam?"

"Thank you, yes," I replied in my best imitation of Suki Fine's upper-class drawl, taking off my sunglasses. "Goodness, it's rather *dark* in here, isn't it?"

"It is a very bright day outside, madam. I dare say after a few moments your eyes will accustom themselves to the gloom."

I blinked, and not because of the dimness of the lighting. Who was this person, Jeeves's twin brother?

"Tell me, would you be the regular person on duty here?" I said, approaching the desk across the wide swathe of green carpet which ran down the centre of the tiled floor. It's very hard to walk in stiletto heels on carpet, especially while wearing a tight skirt. Still, the get-up kept me ladylike; it was absolutely impossible to take large strides in it.

"That is correct, madam."

"But you're not on duty in the *evening*," I said, making this a statement of fact and hoping I was right.

He bowed his head. "I usually leave at seven, unless there is a particular duty that requires my presence."

By now I was close to his desk and could see him better; a middle-aged man, greying hair brushed straight back from his forehead, with a perfectly nondescript face and a mouth that was pursed slightly closed as if to indicate his capacity for discretion. He wore a burgundy uniform with gold braiding, like a flunkey out of *The Prisoner of Zenda*. Behind him stood a large mahogany credenza whose top shelves were a series of neatly labelled pigeonholes, containing what looked like post for the various occupants of the flats.

"No, I thought not," I said. "I haven't seen you before." I hesitated slightly, as if thinking out what I should say. "I used to come here occasionally to visit Mr. de Groot in Flat 3C." I coughed. "Rather later on in the evening than seven o'clock."

His face remained quite impassive, but he tilted his head slightly to one side, as if indicating that I should continue.

"I'm in rather an embarrassing position," I said, lowering my voice. "Mr. de Groot, as you of course know, has very sadly died."

"I was very sorry to hear of his demise, madam. A very amiable gentleman, Mr. de Groot."

"It was a great loss for me." I was beginning to find his way of speaking infectious. "Mr. de Groot and I were very close friends." I cleared my throat. "I'm only speaking to you this frankly because, as I said, I now find myself in a particularly, um, sensitive situation. I have no choice but to confide in you. During my association with Mr. de Groot I wrote him some letters which would prove very . . . problematic should anyone but me read them."

His gaze was full of comprehension.

"But I assume, madam," he said, treading the line between keeping his voice discreetly low and an insinuating half-whisper, "that you are aware that the police have already searched Mr. de Groot's effects? I would have thought that had such letters come to light they would already have contacted you to question you about your, hmm, *friendship* with Mr. de Groot."

"Charles wasn't a complete fool," I said, larding my tone of voice with arrogance. "I have reason to believe that he took great care to hide my letters. Quite frankly, I don't have a great deal of confidence in the ability of a couple of illiterate constables in regulation boots to find something which Charles wanted to keep private."

His mouth twisted into a sour little smile, and he made a phut-phutting sound with his lips which I assumed indicated amusement. I had hit the right note. I only prayed that Hawkins never found out about this conversation.

"I must admit that I am of madam's opinion on this subject," he said. "Mr. de Groot was a very intelligent gentleman. And the policemen who came to examine his flat did not impress me greatly. They were high-handed in the extreme."

He coughed lightly. We were reaching the critical point now.

"Unfortunately," I said, anticipating what he was going to ask, "I don't have a key to the flat. Charles meant to give me one, but we didn't have time, before. . . ." I swallowed and continued bravely: "I wonder if you would be so kind . . . I know that I'm taking great advantage of your good nature, and I would be only too glad to express my gratitude. . . ." I slid a folded twenty-pound note out of my clutch bag and into his hand, which had mysteriously appeared to receive it. It vanished like a magic trick; a second later the hand, empty now, was detaching a pair of keys from a large ring it had produced from a drawer in the credenza.

"The keys are locked up at night, of course," he commented, following my gaze. "You will find the flat as you remember it, though of course I cannot speak for any depredations our flat-footed friends may have committed." That phut-phutting sound came again. "Mr. de Groot's rent was paid up till the end of the year. I believe that the agents are trying to contact his relatives, but since they live abroad the process may take some time."

He placed the two keys on the top of the desk. I palmed them discreetly.

"I take it madam knows the way," he said, with a certain suggestiveness in his look that I thought best to ignore.

"Thank you so much," I said, and walked over to the lift at the end of the hall, an ancient wrought-iron number as antiquated as the hall porter's manners. I had to wrest the doors open when the lift arrived, not knowing the knack, and found him at my elbow, politely assisting me.

"Many of our ladies complain about the lift," he observed. "It is rather unwieldy."

I let out a high-pitched laugh, hoping my ineptitude hadn't made him suspect that this was the first time I'd travelled in the wretched thing. "Charles always operated it for me," I said, hoping he wouldn't remember that I'd said I always visited Charles late at night.

As the lift rose, slowly, and with much creaking and shaking, I glanced down the shaft and saw him standing in the hall, watching my progress upwards. The expression on his face was very strange indeed.

. . .

Charles de Groot's flat was by no means large; for size as well as location he would have had to double the amount of blackmailees on his list. No doubt he'd been working on it. The flat was decorated sparely but the few pieces of furniture it contained were modern classics, like the Le Corbusier Barcelona chair; I doubted it was an original but I had the feeling they were now producing limited-edition copies, which wouldn't come cheap even so. My guess was that Charles had wanted nothing but the best and been prepared to wait until he could afford it. On the stripped-wood floors lay a couple of exquisite rose red carpets which I lifted in order to let me test if any floorboards would come up.

I didn't have much hope for this search; the policemen who came here would have known that Charles had died of an overdose and would have combed the place for drugs. Thank God they hadn't gone so far as to cut open the Barcelona chair. That would have been a sacrilege. I spent two hours looking everywhere I could, shaking open every book and magazine, trying to pry up every floorboard and kitchen tile, without success. It was a tribute to the cleaning service in this block of flats that I hardly even got my hands dirty doing so.

I was dispiritedly poking at the cushions scattered across Charles's bed when a sound like someone clearing their throat in the doorway made me spin round. It was the hall porter. He had managed to come right across the wooden floor of the living room without making a sound.

"I take it that madam hasn't succeeded in finding her letters," he said, and now his voice was definitely laced with insinuation, though not, I noticed with relief, any implication that I might have been looking for something else entirely. He seemed to have swallowed my story only too well.

"I'm afraid not," I said, letting the pillow fall. "I can only hope that Charles had destroyed them. I kept *begging* him to do it."

He pursed his lips slightly, his eyes beady with enjoyment.

"After madam had come up here, I'm sorry to say that it occurred to me that there might be an alternative solution to the mystery of where the letters might be." He coughed. "I don't want to be indiscreet," he said, eyes lowered in what might have passed for modesty had his tone not been so suggestive.

It took me a moment to catch on. I dare say someone who had been brought up with servants wouldn't have been so slow.

"Perhaps this might help," I said, fishing another twenty-pound note out of my bag and crossing the room to press it into his hand. It disappeared as fast as the first one had done. It was lucky I'd stopped by the cashpoint on my way here.

"Is madam aware that Mr. de Groot—well, let me put it this way. I assume you are aware that Mr. de Groot was about to enter the state of matrimony, though I'm sure he would have been careful not to allow it to interfere with his . . . friendships."

"I know that Charles was engaged," I said, raising my chin proudly. "To Belinda Fine. There were no secrets between us."

"Very good. I would hate to have been the bearer of distressing news." He smiled slightly. "Miss Fine naturally made a visit here last week to remove the personal possessions she had left, for convenience, in Mr. de Groot's flat. It is possible that Miss Fine might, while so doing, have come across madam's letters."

I stared at him, thoughts racing through my brain.

"You know Miss Fine by sight, of course," I said.

He bowed his head.

"And you saw her come in that day."

"That is correct. Miss Fine was naturally wearing mourning," he said rather reprovingly. "She looked clearly distressed by her task. Of course," he added, "her distress might to some degree have been caused by her finding of madam's letters. On her exit she kept her head lowered and hardly spoke to me. It would be consistent with having made an unpleasant discovery."

I nodded slowly.

"Thank you," I said. "That's certainly given me food for thought. I'm sure I can leave you to lock up."

I placed the keys in his hand, and made to pass through into the living room, only to find him blocking my path. I looked at him in surprise. His tongue, thin and serpentine, slid out and traced the outlines of his mouth in a particularly unpleasant fashion.

"Will you kindly let me by?" I said with hauteur.

He didn't move aside. Instead, he pressed himself towards me, one hand slipping on to my arm and holding it in an unexpectedly firm grip. His eyes were bright and beady.

"Oh, I locked the door behind me," he said, his voice excited now, rising higher with every word. "Now he's dead, you'll be looking to get your fun somewhere else, won't you? I know your type, you're all the same. I know what you want, don't you worry, and now you're going to get it, you stuck-up little—"

"I think we should stop there, don't you?" I said. "And what happened to the upmarket vocabulary? You're sounding less like Jeeves and more like something out of *The Bill* every minute."

This took him completely aback. His hand froze in mid-air and his mouth remained half open. The sight of his tongue flickering inside it was so nasty that I stamped down hard with one stiletto on his right foot, grinding down the spike heel till he shrieked. While he was still in shock I reached out and twisted his balls round so far they'd need a map to get back to their original location. He doubled over. I put both hands behind his lowered head, overcoming a certain revulsion about getting them sticky with the brilliantine he used on his hair, and pulled it down hard so that his face came satisfactorily into contact with my upraised knee. I hoped I had broken his nose. I thought I heard something cartilaginous snap.

Now I was cross. Bringing up my knee so fast had ripped my skirt, and I hate mending. Looking around me I noticed a very nice piece of Murano glass, a pale pink vase, on the bedside table. He had sunk to his knees in pain, the wimp. I retrieved the vase and knocked it over his head. It didn't break; they blow strong on that island. He crumpled to the carpet and lay there, unconscious. I replaced the vase. The keys had fallen out of his hand; I picked them up and stepped round him fastidiously, out of the bedroom.

His master bunch of keys was in the door. I removed it and locked the door from outside, thus marooning him in an unenviable situation; he wouldn't be able to get out without ringing for help. Unwilling to trust myself to the lift, I tripped down the stairs, able to move more easily now my skirt had torn, wondering what kind of story he would invent to explain his situation. In the hall I returned Charles's keys to the ring and put the whole bunch back in the credenza drawer where they belonged.

Outside it was still a bright day. I pulled on my sunglasses and stripped off my little black gloves with relief—it was too hot to wear them with comfort, even for someone as ladylike as I was. I strolled back to the van, whistling under my breath to calm myself down. I'd have a stiff drink as soon as I got home. That was one of the nastiest pieces of work I'd come across in a long time. He made David Stronge look like Bambi.

But whatever story he thought of would never be traced back to my door. No one but him had seen me, and there was no proof I'd ever been there; when he thought about it he'd realise that I hadn't even left fingerprints. I was completely in the clear.

. . .

"I knew it was you as soon as I heard the description," Hawkins said furiously. "Are you out of your mind? You could be had up for assault, not to mention tampering with evidence."

"Don't be stupid, Hawkins. There wasn't any evidence to tamper with. And I don't think it counts as assault when you're defending yourself against being raped."

"*What?*" Hawkins stared at me in shock, seeing that I was quite serious. "That piece of shit!" He grabbed my shoulders. "Sam, are you all right? Did he hurt you? Oh my God, why did you go there alone! I'll have him up for anything I can. Look, sit down." He led me over to the sofa, one arm around my waist for support, looking at me with as much concern as if I'd just had a tubercular fit. I felt like Greta Garbo in *Camille*. Hawkins made an even more unlikely Robert Taylor.

"Darling," he said, pressing me down. I sat. "Are you all right?" He squatted in front of me as if I were a small child, clasping my hands for good measure.

"Did he hurt you?" His expression was touchingly sweet. "Can you tell me? Is it too difficult? I know, I'll take you round to the counsellor we use, I've heard she's really good. Would you rather talk about it to a woman?"

"Will you let me get a word in edgewise?" I almost shouted. He jumped. "Hawkins, he hardly touched me, OK? He told me what he had in mind and I twisted his balls and nutted him in the face. He's the one that should be seeing a counsellor. In all senses of the word. I'm fine."

"It must have been very unpleasant, though." Hawkins's square jaw was set, his blue eyes blazing with sympathy and the urge to revenge any wrongs done me. Now he was Gary Cooper. I couldn't help relishing the irony; one minute he was berating me for insensitivity and callousness, the next cooing over me as if I were as delicate as one of the girls in the Anaïs Anaïs advertisements.

"It was all over very fast," I assured him. "The main thing is to get them before they get you. That way you have the advantage of surprise."

"Have you had to do this kind of thing before?" he said in horror, before he remembered about my lurid past. "Oh. Yes."

He let go of my hands. I couldn't blame him.

I killed someone once. I didn't mean to kill him but he died all the same. It didn't go to trial; the coroner directed the jury at the inquest to bring in a verdict of self-defence, and from the sympathetic looks they gave me they would have done so anyway, even without his prompting. But it effectively cancelled any credentials I might have had to be treated like a fragile flower.

"It would be interesting to run the guy's record, though," I suggested. "See if he's got any previous. That's how you say it, isn't it? I've been watching *The Bill*."

"So what programme should I be watching to learn how to talk like you, Sam?" he said sarcastically. My efforts to distract him had been successful; he was back to normal.

"*Wildlife Special?*" I suggested.

He grinned and stood up, stretching out his legs.

"How did you find out, anyway?" I asked. "I can't believe he filed a complaint."

"The property agents did. One of them had to come round to let him out—you locked him in, right?—and he spun them some line about having been conned into letting you into the flat and then beaten up. The funniest part is that he seemed to feel obliged to stick to the truth in his description of you—high heels, short skirt and pearls, wasn't it?"

"Thus rendering the entire story about as plausible as if he'd said he was attacked by the ghost of Princess Di. I expect he was so pissed off with me that he didn't stop to think what a wally it would make him look, beaten up by a girl in a linen suit and stilettos."

"Well, exactly. My guess is that's why the agents insisted on reporting it; they wanted him checked out."

He fixed me with one of his piercing stares. "So, did you find what you were looking for in the flat?"

"I wasn't looking for anything in particular," I said. I knew Hawkins' traps too well to fall into them; but he was good, he was very good. "And I didn't find anything. Your lot obviously did a thorough job. I just thought it might be worth a try."

"Right," Hawkins said, not bothering to conceal his disbelief. "You go through all the palaver of dressing yourself up like a dog's dinner and tarting in there to sweet-talk the porter into letting you into de Groot's flat just on the off chance that you might stumble across a vital clue? Come off it, Sam. Let's talk about those names you gave me."

"The people who might have been at the party? They were just names Charles had mentioned."

"In what context?"

"Friendly. I mean, as if he were reasonably close to them. I was just wondering if they were there when he died."

"Hmm." I could tell Hawkins still didn't believe me. "What about the Walters woman? How does she come into it? Don't tell me she was a friend of his—apparently they weren't on speaking terms."

"I heard him talking to Belinda once about the people who annoyed him most at the bank," I said glibly. "I just wondered if there was anything in it. Besides, Nicola Walters wasn't at the party. I don't think the security passes are usually valid for the weekend, are they?"

"You're well informed. This Sebastian of yours keeping you up to date, is he?"

I ignored this. He cast me a sideways glance and continued, seeing I wouldn't be drawn on the subject.

"I bounced the names of— Fuck it, these names are so bloody complicated. Mind you, it's not the worst. Mate of mine was investigating some lorry theft by a group of Tamils recently. They've all got seven-syllable surnames, you know. Does your head in."

"I bet Sri Lankan police have made the same complaint in their time about British holidaymakers with unpronounceable names wearing Union Jack boxer shorts on their heads."

"Yeah, all right. What was I saying? I mentioned the other two names you gave me—"

"Patricia Makamoto and Henrik Claes Smith."

"—thank you, to Brand, seeing as this isn't even my bloody case, and one of his bright young sparks thought she'd seen Makamoto's name in the *FT* diary, or something of the sort. Went off to look it up. I ask you, reading the *Financial Times*! Who does she think she is, the deputy commissioner? Some minor scandal, she thought it was, nothing too important. But it might tie up with de Groot's work, you never know. Especially since you say he knew her—Makamoto, I mean."

"Where did you say she saw the mention?" I demanded, connections clicking together in my head.

"In the diary section. You know, they have little snippets of gossip and stuff, people ring in with the dirt on their colleagues, that kind of thing."

"What's the time, Hawkins?" I said urgently.

He glanced down at his watch. "Nearly three. Why?"

"I've just remembered I should be somewhere now. I'm sorry, I've got to rush."

Jumping up, I grabbed my bag and made for the door, Hawkins following me. I closed and locked it behind us.

"Can I give you a lift?"

"No thanks. It's bad enough you turning up at my place in a squad car without being seen travelling in one. Don't you have an unmarked vehicle you could bring next time?"

"Obviously if I'm expecting to stay a while I'd come in my own car, only it's in the garage at the moment," he said, giving me a meaningful look. "When you say next time, what did you have in mind?"

We were standing next to one another on the step, so close I could feel his breath on my face.

"The next time you come storming round to denounce me for assault, I expect."

"You know that's not what I meant, Sam." He traced the line of my jaw with his index finger, his eyes soft. "I was hoping. . . ."

I brushed his hand away. "Jesus, Hawkins, it's bad enough your coming round in that thing without feeling me up on the doorstep," I hissed. "I really must go."

I hurried over to my van and got in before he could persist. Men, I thought as I drove away. Typical. When they have you, they moan about how difficult things are, and when they don't have you, they'll fall over backwards to get you back so that they can go on moaning about how difficult things are. And they say *we're* the illogical sex.

20

The guard on duty at the *Herald* reception desk let me through the turnstile easily enough once I'd filled out a pass, not bothering to ring up to see if I were expected. The trick, as so often, was for your face to fit and to look as if you knew what you were doing. I took the lift up to the top floor with a lot of advertising salesmen in sharp suits talking at the tops of their voices. Ad types are the same the world over: loud and obnoxious, no matter what they're selling.

As the lift rose I pondered over the tactics I was going to use. I thought short, sharp shock would be best. I wanted to take her completely by surprise, and she could have no idea that anyone had any suspicions. It was a fluke that I did. If it hadn't been for that comment Charles had made to James—"there's something to tell your girlfriend"—that Nicola Walters had overheard, coupled with Hawkins' passing reference to the *FT* diary, the connection would never have entered my mind.

Jordan was off the phone by the time I reached her desk. Her gaze flickered over me curiously but without recognition for a moment; then she realised who I was and it immediately became furtive. She bent over a stack of company reports in an attempt to look industrious. In front of her the computer screen had gone into its standby mode. She hadn't chosen the flying toasters, but a program of flowers budding, blossoming and vanishing in the space of a few seconds. It was more feminine, I supposed.

"Jordan?" I said politely. "I'm Sam Jones. We met in the Cap and Barrel one evening. I wonder if I could have a word with you in private?"

"I'm afraid not," she said, gesturing at the company reports. The screen became momentarily full of red roses, wide open to the world, and then their petals started falling into black space. "I'm very busy at the moment."

I propped myself against the desk, looking down at her. The roses had been replaced by daffodils. I avoided the screen; it was too distracting. "It's about Mowbray Steiner and the article Tim's doing on the death of Charles de Groot. He told me you were working on a story connected with the bank."

"I really can't comment on that. I'm sorry, it's confidential."

"You mean your source is confidential?"

"Well, yes." She made a great play of adjusting the neck of her blouse.

"But if I know who it is, then it stops being a secret, right?"

She darted a glance at me out of the corner of her eye.

"I'm afraid I have no idea what you're talking about."

"James Rattray-Potter," I said. "He's been feeding you diary stories, hasn't he?"

She flushed. "There's nothing wrong with that!" she exclaimed. On the other side of the desk, Anne-Marie looked up from what she was tapping into the computer and frowned. Jordan lowered her voice again. "I mean, every diary depends on people in the know who give you stories. Of course I always check them out before running them."

"Oh yes, I'm not saying that you've done anything wrong. But James has—at least from Sir Richard Fine's point of view. He's very big on keeping the bank's concerns private. If he found out what James had been up to he'd sack him on the spot."

Jordan's façade of professional secrecy crumbled at once.

"You won't tell on him, will you?" she pleaded. "It would ruin James. He'd never get another job."

I studied my fingernails ostentatiously and declined to speak. Jordan's panic grew.

"Look," she said, standing up, "the offices over there are empty for the moment. We can talk in private."

She led me down the central aisle and past the lifts, to the other side of the floor. Here, without the hum of computers and voices, the silence was almost eerie. A series of power points, their white fittings cut into the grey carpet, ran down the floor in neatly spaced aisles; the whole floor had been raised artificially to accommodate the acres of wiring running beneath it. Along the far wall had been built a series of offices with glass walls through which their current emptiness seemed magnified. Jordan walked across to the far windows, which looked over Clerkenwell, and stood there hesitantly, waiting for me to join her.

She was wearing a beige belted suit and matching kitten-heeled shoes, her lank, mousy hair secured as always by the black velvet headband, the gold power earrings matching the buttons on her suit. It was the kind of outfit you needed confidence to carry off, otherwise you looked dressed above your station, like a secretary aping her boss. And at this moment Jordan cut an unexpectedly poignant figure, her drooping stance, her miserable expression so contradicting the smartness of her clothes that I couldn't help feeling sorry for her. It occurred to me that Anne-Marie might be one of those women who, abhorring competition, had deliberately picked a deputy who would never be able to come close to her style and poise, let alone rival them, and that Jordan, aware of this, was constantly insecure as a result.

"You won't tell on James, will you?" Jordan said eagerly, breaking the silence, her voice echoing in an oddly muffled way in the empty room. "It would be so terrible. He'd never speak to me again."

"How did it start?" I said, deliberately not answering her.

"I met him at a party," she said, ducking her head. "It was a friend of mine from school's, and her brother. He's a broker at Hauptmann's. Frances had told James what I did—I'd just started on the *Herald* then—and he came up to me. He was so nice," she added wistfully. "He asked me all about it. And later on he said, sort of jokingly, if he heard of any interesting gossip he'd give me a ring, and of course I said please do."

Looking at Jordan's brown, cow-like eyes, it was easy to see that she had been more interested in James himself than any snippets he could push her way.

"I didn't really think he would. I mean, he was so good-looking and confident," Jordan was saying naïvely. "But he did, a few weeks later. He told me something funny about a reception at the bank, one of the partners getting drunk and making a pass at the wife of the Indian attaché, and it checked out, so I ran it. After that he'd ring me every so often. Sometimes he'd take me out to dinner, or for drinks."

The expense of cultivating Jordan, it seemed to me, would surely have outweighed any payments James might have got from the *Herald* for his diary contributions. Still, I suspected that he had been less interested in the financial remuneration than the opportunity to see in print a few barbed comments on people he disliked. I knew from experience that James had his malicious side. He would crawl to his superiors in public and then happily stab them in the back—with the pen rather than the sword—if he thought he could get away with it.

"And how did Charles de Groot find out about James's connection with you?" I asked.

It had only been a trial shot but it hit the target full centre. Jordan's hands flew to her face as if warding off a dart. Irrelevantly I noticed that her fingers were pudgy but the nails were perfectly manicured, a rosy beige that went with the suit. Behind the hands she was making stifled sounds of misery.

"Jordan?" I said more gently.

"It was all my fault. . . ." She sniffled, still covering her face. She gulped. "All my fault. I should never have told him. . . ."

I fished in my bag. By a hundred-to-one chance there was a creased, half-full packet of tissues at the bottom. Extracting it, I pulled out one of the tissues and tapped her hands until one of them uncurled to take it.

"Thank you," she said automatically, dabbing at her face. It was red and crumpled like a baby's, though she hadn't actually shed that many tears. She looked utterly defeated.

"Look, Jordan," I said sympathetically, "I think you should tell me about it. Hopefully if you do it won't go any further."

Still patting round her eyes as if she were being careful not to drag the skin, she said nothing. Reluctantly I added:

"But otherwise the police might have to be involved."

The tissue fluttered out of her nerveless fingers and fell slowly, drifting on air-conditioned breezes, to the carpet. She stared at me, horrified. I met her gaze levelly.

"You wouldn't do that," she said, but without any conviction. I kept looking at her. After a moment she said in a dull voice:

"All right. But don't ever tell James I told you."

"I won't. I promise."

"It was . . . Charles heard James talking to me on the phone. Just to make an arrangement to meet—he'd never have actually told me anything on the phone because they record the conversations at the bank, they can get printouts of the numbers you've called, everything. But he used my name—just my first name, but that was enough, because Charles overheard him and he must have guessed who I was. My name's on the masthead, you see," she added with a touch of pride. "City Roundup by Jordan Haslett. And it's not a very usual name. Afterwards James thought that maybe Charles had read some of the bits of news he'd given me and put two and two together when he heard James talking to me."

"It was crazy of him to ring you from the office," I said, while thinking that it was James all over; he was too cocky to take seriously the idea of being caught.

She nodded. "Anyway, we met up at this wine bar and after ten minutes or so Charles walked in and came straight over to us, and said hello. He shook my hand and said: 'Charles de Groot, how do you do,' and without thinking I just said back: 'Jordan Haslett.' It was automatic. Then I saw James glaring at me and I realised what I'd done. Charles didn't seem to notice anything, and he left the bar quite soon afterwards. James even offered to buy him a drink but he said no. And we—I mean James, really—thought that it might still be all right. Only the next day he took James aside and said that he'd be in trouble if anyone but him found out about it, and . . . and. . . ."

"And suggested that James pay him a nice sum of money every month by direct debit to keep his mouth shut," I finished for her.

Jordan looked horrified.

"Every *month*?" she said. "I didn't know it was that . . . that regular. Oh, James must *hate* me." She looked as if she were about to dissolve again. "He—Charles—he'd collected together most of the diary clippings and showed them to James. He said that it was obvious I had a source inside the bank and if they traced the phone calls they would tell who'd been passing me information. James didn't have any choice."

"And then Charles conveniently died."

"Yes," she said in heartfelt tones. "It was like a miracle. . . ." Her voice tailed off as she saw the expression on my face. "You don't think . . . you can't think. . . ."

"And you, Jordan? What do you think?"

"I don't know!" she blurted out. "I just don't know!" She gulped, and I thought that her features were going to crumple again. But instead she straightened her shoulders defiantly, swallowing her tears. "And I don't care," she added, finding courage as she heard her own words. "I don't care. He was a blackmailer. People say the police go much easier on you if the person you killed was blackmailing you. I know I've heard that. And anyway, I'd never tell the police what I've just told you, never. So there."

And with that she put her chin in the air and walked away from me, right across the room, never looking back. I watched her go with reluctant admiration, mixed with pity. James would always be out of her league, the kind of man who preferred bubbly, brainless girls out for what they could get to earnest ones who would love him uncritically. Even if he married Jordan—which he wouldn't—he'd cheat on her unmercifully. She was doomed to disappointment at best. And at worst—well, better not to think about that. She might well be in danger if it had been James who killed Charles; James might even decide that Jordan knew too much for comfort.

But there was still a sticking point. I just couldn't imagine Charles de Groot taking heroin from James.

21

"What a glorious day," Suki Fine said. Her hair was loose and fluttered in the breeze off the river like a golden flag blowing behind her. The boat chugged steadily down the river; apart from the traditional raucous noises of City types at play, the only other sounds we could hear were the chugging of the boat and the squawks of the seagulls diving above us, their cry so reminiscent of the seaside and salt water that it was hard to believe we were travelling through the centre of London.

"I'm so glad I came," she added. "I didn't want to, but Daddy rather insisted. I should put some more sun cream on soon. Skin suffers more damage from the sun than anything else, you know, even pollution. You can put on some of mine if you like."

"How's Belinda?" I said, looking down to the other end of the deck where I could just see the slender figure, dressed in mint green, holding court.

"She seems much better." Suki was wearing dark glasses, and in any case the glare of the sun on our faces was dazzling; I couldn't read her expression. But she seemed relaxed, her arms stretched out behind her along the white-painted rail, her head tilted back slightly to catch the sun. "Felix is pleased, anyway," she added.

"Does she talk about Charles?"

"Not at all." Suki sounded slightly wary.

"She's recovered from it very well, all things considered," I observed.

"Well, yes, until they printed that article—did you see it? We don't take the *Herald*. A friend of Genny's rang up and told us about it. Daddy's furious."

"I'm not surprised." Tim had done a good job with it, spread over three pages with plenty of photographs, including one of a younger Suki and Belinda in a wild-child moment, up on a catwalk for a charity fashion show, dressed to kill in matching frocks, both of them looking very much the worse for wear.

"He's going to have a witch hunt to find out who it was," Suki went on. "Because apparently their information is too accurate to sue, or to have a chance of winning, that is, and besides, he doesn't want any more publicity." She turned her head to me. "Did they get in touch with you?"

"No, they didn't," I said truthfully. "They rang my agent, though."

"Your photo came out awfully well," Suki commented. "Belinda said it was that friend of hers' boyfriend who took it. You know, Baby. She's here."

"I know." I could practically hear her, though she was right down the other end of the boat—was it the bow or the stern?—in a skimpy knitted top that displayed not only her midriff but a large portion of her ribcage too, laughing like a drain at something Belinda had just said to her. Trapped on a boat with Baby for three hours. I'd never have insisted we come if I'd known.

"Belinda rang her up when Daddy said we had to come," Suki was saying.

"Why was that?"

"I don't know. Perhaps she wanted some company."

"No, I mean why did he make you all come?"

"Solidarity in the face of trouble," Suki said, as if reciting. "Especially after the article came out. Putting a bright face on it, making it seem as if nothing was wrong. Daddy's marvellous at that. It's his driving force." There was a bitterness to the comment that seemed unwarranted by the simple fact of being made to take a boat trip down the Thames. I wondered about it.

"Dominic didn't make a fuss, of course," she was continuing acidly. "He'd do anything Daddy wanted, on the surface anyway. He knows when he's well off."

"Are you two going to get married?"

Her head snapped round to look at me. Even from behind her sunglasses I could feel her eyes piercing into mine.

"Who told you that?" she said in a harsh voice.

"Your father. And Geneviève," I added, giving the pot a good hearty stir. "They seemed very keen on the idea."

"Oh yes, they are. *Very* keen. God. I can't believe they're talking about it to all and sundry."

"What's the matter? Don't you want to marry Dominic?" I remembered the expression on her face as she looked at Dominic, the night that Belinda and Charles had announced their engagement. At the time I had thought that she was afraid he wouldn't propose.

"Yes—no—*yes*. I can't explain." Suki swallowed. "Yes, I do. In a way. It's just—" She broke off. "I must go and put on some more sun cream, do excuse me," she said, and ducked down the passageway to the lower deck. I stared after her in bemusement.

"Suki seems a little tense," observed Dominic Planchet from behind me.

I swung round, taken by surprise; I hadn't heard him come up. Another romantic hero attribute was moving silently as a cat, if I remembered my childhood reading correctly. He was leaning on the rail, wearing white trousers, a white shirt with the sleeves rolled up and gold-framed sunglasses. He smiled at me.

"She's rather upset about that article in the *Herald* yesterday," I said neutrally.

"Oh yes, the article. It was a fascinating read, didn't you think? Very enjoyable. And so unexpected." He was watching me closely. "Excellent publicity for you, of course. I was only surprised they didn't contact you to ask for your comment."

"My agent wouldn't give them my phone number," I said. "And even if he had, Sir Richard had made it clear he didn't want it talked about."

"And you know which side your bread is buttered on."

"Why not?" I snapped back. "Don't you?"

Dominic laughed, a very pleasant, genuinely amused laugh, showing off his white teeth. "You're quite right, of course," he admitted. "I do. As we all should. I'm sorry if I was offensive."

"Not at all."

"I do like it when people stand up to me," he said. "I tend to be something of a bully otherwise."

"Does that go for your employees as well?" I asked.

"My employees?"

"At your restaurants."

Dominic smiled. "My staff," he said lightly, "do as they're told. Otherwise they're out of a job. I'm afraid I'm rather old-fashioned that way."

"Positively medieval."

Not at all offended, he looked at me with frank appreciation.

"Sebastian's a lucky man," he said. "Not that I mean to imply that you belong to anyone. I'm quite sure you don't."

His ability to show admiration while avoiding either sleaziness, or the implication that it put the admiree under any obligation, was impressive. I looked back at him with the same lack of pretence as he was observing me, the sun beating down heavy on our heads. You could say that we were both wondering what the other would be like in bed.

"Dominic?" his mother called from the passageway.

He remained with his dark eyes on me for long enough for me to wonder whether he had heard her. Then he smiled at me.

"Excuse me, please," he said, and went down the stairs.

I watched him go, sipping my Pimms, which by now was warm, the ice having melted. I wished they wouldn't put pieces of cucumber in it; I never knew what to do with them when I had finished the drink. Being on board ship resolved that question, at least. I chucked the dregs over the side and went into the saloon in search of some more.

It was crammed with men in summer suits and a sprinkling of women, mostly sporting what Laura Ashley considered suitable for garden parties. Personally, I don't think anyone over seven should wear sailor collars. I fought my way through the braying melee to the punch bowl, keeping a watch out for Baby, whom I wanted to avoid, and James Rattray-Potter, whom I wanted to talk to.

On Friday, after my talk with Jordan, I had gone home and on some instinct examined once more the printout of figures and dates next to the names on the list Tim had sent me. Before I had only given it a cursory reading, being more concerned with the identities of the people Charles had been blackmailing and the size of their monthly payments. This time, though, I had discovered that James's last deposit in Charles's account had been almost two months before he died, which was to say that the last payment due had not been made. It could have been that James hadn't had sufficient money in his account to cover the direct debit payment when it came due, but it was hard to believe that someone as methodical as Charles wouldn't have noticed this and pressured James to pay.

Of course, there was another explanation: that James had already been planning to kill Charles and hadn't wanted to lose another month's money into the account of a man who was about to die. It would have been short-sighted, though, putting Charles immediately on his guard; and surely someone who did James's kind of job had to have at least a basic, animal cunning that would have warned him against making such a mistake.

With what I had learned from Jordan, I should hopefully have enough information to lever James into giving me an explanation. And I liked the idea of doing it here, on the boat, with his bosses hovering nearby, their presence reminding him of all he had to lose if I told them what I knew. I'd just have to be careful there were people around. I had the feeling James could be like a raging bull when angry and I wouldn't put it past him to try to throw me overboard without a lifejacket.

"Darling." A pair of arms encircled me from behind. I jumped, even though I had recognised Sebastian's voice.

"What is it?" Sebastian said in my ear. "Am I making you nervous?"

"No, of course not." I turned in the circle of his arms. He was looking down at me fondly, his eyes the colour of gunmetal but distinctly more tender. I reached up and brushed his fringe back. He bent and kissed me lightly on the lips. The boat swayed gently beneath our feet.

"It should be midnight," he said, "not four in the afternoon. And we should be alone."

"Nothing's perfect."

My attention was caught by an unbelievably scruffy-looking man at the buffet table. He cut off a very large piece of blue cheese, speared it on a knife, stuffed it in his mouth and walked away, still chewing. A piece of cheese had fallen on his lapel. I stared after him. One of his sleeves looked as if it had been torn away from the main body of his jacket; there was a good two centimetres of lining showing through, loose threads hanging down.

"He's a director of corporate finance," Sebastian said, his arms still around me. "Turned up looking like that to a meeting we had with someone from the German embassy and the director of a German steel firm. It was pretty important; from our lot there was me, a vice-chairman and one of our directors of equity syndication. Francis turned up an hour late, and he was bringing the presentation. Unbelievable."

"Doesn't anyone tell him to smarten up?"

He shook his head. "Round here, as long as your suit's right, you can wear it into the ground. It's inverted snobbery, really, like saying 'I spent my last bonus on re-roofing the family pile,' or 'We had a lot of money at Lloyd's.' "

"What do you mean, if the suit's right? That it's got to be pinstripe?"

Sebastian drew in his breath sharply. "*Chalkstripe*, please. Pinstripe is for wide boys. Single-breasted suits, plain shirts. Braces at a pinch, but they must be sober."

I was overcome with an emotion I had never expected to feel—a wave of pity for these poor men. How on earth were they expected to express their personalities?

"Unhand that young woman, Shaw," Sir Richard boomed, approaching us. "Pair of lovebirds, eh, Genny?"

Suki had not anointed her father with any of her barrier cream; his face was quite red from the sun. Still, he'd survived better than David Stronge beside him, from whose balding pate flakes of skin were already starting to peel, adding to the dandruff already present. He was escorting his wife, a dumpy woman in a floral sack with a dropped waist to match her own. The two men, in lightweight grey summer suits, were perspiring heavily, both being overweight and accustomed to air conditioning. It was not a pretty sight.

"The young in one another's arms," said David Stronge avuncularly for his wife's benefit.

"I saw your picture in the paper yesterday," she piped up. "It was very flattering."

"You mean you're disappointed with me in the flesh?" I said, sending Mrs. Stronge into a paroxysm of twitters.

"Oh no, not at all, I didn't mean—"

Geneviève said smoothly:

"Actually, Richard would prefer we didn't discuss the article. I'm sure you understand, Sylvia."

"It's just a left-wing rag, after all," David Stronge added quickly. "I dare say hardly anyone we know read it."

"We got about a dozen calls yesterday," snapped Sir Richard. "Then I put the answering machine on and collected hundreds more. Just takes one, y'know. Then they all ring their friends and tell them to go out and buy a copy."

David Stronge cleared his throat discreetly, as if this signalled a change of subject.

"It'll soon blow over," Geneviève said consolingly. "And let's not allow it to ruin this lovely day, shall we?" She finished her drink and looked around her for a waiter. I realised that this was the first social occasion I had attended hosted by Sir Richard Fine where a flunkey hadn't appeared every five minutes to refill my glass with champagne. Most disappointing.

"I'm just going to get myself another glass of Pimms," she said, and disappeared in the direction of the punch bowl.

"The weather's perfect," Sebastian said. "I hope Marcus is enjoying himself."

"The birthday boy? He's earned it." Sir Richard was immediately restored to good humour. "He's had an excellent year so far. A really excellent year." He patted his finger to his nose. "These things are always noticed, y'know."

"Absolutely, Sir Richard," David Stronge said sycophantically.

Richard Fine shot him a look which was not altogether friendly. David Stronge hung on at the bank because he was prepared to carry out a range of administrative tasks which any other director would have considered too menial, but that didn't mean he wasn't eminently replaceable. According to both Sebastian and Simon Grenville, nearly anything was permitted to employees who were making serious money for the bank. I doubted very much that the same licence would be extended to David Stronge.

* * *

I slipped away when Sir Richard and Sebastian plunged into another of their interminable cricket discussions. I quite understood that a man had to do what a man had to do to obtain promotion, but the mechanics, in this case, sounded about as interesting as a discussion about quantum physics and hardly less complicated. Baby was still outside on the deck, and James was nowhere I could see, but in a recessed window seat on the other side of the saloon, drink in hand, watching the panorama of London pass by, was Simon Grenville. I didn't know if he'd welcome my company or not, but I crossed over to him.

"Excuse me, is this seat taken?"

He looked up, eyes far away, as if he had been deep in a daydream.

"Sam," he said. It wasn't a twenty-one gun salute, but nor was it said with the kind of resignation with which I habitually greet Baby, for instance. In the circumstances that probably counted as a welcome. I sat down next to him.

"How are you, Simon?"

"I've been better."

"What is it?"

"Oh. . . ." He made a little gesture with his hands, as if to wave something away. A sprinkling of ash from his cigarette scattered over the table, light as tiny grey feathers. Simon looked paler and thinner than usual; even the light gold of his hair seemed faded to the colour of dull straw. And his manner was withdrawn, distant, the bearing of someone who has retreated into himself and to whom the outside world seems, for the moment at least, quite irrelevant.

"I'll tell you an amusing anecdote, shall I? Look at that bloke over there." He indicated a loud, balding, young-old grey suit, indistinguishable from the rest of his group. "He's on the trading floor. Struck up a feud with another chap, who I can't see here. Maybe he wasn't invited. Anyway, they got more and more competitive, started battling to get in earlier than the other in the mornings. They usually have to be in about seven-thirty, let's say. OK, it gets to the point that one morning they're both jockeying to get into the car park before the other at ten to five."

"*Ten to five?* Is there anything to do at that hour?"

"Well, the Tokyo exchange is open. Anyway, that one I pointed out to you gets through the gate first and parks right there, blocks it off for the other one. The second chap can't just leave his car there in the street, so he has to go through the gate on foot, get the key of the first one's car from the guard and move it before he can drive his own car in. Loses a good twenty minutes, you see. By the time he made it to his desk he was seething mad—they had a punch-up right there in the dealing room."

"What happened?"

Simon shrugged. "They're both heavy hitters, so nothing much. Marcus probably gave them both a wigging, nothing too heavy." He gave me a faint smile. "That's the kind of story that's made me do a lot of thinking recently. Not to mention the conversation you and I had a while ago. I've been thinking about my life, and whether I really want to go on living it this way, with this kind of people around me. The big one."

"Was it something I said?" I doubted it. I wasn't usually deep enough to have that effect on people.

"Not exactly." He took a deep drag at his cigarette. "It was more that I talked about it with you, an outsider, and I realised afterwards that you accepted the Dan thing quite naturally, you didn't seem to disapprove in any way. I began to wonder whether I was in the right place—I mean that metaphorically, of course—to get what I need out of life. And looking around us at my charming colleagues"—he took in with one comprehensive glance the spectacle of Sloane over-indulgence being played out before us—"I doubt very much whether I am."

I nodded understandingly, assuming that Simon meant that to go on living in his current milieu would mean denying his sexuality or having to face the endless disparaging jokes and maybe even bullying that would ensue. How, for instance, could he bring a boyfriend to a party like this? And yet this kind of life was what he knew, the way he had been brought up. I looked at him sympathetically.

"You might not think it, but I'm actually rather ambitious," Simon said in a dry voice. "If it got out it might not actually ruin my career, but everyone would look at me askance. I would never achieve my goals. Which leads me to ask why I want to be here in the first place."

"Why do you hang out with that group, Simon?" I asked him. "The Fine girls and their friends? I mean, I know Sebastian's a friend of yours, but why did you spend so much time in Charles's company?"

He smiled, a tight little smile with only a thread of amusement.

"I was hoping to get some information on him that might cancel out what he had on me. To put it simply."

"And did you?" I asked, thinking that this was probably the explanation why James too had been so determined to form part of that circle.

He shook his head. "I wanted to find out where he was getting his drugs from. I wondered if he was dealing, though that always seemed such a risky thing to do for someone as careful as Charles that I couldn't help doubting it."

"And did you find out?" I said, my heart suddenly pounding.

He looked at me and hesitated for a moment. Then he said, with a certain, almost involuntary inflection: "Where he got his drugs from? No, I didn't."

I believed him. But at the same time I was quite sure that it wasn't what he had been about to say.

* * *

I had seen James cross the room while I had been talking to Simon, but now he seemed to have disappeared again. I made my way through the saloon, passing Geneviève Planchet by the punch bowl, and out on to the deck. The white rails and fittings glittered in the sun, catching the light and throwing it blindingly into my face. A group of young men in shirtsleeves and incipient paunches were horsing around with one of the lifebelts, hurling it at each other like a giant Frisbee, their faces red with sun and drink. Sebastian was talking to a staid-looking couple. Seeing me, he detached himself for a moment, making an excuse, and came over, taking my hand and pressing it affectionately.

"All right?" he said, smiling.

"I am now."

Sebastian rejoined the couple and I headed straight downstairs to examine in the privacy of a toilet the contents of the little packet he had just neatly inserted into my palm. Fortunately there was hardly any wind and the boat was very steady, but it still took me a while longer than usual to decant some coke on to the toilet cistern and sniff it up with a fiver. It had been thoughtful of him to cut it up first. That operation would have been even harder to manage.

The coke was very good. I made a mental note to ask Sebastian where he scored it. Refreshed and clear-headed, I slipped the packet into the bottom of my shoulder bag and flushed the toilet. Nicola Walters was the only other person washing her hands at the sink as I emerged. She caught sight of me in the mirror and did a double take, her eyes widening.

"What on earth are you doing here?" she exclaimed.

Probably she saw me as one of those secret agents in American TV series who manage somehow to infiltrate the most private of gatherings under the most feeble of excuses. I would have to disillusion her.

"Actually, I'm here with Sebastian Shaw," I said apologetically. "Do you know him?"

"Of course. Everyone knows Sebastian," she said with a trace of amusement. "I didn't realise. I'm sorry."

Regaining control of herself, she produced a small brush from her bag and ran it briefly through her hair, the thick wings falling neatly back into place. She didn't touch up her make-up, there being nothing to touch up. Her intelligent, strong features hardly needed it.

"Are you having a nice time?" she said politely.

"Interesting, rather than pleasant. I can't say I think a great deal of your colleagues."

"Nor do I." But she said it very simply; it was just the price she had to pay for her ambitions. She was sure of herself and what she wanted in a way that Simon Grenville no longer was.

"Have you got any further with . . . with finding out where Charles's file might be?" she said, her eyes meeting mine in the mirror.

"I don't know where it is," I said slowly. "But I think I just might know who has it."

"Someone else has it?" Her jaw clenched. "Who is it?"

I shook my head. "I can't say yet. It's just a guess. But I don't think it'll come to any harm where it is."

"But you'll get it? My papers, anyway, I mean. You'll get them?"

"I think so. I'll let you know."

I smiled mysteriously and left the toilets, feeling like a spy who had just successfully completed a rendezvous. Or maybe that was the cocaine. I made a mental note not to consider myself invulnerable. One of the dangers with coke was that it could make you terribly cocky. And as had already occurred to me, on board ship was not the place to make too many enemies. The Thames looked flat and peaceful, as if swimming to shore would be as easy as a couple of lengths in an Olympic-sized pool, but I knew how deceptive appearances could be.

Perhaps I was being paranoid, but that didn't mean people weren't out to get me. So far, at least, no one seemed to realise that I had had anything to do with the newspaper article, for which I thanked God and all her little angels devoutly. I reached the top of the passageway and the first person I saw was Geneviève Planchet, by herself, leaning against the side of the stairhead, sipping a Pimms. There was something odd about this and I realised almost at once what it was: normally at this kind of social function she was in constant motion, talking to the guests, enabling them to circulate, making introductions, being, in short, the perfect hostess. At least for a while she seemed to have abrogated her responsibilities.

I remembered how many times I had seen her at the punch bowl. She wasn't drunk or even tipsy, but she had clearly had a few more glasses than usual.

"Hello, Sam," she said to me as I emerged from the staircase. "Are you enjoying yourself?"

"Oh yes," I said diplomatically. "The perfect Sunday afternoon. It was very kind of Sir Richard to invite me."

"Richard *is* very kind," she said, rather with the air of someone making an announcement. "I should know. I certainly don't know what I would have done if I hadn't met him."

"You mean when you left your husband?"

If nothing else, the coke was certainly making me direct. But it didn't faze Geneviève. Having laid her social obligations to one side she seemed to feel no need to make cocktail conversation.

"That's right," she said, her French accent more apparent now that she had drunk a little, though her English was as perfect as ever. "He was wonderful to us. Dominic was only three when I left Alain, and Richard brought him up practically as his own." She sighed. "I always wished that he would call Richard Papa, but it never happened. Understandable, I suppose."

"Maybe if you had married he would have done."

"Oh, that was never a possibility," she said, raising her neatly plucked eyebrows. "Never. Alain wouldn't dream of giving me a divorce. He's very old-fashioned about that kind of thing."

"Even if he wanted to marry again?"

"Catholics like Alain simply don't marry again. He has his mistresses, of course, but that doesn't count. And we couldn't have fought him through the courts. Think of the scandal it would have caused."

I leaned on the balcony rail, confused. "I'm sorry, I don't understand. Surely . . . I mean. . . ." I tried to think of a delicate way to phrase it and gave up. "Surely your living with Sir Richard the way you do would have been considered much more scandalous than even a contested divorce?"

Geneviève looked thoroughly amused. "I can see you don't understand at all, my dear. The important thing is to get the appearance right and not stir up a fuss. Richard and I have always been very discreet. Adjoining houses, that kind of thing. Of course everyone knew we were a couple, but if you don't draw attention to yourself the gossip fades away faster than you'd think, and soon the situation is simply accepted in society. We knew the rules. Compared to that the mess of a divorce, with Alain fighting every inch of the way, Richard cited as co-respondent. . . ." She closed her eyes and shook her head decisively. "Absolutely not."

A wind had got up and the boat was pitching lightly to and fro. We gripped on to the rail automatically, the breeze lifting my hair off my neck as if it were someone's hand.

"Besides, Richard has been wonderful to me," said Geneviève, returning to her original topic. She downed the last drops of Pimms. "Wonderful. I couldn't have put him through that kind of thing, even for Dominic. The scandal would have been terribly damaging to his career."

"Even for Dominic?" I echoed.

She shrugged, that delicate, comprehensive little movement of hers. "Oh, he would very much have preferred the situation to have been more respectable while he was growing up. Still, it hasn't done him any harm in the end. Hopefully everything will settle down now. Dominic for Suki, and Belinda—well, thank God Charles is out of the way, at least."

"You didn't like him?" A few glasses more than usual certainly had a loosening effect on Geneviève's tongue. But then the sun might be considered a contributory factor; it made one feel tipsier than one was.

Geneviève closed her eyes and shook her head again. It was her way of indicating a categorical "no" more strongly than mere words could do. English people weren't half as good at gestures. "I never trusted him at all. He was completely out for what he could get, a nasty, scheming social climber. Proposing to Belinda was all part of it. He saw his advantage and he took it. I was going to have his title checked out, you know," she added venomously. "I never believed in that either."

She looked down at her glass and seemed disappointed to find it empty. I would have offered to get her some more but I didn't want to interrupt the flow. For a moment I thought she was going to walk away but then she said:

"He was a snoop, too. Poking and prying around what didn't concern him. I think he was one of those people who like to know as much as they can about others; they feel it gives them the upper hand. I once caught him in Richard's study. Oh, he had a perfectly plausible excuse for being there, but I didn't believe it. Instinct, you could say."

She tilted the empty glass in her hand, looking down at it, and when she spoke again her voice was much calmer.

"I go to great lengths to make sure Richard's not upset or worried. His work, naturally, is his territory. But the home is mine. And there I want to make sure that I protect him from any inconvenience I can."

Her eyes flicked upwards to my face.

"Like that article in the *Herald*," she said. "Richard was extremely unhappy about that. It's exactly the kind of publicity he wants to avoid."

I thought of the photograph of Belinda and Suki on the catwalk, drunk as a pair of skunks; Tim had been able to indicate how self-indulgent the twins had been in the past without saying anything directly enough to lay him open to legal action. I grimaced.

"I'm not surprised," I said sincerely.

"You don't know anything about it, do you?" Geneviève was definitely not a fool.

"I knew that they'd rung my agent to get some background and a photograph of me," I said. "But I had no idea it was for anything on this scale, or I would have let you know."

I didn't know whether Geneviève believed me or not; her eyes hadn't left my face.

"Can I get you another glass of Pimms?" I said.

"No, thank you, Sam," she said. "I'll go myself. Remember what I was saying, won't you? I don't want Richard worried by this business any longer. I mean that."

I watched her narrow shoulders in the linen dress cutting a neat path through a crowd of brokers who, despite their raucous and drunken condition, nonetheless parted at once to let her by. I thought they would have done so even if she hadn't been the boss's wife in all but name. There was something about Geneviève's carriage that made you defer to her automatically.

I thought about the warning she had just given me, and winced. I hoped to God Geneviève never found out who had really been responsible for that article. I was sure that her wrath would be mighty.

22

"Sam! Darling!" Baby swooped down on me like a bony, flightless bird of prey. I had been distracted enough to forget to watch my back. Not an omen, I hoped. How she managed to walk, let alone run, in those knee-length high-heeled boots on board a boat which was rocking, albeit gently, back and forth, passed all understanding. "I've decided at my next party we're going to have Pimms," she declared enthusiastically. "It's just too fabulous!"

"How's your boyfriend, Baby?" I said in an attempt to be friendly. "I must thank him for those photos he did of me."

Baby's forehead creased in puzzlement. "Boyfriend?" she repeated.

She couldn't be that drunk. She wouldn't still be vertical.

"Tony Muldoon," I said. "The photographer."

"Oh, him!" She let out a tinkly laugh. "It was absolutely impossible. I told him to go back to his girlfriend."

Decoded, I presumed this meant that he had never had serious intentions towards Baby. Behind us the group of drunks who had been playing Frisbee with the lifebelt had now unzipped their trousers and pulled their penises out. They dangled down rather sadly, like worms who weren't that happy to be taking the sun. Probably afraid of the seagulls. I hoped they had been duly smeared with sun cream. Suki Fine would be pointing the necessity out to them any minute now.

"He was just a druggie," Baby was saying. "I mean, syringes all over the floor. If I'd trodden on one I could have caught God knows what."

The flashers were standing in a circle now, hands on their love-handles, wiggling their hips back and forward, their penises bobbing up and down with the movement. Perhaps it was some kind of Sloane fertility dance. I expect a social theorist would have read their behaviour as a powerful statement about the invisibility of the male member in modern society, a daring attempt to confront its reality. For some reason the word "pathetic" sprung more easily to my lips.

"I mean, it's all very well if you're not having sex with the person," Baby continued, magnificently unaware of my divided attention. "I'm not at all prejudiced about that kind of thing. I mean, it's very cool at the moment. Everyone's doing it. But there are limits. God, I remember when we were at school we tried everything that was going, me and Belinda. She'd come in with something new every day and make us all try it out."

A loud cry suddenly arose from the group of fertility riters. James was emerging from the staircase and behind him was Susie, the receptionist. They both looked flushed and tousled. It was lucky for James that Jordan wasn't here.

"Weh-eh, weh-eh, weh-eh," chanted the band of floppy penises, moving to encircle James and Susie and making their hip-jerking gestures even more explicit than they had been before. If an anthropologist had happened to be present they would have had a field day.

"God, look at that," said Belinda Fine, approaching us. "Pathetic, isn't it?"

Finally Belinda and I agreed on something. I grinned at her. "Especially when they're that size," I added.

She stared at me blankly. "Oh, you mean the boys getting their willies out! They're just letting off steam, you know. They often do that when they get pissed. Daddy thinks it's terribly funny. As long as they don't start mooning. That would be a bit much. No, I meant

James and Susie. Screwing the seccy in the toilets at a party. How *common*."

"I've decided I'm going to have Pimms at my next party," Baby informed her. "It'll be fab. I want to start a whole new trend."

James and Susie broke free of the group of exhibitionists and started unsteadily round the deck, bumping into people as they went. James was holding a half-full tumbler and was trying not to spill it; Susie, clutching on to his other arm and giggling madly, wasn't helping. Dominic and Sebastian, who were leaning against the rail, nearly got knocked overboard by an unsteady lunge of James's to save his glass. Since he had no hands free to steady himself, it wasn't easy; there was a scuffle in which the glass nearly went flying. Sebastian caught it just in time. They righted James with considerable difficulty and sent him on his way. Dominic, looking after him, curled his lip in his trademark cynical smile and said something to Sebastian which made him laugh.

James and Susie disappeared inside the saloon. I was tracking their progress, though the hope of catching James alone and sober enough to talk was looking increasingly remote. They stopped by Suki, Sir Richard and Geneviève, who were talking to an unknown couple. James had put his glass down to shake the hands of the strangers, Susie still attached to his left arm like a limpet. My attention wandered back to what Baby was saying to Belinda.

". . . when he told them that flesh tones were absolutely out. Salmon or nothing. And in any case those breast pockets were so last year. He was wonderful, there was nothing they could say."

"So did they take it out of the collection?"

"Oh, *absolutely*!"

James and Susie, with many hitches, were staggering out of the saloon roughly in our direction.

"B'linda!" James exclaimed. "Lovely B'linda! Lovely party!"

Susie made an effort to shake her curls coquettishly but stopped halfway through, looking as if it had hurt her head.

The tumbler in James's hand looked even less full than it had been before. "Careful," he said, gazing down at it. "Careful with the whisky. Oops!"

Susie caught her high heel on the wooden floor and stumbled, pulling James with her. I grabbed Susie, and Belinda and Baby caught James, putting them back on their feet. Why we bothered I don't know. Instinct, I suppose.

"Thank you, girlsh," slurred James. "Nishe girlsh. Thank you. Say thank you, Shushie."

"Thank you," Susie giggled.

James tilted his head back and brought the glass up to his lips. "Funny smell," he said, frowning. "Oh well, down the hatch." He downed the whisky in one go and looked around him, smiling. Then the glass fell from his hand.

"Oh, for God's sake, James," said Belinda, irritated. "Look at the mess you've made."

Broken glass littered the wooden floor around James's feet. He ducked his head as if to look at it. Then his hand darted to his throat and he made a choking sound.

"And don't start playing the fool," Belinda said snappishly.

But James was still choking. His other hand had jerked convulsively free of Susie's clasp and now he was doubled over, clutching his stomach.

"Jamie!" Susie wailed.

"Is he all right?" Baby said, finally catching on.

"Of course he's bloody not!" I snapped.

James was retching, but in a dry, stifled way, as if he couldn't bring anything up.

"He's just drunk," said Belinda dismissively.

Ignoring her, I grabbed James's shoulders, pulling him up so I could look into his face. The smell hit me at once, but I didn't yet recognise it.

"What is it, James? Where does it hurt?"

He tapped his chest and stomach. One hand was clasped round his neck. "Burning . . . burning . . . can't breathe . . ." he gasped out. His eyes were terrified. Under my fingers his shoulders, through his shirt, were hot as coals. Beads of sweat formed on his face like tears. I couldn't hold him up. His legs gave way under him and he collapsed to the deck. Looking around me desperately I waved to Sebastian and Dominic, who were already staring curiously in our direction.

"For God's sake get out of the way, Sam. He's going to spew and you'll be directly in the firing line," Dominic drawled, strolling over.

"He's been poisoned!" I snapped. "Get me a glass of milk. Both of you, go on!"

Over Sebastian's face flashed a series of expressions, from bewilderment to doubt to shock. "Come on, for Christ's sake," he said to Dominic, heading into the saloon.

James was doubled over now, his arms wrapped round himself, sweat streaming down his scarlet, agonised face, gasping for breath and retching simultaneously. He looked like someone who had run a race and nearly killed himself in the process. Susie was screaming, predictably enough, a series of short, puppyish yelps, which were horrible because in other circumstances they would have been funny.

"Take her away," I said to Baby and Belinda, but they were both transfixed, staring down at James, and seemed not to have heard me. A crowd was forming around us and I saw Geneviève Planchet's face in the circle. I nodded at Susie, calling to Geneviève: "Get her out of here, for God's sake!"

Out of the corner of my eye I saw Geneviève go over to Susie and say something to her, turning her away. Her screams abated. Sebastian returned at a sprint with a half-full glass of milk.

"This was all they had," he said, handing it to me. "The rest was cream. I can get some if you want."

"James. James, drink this." I held the glass out to him. "It'll help."

He made a sweeping gesture that nearly knocked the glass out of my hand.

"Hold his head," I said to Sebastian. He knelt down beside me and took hold of James.

"James, old chap. Get this down you. It'll do you good. Come on."

He was better at it than I was. James sat up, raising his face, which was terrifying, crimson and agonised, running with sweat, his eyes bewildered. He managed to drink down the milk and gave the glass back to Sebastian.

"How do you feel?" Sebastian said urgently.

"Better . . . cooler . . ." James took a deep breath, and everyone around us let theirs out in relief. "Better," James croaked, "doesn't hurt so much. . . ."

Then, as if kicked in the stomach, he doubled over, retching again and again. Geneviève, her arm around a sobbing Susie, was trying to get her to drink something—brandy, I assumed—but Susie was refusing hysterically, pushing the glass away. One couldn't blame her.

Dominic came out of the saloon, half-running.

"I've spoken to the captain," he said, bending over us. "We should be stopping soon. He's radioing the emergency services for an ambulance."

"Shall I get him some of the cream to drink?" Sebastian said to me desperately.

"It can't hurt," I said, frowning. James was curled on the floor, coughing and choking. The circle of people around him had doubled in size; most people by now had realised there was something going on. Geneviève had managed to draw Susie right out of the throng, though I didn't know if she had succeeded in convincing her to drink the brandy. Sir Richard Fine elbowed his way to the front. Beside him was another man whom I recognised as Marcus Samson, whose birthday we were celebrating.

"My God!" said Richard Fine. "What the hell has happened to him? Not a bloody epileptic, is he?"

"Rattray-Potter can usually hold his drink," Marcus Samson said, frowning.

"Someone seems to have spiked it," Sebastian said.

Sir Richard looked round him urgently. "Shaw," he said in a lowered voice, "round up the clients and take 'em into the saloon. Give 'em some brandy, there's a good chap. Tell 'em he's had a bit too much to drink. Happens all the time."

"What the hell has he taken?" Marcus Samson exploded. "You'd think he'd been poisoned!"

James's heels drummed on the floor with the violence of his convulsions. He opened his mouth to retch and I saw with horror that his tongue and lips were turning blue. God knew when we'd be able to pull into dock and get him to a hospital. The longer this went on the more dangerous it was for him.

Dominic was by Sir Richard, muttering something about an ambulance. He was the only person talking. The group of onlookers had gone silent when their bosses appeared, and Samson's words had fallen into a stillness broken only by the terrible sounds James was making. The word "poisoned" hung in the air above James's head. People shuffled a few paces back, as if afraid of contamination. Out of sight, behind the crowd, Susie was sobbing, long, terrified, panic-stricken sobs like a counterpoint to James's groans of agony. Everyone was looking at Marcus Samson as if he were their spokesman. But he wasn't looking anywhere but at James, and he was white as a sheet.

I expect he hadn't watched anyone die before.

23

It was the first time I'd ever seen Baby decently covered. She was wearing a man's shirt hanging loose over jeans and would have looked much more attractive than she usually did in her skintight outfits if it weren't for the deep grey circles under her eyes. The fact that she hadn't bothered to paint them out spoke volumes. She was chain-smoking and her face was drawn.

"I've never seen anything like that before," she said for the fifteenth time, her hands shaking on the cigarette. "I couldn't sleep all last night for remembering."

"Why did you come into work?"

"We've got this big promotion on and I'm the only one that knows about it," she said, extraordinarily enough without a trace of self-importance. Baby had been shocked so badly by James's death she had reverted to normal behaviour. Doubtless it would only be temporary. She lit another cigarette from the first one, though it was only half smoked. "You could tell he was going to die," she said, shivering. "The way he looked . . . the sounds he was making. . . ."

"If we hadn't been on a boat he might have survived," I corrected her. "One of the doctors had rung Guy's—they have a special poisons unit there and they'd told her what antidote to use. They had it all ready and waiting for him at the hospital. Only it was too late. He died in the ambulance."

Baby had been too hysterical yesterday to realise what was going on. They'd had to give her a sedative. And she hadn't been the only one.

"What *was* it?" she said now. "What had he taken?"

"Poppers. I smelt them almost at once."

"Poppers?"

I nodded. "If you drink amyl nitrite it goes into the bloodstream and burns out the internal organs. That's why I gave him the milk, to line his stomach. It helped. But it wasn't enough."

"How did you know what to do?"

"The same thing happened to a friend of mine at a club, years ago. Some wanker she'd just turned down spiked her drink. She'd have died if one of the bouncers hadn't got a pint of milk down her. As it was she could have serious liver damage, and it's played merry hell with her immune system."

"My God."

"We beat the crap out of him a few days later. He won't be trying that on anyone again." I stood up. "Thanks for answering my questions, Baby. You've been a lot of help. I expect you'll want to be getting back to work."

"Yes, I should, really. Not that I feel like it." Baby stood up too. Behind her the receptionist looked at us curiously. We'd been speaking low but it was clear that the conversation had been serious.

"There've been a couple of calls for you, Baby," she said.

Baby held out her hand for the messages, still looking at me. She blurted out:

"Do you think—I mean—do you think—what you asked me just now. . . ." Her voice tailed off. She didn't want to say it aloud. And she didn't want to look at my face either. "I've got to go," she said. "Look after yourself."

Then, unexpectedly, she gave me a quick hug, holding me for a moment, before she ducked away down the corridor that led to her office. I stared after her for a moment, feeling ridiculously touched.

All I wanted was to sit back down on the sofa and leaf through the sheaves of glossy magazines and forget what I had to do now. It was hard to make myself move out of the door, into the street, to unlock the van and drive away. It was made harder by the beauty of the day, warm and balmy, the sky clear and blue. The offices of Baby's PR firm were in a little alley off Bond Street. I navigated myself across Grosvenor Square and down Park Lane, feeling like a zombie, my hands moving on the wheel, my feet on the pedals, as if I were on automatic pilot. There was a cold shiver down the back of my neck and despite the sun on my skin it felt icy, like something resuscitated from a morgue.

Through Knightsbridge, down Sloane Street, into the King's Road. By the time I'd parked and was ringing the doorbell my heart was beating unpleasantly fast and the chilliness hadn't abated. Suki Fine opened the door and looked very pleased to see me.

"Sam! Come in! My God, your hands are cold!"

It was nice to know that I wasn't hallucinating, anyway. I moved inside the house, Suki shutting the door behind me and bustling us through into the kitchen. All the while I felt strangely detached, as if there were a glass wall between me and the rest of the world. Sunlight, dappling the yellow-painted kitchen, pooled becomingly on the handmade terracotta floor and the blonde hair of Belinda Fine, who was standing at the stainless steel counter, slicing an apple. She was wearing a pink silk dressing gown, her feet were bare and the breadboard was of olive wood. My mind was sharp, noticing every detail, no matter how pointless.

"Are you all right?" Suki was saying. "You look strange."

"I feel strange."

She sat down at one of the chairs round the kitchen table and indicated another for me. I shook my head. There was a cafetière on the table, half full of rich-scented black coffee. Suki poured herself some.

"Do you want some coffee, Sam? Bells?"

"Got some already," Belinda said through a mouthful of fruit.

"Is there anyone else around?" I said.

Suki, looking puzzled, shook her head. "Mrs. Hermesetas only comes in the mornings."

"Good," I said. "Because I want to talk to you both. Or rather Belinda."

"What do you want to ask Bells?" Suki said, immediately on the defensive.

Belinda waved her concern away. "Don't worry, Suki. She can ask away as far as I'm concerned. Well, what is it?" She stared at me, and her eyes were bright, challenging me. It was almost as if she knew what I had to say and was perversely enjoying the anticipation.

"Your sister's been doing her best to suggest that it was Charles who corrupted you into evil ways, hasn't she?" I said, not mincing my words. "It was Charles who did drugs, who gave you heroin. That's what you told the police, and that's what people believe. I accepted it at the time, but the more I thought about it the less it rang true. Charles was so organised, so self-controlled, that he could run a thriving blackmail business as an extra to his work at the bank. It was hard to believe that he'd do something as stupid as seduce the boss's daughter into doing junk. While if it was the other way round, it would make complete sense. You tempted Charles in over his head. He was a social climber, using a title he may not have had; his Achilles' heel was the kind of life you represented. You would have loved making him do what he didn't want to just to please you."

I was guessing, but Belinda didn't challenge anything I had said. It was Suki who exclaimed:

"*Blackmail!* Bells, what *is* this? Tell her it's not true! It was Charles who made you do smack, wasn't it?"

Neither of us listened to her. My eyes were fixed on Belinda's and hers on me. I continued:

"But Charles, however much he enjoyed it—and he must have enjoyed it, or he wouldn't have done something as damn silly as to shoot up at your engagement party—couldn't let an opportunity slip to earn some money on the side. He found out where you were getting your drugs from, didn't he? Exposure wouldn't have hurt him—he would have denied that he was using himself, and looked like a hero who was saving you from a fate worse than death. But your supplier would really have been in trouble. He told you that Charles was getting ready to milk him for a lot of money, didn't he? It was you who gave Charles the uncut heroin; it must have been. Charles wouldn't have trusted him. He wasn't a fool. Or maybe he *was* a fool, for trusting you." I paused for a moment, remembering again Sebastian passing me the coke yesterday, so long ago, on the boat. "I saw you and Charles holding hands for a moment at your engagement party. You were passing it to him, weren't you, getting a kick out of doing it in front of everyone without their knowing—"

"Bells didn't know!" Suki sprung out of her chair, almost knocking over the table. "She didn't know it would kill him, I swear! She was absolutely terrified when she found Charles, she had no idea what it was she had given him!"

"Fucking shut up!" Belinda snapped at her sister. "Can't you see she's trying to make us talk!"

But Suki was unstoppable, defending her sister with passionate conviction. "She'd already pulled him out of the loo and into the corridor

v ut what she was doing, she'd been a k for her, I knew where they went t

ued: "And by that time it was too la and the syringe had fallen out of his o leave him there but Bells was det nobile and drop it on him, she tho ng enough for her to get herself clea t away that there was smack invo

"S uriously on her sister.

"—It was so frightening, I had to go up and undo the chain, I nearly left my fingerprints all over it, I just remembered in time, and then when we were going up the stairs there was Simon coming up behind us and we were sure he'd seen us, but he can't have done. God, I was so terrified, but I didn't know then it had been deliberate, or I wouldn't have helped her—I thought it was an accident, the dose was just too strong. Well, it does happen sometimes, doesn't it?" Suki said pathetically, her voice pleading. "Everything was going so well, Felix was treating Bells and she seemed so much better, and I thought it was all behind us. And then James died, oh God, and now I just don't understand what's going on. . . ."

"You really don't know, do you?" I said, looking at her with pity. "You don't know where Belinda was getting it from? Where she's always been getting it from?"

Suki started to cry, terrible, high-pitched cries like a bird in distress. She clapped her hands over her ears. "Don't tell me," she wailed. "Don't tell me—"

"*Will you shut up!*" Belinda crossed the room, the silk of her dressing gown swishing round her, and slapped her sister across the face. Suki drew in her breath with a gasping sound and the cries stopped as abruptly as they had started. In the silence Belinda said to me, her eyes angry:

"You're just guessing. You don't know anything worth knowing."

"I've just been talking to Baby," I said. "She said you were the girl at school everyone wanted to be friends with, because you always had a supply of whatever anyone wanted. You were very careful not to tell where it came from but one night the two of you got drunk and did too much coke and you confided in her about your wonderful stepbrother who ran these open-all-night restaurants which were the perfect cover for selling lots of drugs to rich Sloanes with nothing better to do. . . ."

Suki's hands had fallen to her sides. Her face was as pale as a sheet of paper, making the red mark where Belinda had slapped her stand out like a port-wine stain. She was staring at me, but then her eyes shifted slightly, behind and above me. I swung round but I wasn't fast enough. Two strong hands gripped my upper arms, stopping me in my tracks, turning me back to face the room.

"I expect I should say something clichéd, shouldn't I, like: 'How very clever of you, Miss Jones, but not quite clever enough?'" Dominic Planchet's well-bred tones drawled in my ear.

. . .

He had come up the corridor behind me without making a sound. I didn't even bother to kick myself metaphorically for letting myself be caught like an idiot. I had other things to think about.

"Of course, you don't have any proof," he was saying quite amiably. "I expect you could be recording this conversation. Not that it would be admissible. I might get Belinda to check if you're wearing a wire or something of the sort."

"Dominic!" Suki said, still rooted to the spot, the slap mark burning on her cheek. Without taking her eyes off him she said to Belinda: "Tell me it's not true, Bells?"

"Of course it is," Belinda said, irritated. "Only someone as stupid as you wouldn't have realised it. God, you didn't even know I was doing drugs for years. I could come downstairs, off my face, giggling madly, and all you'd do was ask me if I felt OK."

Suki didn't seem to be taking this in; she was thinking about something quite different. After a moment she said to Dominic: "Where have you just come from?"

"Across the garden," he said. "I heard you girls talking and came round the front—"

"No you didn't. You must have come down the main stairs. We would have heard the front door if you'd come in that way. *Where were you?*"

"Oh, for God's sake, Suki, stop making such a fuss about something like this! Dom was with me, if you want to know, OK?" Belinda said. "We were fucking each other's brains out. Satisfied now?"

Suki's face flooded with colour, as if Belinda had slapped her again. "You haven't told her, have you?" she said quietly, looking at Dominic.

"Told me what?" Belinda said curiously.

I felt Dominic shrug, but the hands on my arms didn't lessen their grip. It was beginning to hurt. Still, I didn't want to move yet. I wanted to hear what they were about to say.

"Oh, it's a sad little story," Dominic said lightly. "Suki and I had a childhood romance and rather unfortunately she got pregnant. Neither of us thought that might happen. Geneviève whisked her away to a nice private clinic and it was all over before we knew it, only ever since then Suki's been terribly guilty about the whole thing. Keeps trying to engage me in conversations about whether we did the right thing and plenty more sentimental rubbish of the sort. That's why Genny and Richard want us to get married. Redeem ourselves, have babies, save Suki's soul and all that."

"I never knew about this!" Belinda sounded merely offended, as if she'd been left out of the excitement.

"We didn't have an affair," Suki said in a low voice. "I was only fourteen. You raped me. That's what my therapist calls it, and she's right."

"Pity you aren't Catholic," Dominic observed. "You could go to confession. As it is you've had to have your head shrunk. You were always neurotic, Suki. You wanted it as much as I did at the time."

"I wanted you to stop! I begged you, but you wouldn't listen to me!"

"Oh come on, you had a fine old time. You were just playing hard to get. Added to the fun, didn't it?"

"It's not true! I wanted you to *stop!*" Suki screamed at him, her face a mask of pain. "You were jealous of Daddy, you were furious when you found out he wasn't really your father! That's why you did it to me, you wanted to punish me for being his flesh and blood when you weren't! And that's why you've been feeding drugs to Bells, isn't it? It's all been for revenge, to drag us down. . . ."

She had hit a nerve. Dominic's grip loosened slightly on my arms as he snarled at her:

"I've had enough of these pathetic little shrink-wrapped fantasies of yours—"

I bent my legs suddenly, ducking down, his fingers slipping out of their grip on the sleeves of my shirt, and took a couple of quick paces forward before he could catch hold of me again.

"There's no need for this, Dominic," I said. "As you said, I don't have any proof—"

"You killed James too!" Suki said, suddenly realising what had been obvious to the rest of us for some time. "Why did you kill him?"

"He'd found out that Charles was doing smack," Belinda said. "Charles was getting money out of him and James didn't like it. He told Charles he wasn't paying any more because now they'd evened up the score, and he wanted his money back besides. When Charles died, James came to me. He'd guessed about Dominic. He overheard a conversation we had once and put two and two together later. He wanted Dominic to pay what Charles owed him."

"Only I don't believe in paying blackmail," Dominic said smoothly. "James should have learnt his lesson from what happened to Charles." He looked at me, his black eyes gleaming. "And what does Miss Samantha Jones want? I don't think money, do you? I think Miss Jones wants justice. But there's not much of that around these days, I'm afraid." He paused for a moment. "And I think she wants something else. She wants teaching a lesson, just like Charles and James did, to keep her mouth shut about what she knows. I would have thought the way James died would have been enough, but obviously you're quite persistent. And I think you have what Belinda and I have been looking for. I think you've got Charles's file and now you're going to tell me nicely where the fuck it is."

I should have hit Dominic while I had the chance. He started to walk towards me, slowly, savouring it; I knew he wanted to see me back away, pleading for mercy. I was in a lot of trouble. Dominic was several stone heavier than me and from the gleam in his eyes, the set of his jaw, nothing I could say would stop him. He wanted to hurt me. He had a taste for it now. Maybe after having killed two people at a distance he wanted something more close up, more hands on.

"Are you going to hand over the file like a good little girl?" he said smoothly. "I'm much nicer to girls who behave themselves. Ask Suki."

Just then the doorbell rang. The sound startled all of us, but Dominic, stronger and larger than I was, had less to lose by being distracted and allowed his head to swing round for a moment in the direction of the front door. Seizing my opportunity, I took a quick step towards him and boxed his ears with all the strength I had, feeling my fists slam into their target, though not hard enough to shatter his eardrums. He was too tall for that. I was close enough to clasp my hands together and double-punch him with each of my elbows in turn before I jumped back again, out of his range.

He lunged for me, hitting me on the side of the face. I saw it coming and swung with it but he was strong and it hurt all the same, throwing me to the side, and before I could react he caught me on the ribcage, his fist grinding into me as I twisted away. If I hadn't got in that punch to his ears the fight would have been over now; he'd have hit me hard enough to knock me out. But he was still groggy, his ears would be ringing, disorientating his balance, and if I could only capitalise on that. . . .

He came at me again, and now his eyes were mad, narrowed in fury; he couldn't understand why he hadn't put me down yet. If he landed a punch on me now I was out. He was strong enough to kill me. His breath hissed out between his teeth, the only noise in the room apart from the constant ringing of the doorbell.

He lunged again, but he was slow and signalled the blow far enough in advance for me to duck back; the counter was behind me but I had plenty of space to move. Then my foot caught on something that shouldn't have been there. For a moment I staggered, nearly managing to recover, but the something knocked back against my ankle and sent me flying. Even as I fell I knew what it was. Belinda Fine had stuck her foot behind mine and tripped me up.

There wasn't time to jump to my feet; Dominic was already kicking out at me, his face contorted with anger. Scuttling back on my hands, I blocked his kicks with my own, not allowing him to get round me, not letting myself feel how much he was hurting me, till I had manoeuvred myself round to the right place. In the process, one of his kicks landed on my thigh, but thank God it was my left leg, the weaker one. It hurt bad enough as it was. The side of my face where he had hit me before was swelling up, puffing out my eye so I had to squint to see, and it was better not to think about the damage to my ribs. Pushing all this from my mind, I concentrated everything I had in a laser beam of aggression and sent out a roundhouse kick that caught him squarely just above the right knee, pushing him sideways, while my left ankle twisted around the back of his right ankle, knocking it in the other direction, forcing him to fall over to avoid having his knee joint broken.

As I kicked him all my breath shot out in a noise between a grunt and a shout, and I felt the blow land just where I wanted it. For a moment I thought he wouldn't go down, and I threw myself upwards, bringing all the weight I had to bear on his right knee, trying to break it, to smash it into pieces, holding in my mind an image of the joint snapping like a stick, torquing it round and under him till his foot slipped and he went over. At the last moment he caught at the table to break his fall, but it was too late. The table came down with him, glass and china sliding across the surface and smashing over us.

I didn't give a shit about a bit of broken glass. I had his foot trapped under my body, his knee twisted in the grip of my right leg, so that I could break it if I wanted to, and I was rising up over him, not giving him time to swivel round, unstoppable now. I grabbed my fists together and jabbed him in the face once, twice, three times, all the strength of my right elbow with both my arms behind it, not letting up, smashing it into his face, my legs still holding his tight as a vise, and the more I came up the more it pulled his knee round under the weight of both our bodies, nailing him to the ground, putting an agonising pressure on the socket.

Every time I hit him I grunted, a rough, raucous sound that filled the air around us. My world seemed to have shrunk to our two bodies, twisted together in a ghastly parody of intimacy, but all my senses were on full alert still. As soon as Belinda moved I heard her.

"Stay right where you are or I'll break his leg!" I yelled, not taking my eyes off Dominic's now-bleeding face. "Tell her to stay where she is, Dominic, or by God I'll break your knee for you!"

I tightened my grip on his knee still further. It hurt me too but it made him cry out in pain.

"Stay back, Belinda!" he shouted, "I can deal with this little bitch."

God damn him, that was the last straw. We had ended up against the counter, our bodies caught against it; looking up for a weapon I saw the breadboard Belinda had been using to cut her apple projecting slightly over the edge. With a surge I reached up, grabbed it and brought it down over Dominic's head, sideways on.

I let the board fall. His head slumped to the side. He wasn't faking, either. I'd hit him hard enough to put him out for a good ten minutes at least.

"You've killed him!" Belinda screamed.

"Don't be bloody stupid." I caught my breath, disentangling myself from Dominic, standing up slowly, still holding the breadboard in case Belinda had any more clever ideas. My right leg hurt like hell but it wasn't broken, which was more than I could say for one of my ribs. I patted my face gingerly. The pain was searing but the bones seemed OK. The persistent shrilling of the doorbell made itself heard through the blood rushing in my ears. I realised it must have been ringing all this time. Whoever it was had started banging on the door as well.

"Get the door," I said to Suki. "Go on, do it!"

She stared at me for a second and then obeyed. From the blankness in her eyes I could see that she had gone into a sort of suspended animation, like a zombie; she would comply with whoever gave her an order first. She disappeared down the corridor, and I heard an upraised voice I recognised, someone pushing roughly past Suki and sprinting through the house, into the kitchen. Sebastian emerged on the threshold and stopped as dead as if he'd walked into a wall.

"Sam, your *face* . . ." I watched him take in Dominic, slumped at my feet, the table he had pulled down with him, everything that had been on its surface smashed on the tiles, the smell of coffee all around us from the broken coffee pot, shards of glass stained with coffee grounds thrown across the floor by the impact. Then he saw Belinda, standing frozen against the far wall. His eyes rose to me again, incredulous.

"I was worried about you," he said simply. "I knew you were going to see Baby, so I rang her, and she said she thought you were over here. I came straight away to see if you were all right. . . ."

He looked down at Dominic again. Words seemed to fail him.

"I wouldn't have been all right if you hadn't rung the doorbell," I said. "He'd have hammered me."

"Sam—my God, your *face*—" He came towards me.

"Don't touch me!" I said quickly, backing away. "I think I've broken a rib or two."

"*Christ*—"

"It was Dominic you got the coke from, right? I should have asked you ages ago." More pieces clicked into place. "You must have had some idea that he was dangerous."

He nodded. "I started putting two and two together. The way he looked at James yesterday, when he was dying—I guessed. But I didn't have any proof."

"Join the club. What we need is a witness. How about it, Suki?" I looked at her. "Will you testify against him? I'll see you're looked after. You can stay with me, if you want to. You'll be safe there. No one'll get at you if you don't want them to. I promise you that."

Suki stared at the hand I was holding out to her.

I held her eyes with mine, willing her to agree. "You trust me, don't you? Look at what I've just done. You'll be safe with me. I can protect you. He won't be able to hurt you."

I put everything I had left into that look, and she must have seen I meant it. Slowly she started across the kitchen towards me, her feet crunching on the broken glass and china.

"Suki! What are you doing!" Belinda exclaimed. "You can't go with *her!*"

Suki kept looking at me.

"Come on, Suki," I said slowly, quietly, as if I were gentling a horse. "Just a few more steps." I was sure that once she took my hand I would have her.

"*Suki!*" Belinda's voice lifted. "Suki, you can't go! You can't do this! Think of the scandal! Daddy would go mad!"

She pushed forward, past Sebastian, confronting Suki directly, hands on her hips.

"Let's just go, Suki," I said. "We can talk in the car."

"No!" Belinda stamped her foot. Realising that her tactics weren't working, she changed them, softening her voice to a little-girl whine. "I won't let you! You need to stay and look after me, you can't leave me, you can't! Suki, you can't do this, you've always looked after me!"

Suki's gaze dropped to the ground between us, as if avoiding Belinda's insistent stare. She was nearly close enough for me to touch her. And then she said, in a half-whisper:

"Bells, look at the glass on the floor. You'll cut your feet. You should be more careful."

"Suki—" I made a last effort. Belinda snapped her head round to look at me, knowing that she had won her sister.

"And you can get out of here! Get out!" she shouted. "Get out of my daddy's house!"

"Yes," Suki said suddenly, her voice rising in hysteria. "Do what Belinda says, get out, get out!"

Both of them were screaming at us now, their pretty faces convulsed in identical ugly expressions of hate, venomous as snakes. Belinda's lips were drawn back over her teeth, her hands rising up towards me, the fingernails like claws to rake down my face. It was harrowing, terrible, this sudden transformation—in particular of Suki, who had nearly broken free only to fail at the last moment and was rejecting the person who could have saved her—if she'd let me. But now she was coming towards me, face suffused with blood, hissing at me from between clenched teeth:

"Get out! Get out!"

This was how the maenads must have looked. I couldn't move. I was paralysed. It was Sebastian who saved me, pulling me back as they advanced on us, dragging me down the corridor.

"Get out and never, ever, ever come back!" Suki was screaming, like a broken record. "I hate you, I hate you! Get out of my daddy's house!"

It wasn't what she was saying that was so terrible so much as her face, torn and tortured with emotion, swollen with the tears streaming down her face. Sebastian, behind me, was fumbling with the front-door latch. Belinda tried to claw at me, her eyes quite mad, and I had to block her with one hand. If they had spat poison at us I wouldn't have been surprised.

"*Get out!*" they screamed. "Get out of our house, get out, *get out!*"

Sebastian hauled me through the door, slamming it behind us. The sunshine hit us in the face, blinding me for a moment, and that must have been why I started to cry, because of the brightness of the sun, the contrast of its dazzling light after the darkness I had just confronted. Though that makes no sense when I remember it now. None at all.

24

"Where had Charles hidden it?" I said, looking down at the file I held in my hands.

"Right under his desk," Simon said. "He'd cut a slit in the carpet, next to the electrical socket for the computer, and slid it underneath. It took me ages to find it."

"And then you hid it yourself and came up by the fire stairs, hoping no one would notice you'd been away from the party. Did you hear Suki and Belinda? They must have been a few flights above you. They saw you, you know. That's how I finally worked out where the file was—realising that you'd taken the opportunity of the party to search Charles's desk for it."

Simon grimaced. "I heard them, yes, so I ducked back into the stairwell. Actually, I didn't think they'd seen me, so when they didn't say anything about it I thought I was in the clear."

"You must have been shitting bricks when you heard Charles was dead."

Simon nodded. The strain I had noticed only a few days ago was gone from his delicate features; he looked infinitely more relaxed, as if handing the file over to me had taken a disproportionate weight off his shoulders. He glanced briefly at my bandages and then away again. I'd already discouraged any attempts to ask how I felt. I was in retirement in my studio, licking my wounds, till I felt ready to go out and face the world.

"The police weren't searching for papers, though, only for drugs," Simon continued. "I was pretty safe, as long as anyone didn't look too closely."

I tapped the file with one finger. "I'll send this stuff back to the people it belongs to." Yielding to curiosity, I opened it. It was thicker than I expected. There were photographs of Nicola Walters and the others on the list, each with its documentation clipped to the back, direct debit forms, agreements to repay loans, and so forth. The saddest thing was the photocopy of the letter informing Charles that Bill had been kicked out of the army for being drunk on duty. Poor Bill, how he would have hated to have that known. I paused too over the photograph of David Stronge dousing his car with petrol. Clipped to it was the loan agreement and direct debit form, made out in David's name, but not yet signed. If Charles had died a few days later, David Stronge would also have featured on the list Tim had sent me.

"Look at the photo closely," Simon said dryly.

It was dark, but poring over it I made out someone else in the background, leaning against a wall, watching David at work. I squinted over his features and did a double take. The original was sitting next to me on the sofa.

"I would have told you," Sebastian said apologetically. "I was pretty drunk in a bar and bumped into David, and for some reason it seemed like a wonderful idea to torch his car. I didn't actually do the work. You could call it moral support."

"Did Charles try to blackmail you?"

"Of course he did. I just told him to piss off. It wasn't even my bloody car. And I'd had a damn good year. I told him if I heard another word about it I'd tell Richard what he'd tried to do. That shut him up all right."

I turned the picture over. David and Sebastian's names were written on it; through the latter Charles had ruled a neat line. I tossed it over to him, saying:

"Want a memento?" Turning to Simon, I said: "I expect you've taken your stuff out already."

He nodded. "Shots of me coming out, close-ups of Dan—Dr. Goldman's—name on the bell—"

"Dr. Goldman?" I stared at him. "Do you mean—" God, I was slow. "Do you mean you were seeing an analyst?"

"Well, of course! He's my therapist! I thought you knew all about it. . . ."

I bit back anything I'd been about to say. I'd been an idiot once more. Why else did people go to NW3, if not to be analysed?

"What did you think I was talking about?" Simon said incredulously.

"Umm . . . never mind. But look, I don't understand," I said quickly, before he could press me on the subject. "Why would going to an analyst get you sacked from the bank?"

Simon and Sebastian exchanged disbelieving glances. "Are you serious? It'd question his whole mental stability!" Sebastian said. "Get him labelled as a nutcase."

"But that's insane! I mean, surely someone's more stable if they admit they have a problem than if they just bury their head in the sand. . . ."

My voice tailed off. Both men were staring at me pityingly.

"You just don't understand how the City works, Sam," said Sebastian.

"I'm leaving the bank and staying with Dan," Simon said. "It seems the right way round."

Still baffled, I went on leafing through the file.

"You haven't reached the best bit yet," Simon said.

I delved deeper into the file and at last hit pay dirt. Photographs of Dominic and Belinda, neither of them wearing very much clothing, sprawled on what I recognised as the carpeted floor of Belinda's bedroom, the low glass table in front of them littered with drug paraphernalia, a roll of kitchen foil, torn-up, scorched pieces that had been used to smoke junk, an open clingfilm-wrapped packet and a mirror with a couple of lines on it, ready cut.

"His and hers," I commented. "I don't see Dominic doing junk, but you never know. How the hell did he get these pictures?"

I passed them to Sebastian. "He must have had a key to the house," he suggested. "Belinda gave him one or he copied hers without her knowing. Opened the door a crack while they were otherwise occupied and ran off some photos."

"What a risk!"

"It wasn't the only one he took, though, was it?"

"I'll send these to Sir Richard, anonymously," I said. "That should stir up trouble for Dominic. And I spoke to a policeman I know. Apparently Dominic's business partner has been under suspicion of importing heroin for some time now. They're going to raid the company offices. And they might be able to nail them through their tax declarations. Both Dominic and his partner have been spending much more than they've declared as earnings."

"No hope of his being arrested for killing Charles and James?" Simon said.

I shook my head. "Where's the evidence? Even with Suki to testify it would have been slight. As it is. . . ."

I came to a halt.

"You look tired," Simon said, which was tactful under the circumstances, considering that the right side of my face was still swollen and bruised like something which had fallen from a tree last autumn, and my ribcage was bandaged up so tightly that it hurt because of the pressure alone. "Shall I be going?"

"Yes, thanks," I said gratefully.

"Would you rather I went too?" Sebastian said.

I nodded, though it hurt to move my face. Sebastian had been doing his best to cosset me for days now and it was getting on my nerves. He looked wistful, but, thank God, he didn't make too much of a fuss, just kissed me on the side of my mouth that wasn't puffed up like a balloon and told me to ring him soon. I wondered if I would.

I locked the door behind them and went back thankfully to lie on the sofa. It was time for my painkillers. I washed them down with some vodka and propped my head on a pair of cushions. Across the room lay Floating Planet, even more smashed up than I was but with no chemicals to take the pain away. A couple of art world entrepreneurs, alerted by Tim's article, had rung up Duggie to ask him whether it could be included in an exhibition they were planning entitled "Art That's Killed." It would be stretching a point, since the sculpture hadn't directly been responsible for Charles's death, but they hadn't seemed bothered about that. Well, it was something to think about when I felt better. As was the one-woman show Duggie had promised me in the new year. . . .

Closing my eyes, I sank back gratefully against the cushions. In the dark behind my eyelids appeared Suki Fine's face as I had last seen it, distorted and sobbing, complicit with everything she hated, and I felt sick to my stomach. I had failed. I hadn't been able to pull her out of the broken glass. For Belinda I didn't give a damn; she would probably drug herself to death and the faster she did it, the better I'd feel.

The painkillers had lodged in the back of my throat, sending up waves of sour, acid taste as their coating dissolved. Coughing, I sat up again and took a swig of vodka, and then another, till I had drowned them thoroughly in my stomach. The taste still remained, though, bitter as aloes. I took a final pull at the bottle, enough to give me a temporary *coup de grâce*. Gradually I felt the pills taking effect, waves of sleepiness washing over me, and I lay down again and closed my eyes, retaining just enough sense to wedge the pillows firmly under my head, propping it high enough to stop me choking.

Darkness drew around me as smoothly as a velvet curtain on a four-poster bed, and I was only too grateful for it. I would have been grateful for anything that would close over my head, take me away from here, and stop me remembering.

Sam Jones is back and this time she's raising eyebrows in London's exclusive theater world. A chance meeting in a fetish club leads to a job as a set designer for a new production of *A Midsummer Night's Dream* in *FREEZE MY MARGARITA,* the latest Sam Jones novel, coming in March from Crown:

The man on his hands and knees in front of me had been there for a few minutes already, but in this establishment that was nothing out of the ordinary. I didn't realize at once that he was asking me something; the Velvet Underground were pounding lugubriously out of the speakers at a high enough volume to drown out anyone speaking in an appropriately servile tone of voice.

"Can I lick your boots clean?"

"I'm sorry, what?" I ducked my head. Rearing up on his knees, he said more loudly:

"Can I lick your boots clean?"

I shrugged. "Be my guest." His face fell. "You filthy little piece of scum," I added, not wanting to disappoint. He cheered up at once and ducked down, tongue poking out of the slit in his leather mask. But just as I turned back to the conversation he had interrupted, a horrible realization struck me.

"Oh my God, they're suede! Stop it! They'll be ruined!" I kicked out involuntarily. He curled over on one side and started moaning:

"Sorry, mistress, sorry, I'm a bad slave, do with me what you will. . . ."

"Do with me what you will?" I said sotto voce to Janey. She shrugged.

"Been reading too much Anne Rice."

"Mrs. Radcliffe, more like." I looked down at the bad slave and, feeling guilty at having deprived him of his fun, prodded his rubber bodysuit with the heel of my boot. He whimpered in ecstasy.

"I never know how they manage to let the sweat out in those things," I said to Janey.

"Probably don't."

"Ick."

"Oh well, at least he didn't claim to be the slave in *Pulp Fiction*," she said. "I've had three of those already this evening. So unoriginal. I like your dress, by the way."

"Thanks." I looked down at myself complacently. "Makes me feel like Scarlett O'Hara."

She gave me a frankly uncomprehending stare. "Ran it up out of a pair of old curtains, did you? I'd like to see the room they were hung in.

"The lacing, idiot." Without a Mammy to pull me in while I gripped onto the bedpost, I hadn't quite achieved an eighteen-inch waist, but it was still considerably restrained. And my bosom, never insubstantial at the best of times, was now resting precariously just under the top of my leather corset, propped up by what felt like most of the flesh that should have been covering my ribcage.

"Sam!"

I looked around to see a slave heading towards me at full lick, rather like an out-of-control Labrador, dragging his handler behind him on the leash. At first I didn't realize who he was; his features were obscured by two wide strips of leather, one over his eyes, the other over his mouth, secured at the back by a cross-piece. The zips that would have made him blind and dumb were hanging open, and squinting through them I began to distinguish a familiar face. He was wearing a black rubber sleeveless bodysuit, which at least allowed the air around his armpits to circulate.

"Eet's been so long!" he was exclaiming. "How are you?"

With the clue of the accent, I pinned down his identity: Salvatore, Sally to his friends, one of a gang of gay Sicilians who had for that very reason emigrated en masse to London. We had been at art school together, but our paths hadn't crossed for years.

"Hi, Sally." I did my best to kiss him hello, though the straps kept getting in the way. Janey had meanwhile struck up a conversation with some guy who'd been trying to catch her attention for the past half an hour and was now deep in a monologue about the latest power politics at Channel 4; she was a TV script editor. Disturbing her to introduce Sally would have been like breaking into the middle of Mass to ask the priest what the time was.

Sally looked round pleadingly at his handler. "Meestress, thees ees an old friend. May I harmbly talk to her for a few minutes?"

"Only if you obey her every command," said his mistress, handing the leash over to me. Her heels were so high that her calf muscles stood out like clenched fists. I took it gingerly. I've never really liked being responsible for other people.

"Um, buy me a drink," I suggested. "And that's an order."

"Two of the usual," Sally said to the barman. "On my account."

"You have an account here?"

"Not really. I give heem the merney at the end of the evening. I can't carry money een thees." He indicated the latex bodysuit. I saw what he meant.

The barman was already placing two identical concoctions in front of us, the salt rim to the glasses contrasting prettily with the pale aquamarine liquid inside.

"What's that colour?" I said warily, reminded of mouthwash.

"Blue curaçao," said the barman proudly. "Half and half with the triple sec. They're blue margaritas."

"Aren't they fabulous!" Sally enthused. "Eet's my dreenk of the year."

"Ever since the time some wally brought a bottle of crème de menthe to a cocktail party and made us Peppermint Somethings that tasted like toothpaste and cream, I've stuck to the whisky sours," I said, picking up my glass. I sipped tentatively. "God, this is *delicious*." Instantly converted, I took a good pull at my straw.

"So, tell me everysing you have been doing," Sally said.

"Oh, it's going OK, I suppose. I've got an exhibition coming up soon and I've finished most of the pieces for it. All of them, really. I'm just tinkering around now."

"Who are you weeth?"

"The Wellington Gallery."

"But that's excellent!"

"I know," I said gloomily. "It's hard to explain without sounding spoilt, but the trouble is . . . Sally, do you remember Lee Jackson, who taught us sculpture? I know you only did it for the first year—"

"How do I forget a woman like that?" said Sally rhetorically, lapsing for a moment into the traditions of his culture.

"She said once that the two responses of the hack sculptor, if a piece of work isn't going well, are either to make it big and paint it red, or make loads and fill the room up with them."

"So you are making everysing raid?"

"Nope, it's the second one. I see fifteen mobiles hanging together and I just don't know if I think they're good any more. They look really striking *en masse*. But anything looks good if you multiply it by fifteen and hang it from the ceiling: goldfish bowls, bits of ironmongery, even cocktail glasses—why are you staring at me like that?"

Sally's eyes were bugging out through the zips as if he were a Hanoverian king with water on the brain. The very small part of my mind which was not occupied with the misery of my artistic crisis wondered how he zipped his eyes shut without catching those long Sicilian eyelashes in the teeth. Be a waste to pull them out.

"You said you are making mobiles now?"

"That's right."

"*Guarda bene*, we must meet up and talk about thees. Can I come round to your stoodio? Are the mobiles there?"

"Yes, but—"

"I remember your work well. I liked what you did very march. *Very* march."

"Well, it's completely changed," I said instantly, not being one of those people who hoards their juvenilia. I'm the opposite: I need to keep moving on. Preferably as Juggernaut, with spikes on my wheels to shred my old work as I go. At art school our painting teacher made us bring in what we considered the best of our current work, then announced that we were going to build a bonfire in the yard with the paintings as fuel. I was the only one who jumped at the idea. Move on or die. Thank God I had a gallery and could get rid of my mobiles. I knew artists who, still unrepresented, lived with the pieces they had made years ago, unable to sell them. As far as I was concerned, they might as well have been living in crypts surrounded by mouldering corpses.

Sally shrugged his shoulders, raising his hands, palm up, in a gesture I remembered well. It meant, "So what?"

"Why do you want to see them?" I asked warily.

"I am set designing now, and I am doing well." Sally had none of the English inhibitions about blowing one's own trumpet. It was very refreshing. "I am just to start—just *about* to start," he corrected himself, "to wairk on a new production of the *Dream*. That ees *Midsummer Night's Dream*, if you do not wairk in the theatre."

"Thanks, I didn't think you meant *I Dream of Jeannie*."

"*Cosa?* Anyway, we want it to be modern, modern, modern. Also we have some money, we have thees nice big theatre with a *proscenio*—the Cross—and so for instance we can permit oursailves to fly some people. I have been theenking about thees for a long time, how to do it in an interesting way, like Peter Brook with the trapezes. And now you come to tell me that you are making mobiles, and this whole idea explodes in my haid. . . . They are beeg, aren't they? You always make theengs beeg."

"Pretty big. But Sally, even if you like them, the last thing I want to do is start making more for a theatre production. I was thinking about a holiday. Somewhere warm, where the boys are pretty and the drinks are cold."

"I come weeth you! I know just the place. *After* we've done the show."

"Oh, for God's sake—"

Sally's leash was abstracted from my hand.

"Was he well behaved?" his mistress asked me. Her lipstick was dark plum and so fresh that it glistened stickily, even in the dim light. Either she had touched it up recently, or she had been at the newly tapped virgin's blood in the back room.

"Not at all," I said vindictively, "he's been nagging at me and won't take no for an answer."

She drew in her breath sharply and tugged Sally's collar so hard he nearly fell off the bar stool.

"I see you still wilfully fail to respond to discipline!" she said, dragging him off with her. It was a choke leash; his half-strangled gurgle of pain wasn't faked. "Down!"

"I'll reeng you!" he croaked at me, hobbling off on all fours, and providing me in the process with a nice view of his bottom through the lacing on the back of his suit.

I stared after them, knowing that he would. Sally didn't have my number, but that wouldn't stop him; he'd just ring round everyone he knew till he found someone who did, persistent little bugger that he was. Well, he would just have to take no for an answer this time. There was no way I was making any more mobiles for a very long time, let alone ones specially customized so that people answering to the names of Peaseblossom and Mustardseed could use them as tarted-up hoists. I had my pride.